Sing a New Song

Tales from Grace Chapel Inn

Sing a New Song

SUNNI JEFFERS

Guideposts
New York, New York

Sing a New Song

ISBN-13: 978-0-8249-4917-4

Published by Guideposts
16 East 34th Street
New York, New York 10016
www.guideposts.org

Distributed by Ideals Publications, a Guideposts company
2630 Elm Hill Pike, Suite 100
Nashville, TN 37214

Cover Illustration by Deborah Chabrian
Interior Design by Marisa Jackson
Typeset by Müllerhaus Publishing Group | www.mullerhaus.net

Printed and bound in the United States of America
10 9 8 7 6 5 4 3 2 1

GRACE CHAPEL INN

A place where one can be
refreshed and encouraged,
a place of hope and healing,
a place where God is at home.

Acknowledgments

Sing a New Song is dedicated to Regina Hersey, a great editor and friend. You take my rough stones and cut them into diamonds. Thank you!

To the Booher family, who offers a wonderful family music camp experience each summer. The love of the Lord shines out from you. I hope this little book brings a song to your heart.

To Floyd Domino, a remarkable piano artist and teacher. Your passion for music and your energy amaze me. Thanks for your help.

And to my nephew Nathan. Without your help, I'd never get the keys right. Any errors in the musical renditions are strictly mine.

—Sunni Jeffers

Chapter One

"Would you care for more coffee?" asked Louise Howard Smith as she attended to the guests in the dining room of Grace Chapel Inn. Dressed for Sunday services, she wore a brown tweed skirt, dusk-blue cardigan sweater and her signature pearls. Her short silver hair glinted in the late October sunshine that shone through the windows into the pleasant room.

Garrett Yeager gave her a grateful nod and said, "Thanks," as she refilled his cup. His reading glasses sat atop a folded copy of a financial newspaper next to his plate. Louise had overheard snippets of his conversation with Ed Gladstone, another inn guest, regarding the stock market. The Gladstones were vacationing, yet the man looked dressed for a corporate boardroom. Garrett, on the other hand, was staying at the inn on business. He had a project in the neighboring town of Riverton requiring him to remain in the area for a month. He wore his brown hair in a casual style and had donned a collared navy knit shirt and chinos, giving him the appearance of a man on vacation.

Mrs. Gladstone paused, holding a spoonful of apple, pear and blueberry compote midair, and smiled up at Louise. "Breakfast is delicious again, and I'm feeling thoroughly spoiled. I adore historic homes, and you have a perfect mix of Victorian atmosphere and modern comfort here. I hate to leave today. I can't remember a weekend I've enjoyed more."

"I agree," her husband said, "but I must get home in time for work tomorrow." He smiled at his wife. "Perhaps we can reserve a room in December. I imagine Acorn Hill is beautiful in the winter."

Mrs. Gladstone's eyes lit with excitement. "Oh, let's do!"

"The inn is lovely at Christmastime. I'm sure you'd enjoy it here," Louise said. "I can reserve a room for you before you leave. Would you like more of anything? Another waffle perhaps?"

"No, thank you," the woman said. "I couldn't eat another bite. In fact, I must excuse myself now to go upstairs and pack. The pumpkin waffles were wonderful, though."

"I must be leaving too," Garrett said. "Time to get to work."

"Too bad to spoil a beautiful Sunday with work," Ed said.

"You're right. I don't intend to work all day," Garrett replied. "I must compile my notes before a meeting tomorrow, but then I intend to check out the countryside. Is it all right if I work here at the inn during my stay?" he said, addressing Louise.

"Certainly," she said. "There's a desk in the library, but feel free to use any of the public rooms. I give piano lessons in the parlor after school during the week. The room is soundproof, but the children can be a bit noisy coming and going. I hope that won't disturb you."

"No, it won't I'm sure. My work is portable. I use my lap-top, and with wireless cell-phone Internet access, I can work anywhere."

"Oh dear, we don't have good cell-phone reception here,"

Louise said. "It's better outside. You could use the front porch if it's not too chilly."

"Maybe there's somewhere in town where I can get better reception. I'll check around."

"You might try the library or the Coffee Shop," Louise suggested.

"Thanks. I'll find a good reception area somewhere."

"What kind of work do you do?" Ed asked him.

"I install wireless communication systems. I'm setting up a system for a commercial trucking company out of Riverton."

"Like satellite communications?" Ed asked.

"Yes. In this case, we're integrating phone and computer systems to track loads and consolidate freight pickups and deliveries."

"Interesting. My firm's internal communications could use a facelift. Perhaps you could give me one of your cards before we leave."

"I'd be happy to," Garrett said as he plucked a card from his wallet and handed it to Ed.

"If you don't need anything else, I'll leave you to your conversation. My sisters and I will be going to church in a short while. You're welcome to join us if you'd like."

"Thank you," Ed said. "Perhaps the next time we visit."

Garrett said, "Thank you," but he didn't comment on her invitation. Louise left the men talking. Her knowledge of such technological advances was nonexistent, but she was pleased that their guests were interacting so well.

The phone rang as Louise went through to the kitchen. Her

sister Jane Howard had her hands in soapsuds, washing a baking dish. Jane was the inn's chef. Her other sister, Alice Howard, was upstairs preparing for church. The three sisters owned and operated the inn together. Louise set the coffeepot down and answered the phone on the third ring.

"Grace Chapel Inn, Louise Smith speaking."

"Hello, Mother. It's Cynthia. I was hoping to catch you before you went to church. Is this a bad time?"

"No, dear. This is fine. How are you? How is work? It's so good to hear your voice."

"I'm fine and work is busy. Actually, that's why I called. How would you like to get away and spend a week in California with me? I have an assignment that is right up your alley."

"I'd love to, but when? I don't know if I can get away for an entire week."

"Of course you can," Jane said from behind her.

"I heard that," Cynthia said. Louise could hear a smile in her voice. "I'm talking about early November."

"That looks like it's going to be a slow time this year. A storm blew through here last week and took most of the beautiful leaves with it. We had cancellations from leaf peepers because of that. So perhaps I could spend some time away. I don't like to leave Jane and Alice with all the work. And I'd have to reschedule piano lessons."

"Please consider it. You'd be doing me a favor. I'm researching a family music camp for a new children's book series that I'm developing on family activities. You're my expert when it comes to musical training. If this works out, I may get my own imprint."

"That's wonderful, honey. Of course I'll help you. Northern California? Where? San Francisco?"

"No. Actually, it's at a ranch in the foothills outside a little town called Nevada City. It may be a bit rugged, but it's steeped in western history, so there are many interesting sights to explore. This is gold-rush country. Many of the attendees come in trailers and motor homes or set up tents. The ranch has a bunkhouse where students can stay."

Louise's mind whirled with images of cattle, horses and dust. What was she agreeing to? "Do you have access to a motor home?" she asked, hoping Cynthia didn't expect her to sleep in a bunkhouse or a tent. Camping was not her idea of a grand vacation.

"No. I found a Victorian bed-and-breakfast near the ranch. We'll fly to Sacramento and then rent a car for the week. That way we can go back and forth to the ranch. I convinced my boss that I need your input, so he agreed to pick up the tab. I hear the town is charming."

"That sounds nice. What is my role? How can I help you with your project?"

"The camp offers classes in fiddle, guitar and piano from beginner to advanced. Their staff has an excellent reputation. I want to observe many of the classes and get an overall picture. I was hoping you would go as a student, so I can get the perspective of a student. The class should be a breeze for you, Mother."

"A student? Won't they think it's strange for a music teacher with an advanced degree to attend as a student?"

"Not at all. They teach bluegrass and western-style music, so it will be different from what you teach."

Louise loved old gospel music, but she didn't care for the western genre. "I'll do it for you," Louise said rather hesitantly. "How do I register?"

"I'll take care of everything. I'll drive down and pick you up, and we'll drive to the airport from there. Thanks, Mother. I'll send you a brochure that tells what to bring and gives the details. I can't wait to see you."

Louise smiled. The anticipation of a week with her daughter would fill the next few weeks with joy. "And I can't wait to see you. Being with you will make this adventure special."

"I'll talk to you soon. This will be fun, I promise."

Louise said good-bye and hung up. She turned to find Jane watching her expectantly.

"What's up?" Jane asked. "You're going to California with Cynthia?"

"We're going to a music camp. Cynthia has an assignment that could lead to her own imprint. She's developing a series of books for children that involve family activities."

"She must be thrilled. What's your role in the trip?"

"I'm not exactly sure, but she wants me to learn to play bluegrass and some kind of western music. As you know, that's not exactly my cup of tea, but music is music. Learning new styles shouldn't be too difficult." At least in theory, she should be able to play anything, Louise thought. After all, she knew the piano intimately, and she knew theory and how to sight-read music and count tempo. How hard could it be?

"Why would you need a motor home in San Francisco?" Jane frowned as she pushed back a loose strand of hair that had fallen out of her dark, glossy ponytail.

"We're not going to San Francisco. We're going to some mining town in the mountains. Fortunately, we're not staying in a motor home. Cynthia found an inn for us."

"I don't know, Louise. I can't picture you playing bluegrass. I mean, you can play anything beautifully, but that just isn't you."

"I'd learn to play boogie-woogie for a chance to spend a week with Cynthia. I'm sure it won't come to that, though."

"So what exactly is a book imprint? Is Cynthia going to start writing children's books?"

"She won't write, but she will have a certain type of book under her supervision, and she'll decide the subject matter and content. Then she'll work with different authors and artists to develop the books."

Chapter Two

*T*hat sounds like quite an opportunity for her. So she wants books featuring family-oriented activities?"

"That's what she said. I don't know any details. It sounds like this could be the first project of many, so she's doing a lot of research."

"*Hmm.*" Jane returned to her task.

Louise picked up a dishtowel and dried a spatula. "I'll have to go through my music and see if I have some bluegrass pieces. Maybe I'll go to Potterston and see what's available at the music store."

"I'm sorry. What did you say?"

"Nothing important. I was just thinking out loud about what I might need to prepare for the music camp."

"Oh. Won't they have a curriculum?"

"I'm sure they'll supply basic music, but I like to be prepared," Louise said.

"Yes, of course."

Jane rinsed a saucepan and handed it to Louise. They finished the dishes in silence. Jane seemed unusually quiet, but Louise didn't mind. She had plenty to think about.

Jane's mind turned over an idea as she wiped her hands on a red and white striped towel. Removing the chef's smock that she wore when cooking and serving guests, she carried it to the laundry room. Louise had finished putting the dishes away and left the kitchen. So, Jane thought, Cynthia was developing a children's book series structured around family activities. Cooking together would be a great activity. Perhaps she could help Cynthia with an idea for her book series. A cookbook for kids would involve families. *The Minigourmet. The Junior Chef. The Young Epicurean.* None of those sounded intriguing enough, but the title could wait.

Jane glanced at her watch and then hurried up the stairs. She barely had five minutes to get ready for church. It was time to stop daydreaming.

Jane slipped on a multicolor jewel-toned broomstick skirt and an emerald peasant blouse that she'd laid out on her bed before breakfast. As she twisted her hair and pinned it on top of her head with decorative clips, a phrase popped into her head. *Visions of sugarplums danced in their heads*. She had no idea what made her think of a Christmas poem, but the phrase was catchy. She had a great recipe for making candied plums that would work for the cookbook. *Visions of Sugarplums* would make a great title, except it seemed to indicate Christmas. She didn't want to create a Christmas cookbook. She wanted something that fit any season.

Jane jotted the word *sugarplum* on a small notepad and tucked it in her purse, picked up her Bible, then headed downstairs.

The Gladstones were talking to Louise at the reception desk in the hallway, so Jane went through the dining room. Alice was there, putting away the sugar bowl and salt and pepper shakers.

"Need any help?" Jane offered.

"No. I'm finished. I'm just waiting for you and Louise."

"She should be done in a minute. Let's wait in the kitchen." Jane opened the swinging door between the two rooms and let Alice go through.

Louise came in just as Alice put on her jacket and picked up her Bible.

"It looks like we'll have guests in December. The Gladstones booked a week ending on Christmas Eve," Louise said. "Shall we go?"

As the sisters walked toward Grace Chapel, Jane hummed a tune.

"What is that tune?" Alice asked. "It sounds like a Christmas carol."

"Are you talking to me?" Jane asked.

"You were humming something," Louise said. "I didn't recognize it either."

Jane laughed out loud. "That would be my singing, not the song. Furthermore, I didn't realize I was humming, so I don't know what it was."

Louise shook her head. "You seem preoccupied this morning. Is anything wrong?"

"No. I was just daydreaming," Jane said.

"Perhaps my mention of Christmas guests planted a song in your mind," Louise said. "Let's not rush it, please. I'm not ready for the holidays. I have a music camp to get through first. Right now, I need to warm up the organ for church, so we'd better step up our pace."

As they neared Grace Chapel, Jane passed her sisters. Besides being fifteen years younger than Louise and twelve years younger than Alice, Jane walked and jogged regularly, so the slight uphill pathway presented no challenge. She arrived at the church steps and held the door open for her sisters. *I can include cookie recipes*, she thought. *They're fun to make, and everyone in the family can get involved.*

After the service, Alice stood outside on the church steps, waiting for Jane and Louise. She pulled up the lapels of her jacket to cover her neck against a sudden, chilling wind. She loved autumn, when the air seemed sharp and clear. She loved the texture of soft knits and woolens cuddling against her skin like a warm hug, and fall colors complemented her reddish-brown hair and her fair complexion. She'd always thought her coloring clashed with the other seasons.

"Oh, Alice, do you have a minute?"

Alice turned and smiled at Penny Holwell, who had just stepped through the door. The wind caught a wisp of Penny's shoulder-length blond hair and whipped it across her eyes. She pushed it behind her ear. Penny was a trim, energetic mother of a teenaged son, Bart. Her husband Zeke ran his own construction company.

"Bart and Zeke will be out flying their new kite this afternoon for sure," she said. "I went to a scrapbooking party last night," she added, changing the subject abruptly. "Have you ever gone to one?"

"No. I haven't," Alice said, wondering if Penny was going to invite her to one. Alice didn't have time for a lot of hobbies. Other than a bit of knitting and making a couple of small quilts, she devoted her efforts to her patients at the hospital where she worked part-time; to the ANGELs, a group of middle-school girls she led at the church; and to helping her sisters run the inn.

"Scrapbooking is the current rage," Penny said. "I started the neatest album. I want to finish it, but there's so much more to learn. I had an idea. There's a gal from Potterston who leads scrapbooking retreats. I was thinking it would be great to have a retreat here in Acorn Hill, and the inn would be the perfect place to have it. Lots of women in town would come, and I know it would attract out-of-town guests if it was advertised." Penny stopped to take a breath. "What do you think?"

"I...it sounds interesting. I'll have to talk to Jane and Louise about it. Do you have information about what such a retreat entails? And when would you want to hold it?"

"We'll need a couple of weeks to put it together, but I'm thinking as soon as possible. Otherwise, we'll run into the holidays, and also, I can't wait to finish my scrapbook."

"I'll talk to my sisters this afternoon and see what they think."

Jane and Louise came through the door as Penny said, "Great. I'll call you tonight." Penny saw them as she turned to leave.

"Hi, Jane. Hi, Louise." She looked at Alice. "Don't forget," she said as she hurried off to catch up to her husband, who was walking toward their car.

The sisters greeted several people as they began strolling down the path to the inn. Just out of earshot of their friends, Jane turned to Alice. "I don't want to be nosy, but what is it that Penny doesn't want you to forget?"

"She wants me to talk to you about using the inn for a scrapbooking weekend."

"When?" Louise asked.

"Soon, before the holidays begin. She knows someone in Potterston who leads retreats and parties."

"What a wonderful idea!" Jane said. "I've seen some of the scrapbooks that have been made at those parties. They can be so beautiful and creative. I can just picture a group of women sitting around our dining-room table making albums."

"We must check our schedule. Remember, I'm going away for a week with Cynthia."

"No problem," Jane said. "I've been to a craft retreat. They work on their projects, laugh and talk a lot, and snack as they work. We just have to give them the space to work and keep the snacks coming."

"What about meals?" Louise wanted to know. "They won't want to go out to eat."

"True, but food isn't their main concern. A tureen of soup and trays of sandwiches or finger foods would suffice. We just build it into the cost of the retreat. I vote yes. Let's do it," Jane said.

"We'll look at the calendar and see," Louise said. "Don't forget, Garrett Yeager has a room reserved for a month. That leaves just three rooms for a retreat."

"Penny thought that most of the women would come from

Acorn Hill, so they won't need rooms, but the retreat could attract a few women from out of town," Alice said.

Louise shook her head. "I just don't know about the timing. Our rooms are booked for the next three weeks, and then I'll be gone the early part of November."

"We'll be fine without you," Jane said. "You just go have a good time."

Alice thought Louise appeared taken aback by Jane's seeming flippant dismissal. "Of course, we'll miss having your help, Louise," Alice assured her. "You're so organized and efficient. But perhaps we can get someone attending the retreat to help during the meals."

"Great idea, Alice. And we'll keep it really simple. We'll manage."

Jane's imploring look took Alice back forty years. She could remember Jane entreating her with just such a look, and Jane generally succeeded. Their mother died when Jane was born, and Louise and Alice had helped their father, Rev. Daniel Howard, raise their baby sister. Alice almost laughed at Jane's wide-eyed plea. Neither Louise nor Alice could resist her at age ten, and they couldn't resist her now. Some things never changed.

"How many are coming to dinner?" Louise asked as she took a pile of plates out of the cupboard. "Aunt Ethel told me she and Lloyd will be here. Any others?"

"I invited Pastor Ken and our guest Garrett Yeager," Jane

said. "Since he is with us for a month, I thought it would be nice for him to meet some of the local men."

Louise nodded as she counted out seven dinner plates. Though breakfast was the only meal included in the inn's rates, the sisters sometimes invited guests to join them. Jane always cooked a large Sunday-afternoon dinner, and she and her sisters liked to share their table with friends.

"I invited Cyril Overstreet, and Lloyd promised to pick him up," Alice said. "He looked a bit frail today. I'm afraid he's been sick. He missed church last week, you know. It's hard to see him getting frail. He has always seemed so healthy. Of course, he must be in his late eighties by now. I remember Father and him playing chess every Thursday afternoon."

"I used to think Cyril was older than Father," Jane said. "I remember thinking he was ancient when I was a teenager."

"What about the Kirkwoods?" she asked, referring to their other inn guests.

"They're touring the countryside today, so they won't be back until evening," Louise said, taking out another plate for Cyril. "The Kirkwoods are staying tonight, though, so plan on them for breakfast."

"Right." Jane opened the oven and basted the ham with a rich, thick glaze.

"That smells wonderful," Alice said.

"Thank you. Would you open a jar of cranberry chutney, please?" Jane asked.

"Glad to." Alice went into the pantry and returned with a jar of Jane's home-canned chutney. She opened the jar and scooped the contents into a glass bowl.

The kitchen door opened. "Yoo-hoo," Ethel Buckley called as she made a grand entrance, removing the russet-colored jacket that almost matched her hair.

"Hi, Auntie. Where are Lloyd and Cyril?" Louise asked, accepting her aunt's jacket.

"They'll be along soon. I told Lloyd I'd come ahead and see if you girls need help." Their father's younger half sister, a widow, lived in the carriage house behind the inn. Lloyd Tynan, the town's mayor, was her special friend.

"We're ready," Jane said. "We can eat as soon as the guests arrive."

"In that case, I'll go to the living room and wait to greet your guests. I do miss entertaining. When Bob was alive, we always had a crowd for Sunday dinner," she said, sailing through the doorway into the hall.

"I remember Sunday dinners at Aunt Ethel's house," Jane said. "Even out on the farm, she always decorated the table and used formal place settings. She was quite the hostess. I loved her fried chicken, although watching Uncle Bob clean a freshly butchered bird from the chicken house nearly turned me against poultry for good."

Alice laughed "Fortunately, you overcame that aversion. You've even improved on Aunt Ethel's fried chicken. In fact, now you've got my mouth watering. We haven't had that dish for some time."

"Maybe I'll make some this week," Jane said. At the sound of voices in the front hall, Jane pulled out the ham from the oven and set it on a carving board.

Louise and Alice went to greet their guests and then returned to carry the bowls of hot food to the table.

Garrett Yeager stood next to Rev. Kenneth Thompson at the dining-room table. Ethel was trying to convince Cyril to take a seat, but he stood with his hands folded together, waiting for his hostesses. Ethel took a place between Lloyd and Cyril.

Louise and Alice set their dishes on trivets, then sat at either end of the table as Jane came in carrying a platter of sliced ham.

"I do hope we will be able to feast in heaven," Cyril said, sniffing appreciatively.

"I do believe we will," Rev. Thompson said. "Although out-shining your cooking will not be easy," he added, smiling at Jane.

"Ah, but with God, all things are possible," Lloyd chimed in.

"Yes indeed. The Bible says so in Mark 10:27," Cyril agreed.

"Oh my. Please forgive our banter, Garrett," Louise said to their guest. "I'm sure you must think we are quite irreverent."

Garrett's eyes twinkled as he laughed. "Not at all. After all, God is the creator of humor."

"I quite agree. Pastor Ken, would you ask a blessing on this meal?" Alice asked.

They bowed their heads and gave thanks, then Jane passed the meat platter.

As they ate, they discussed a wide variety of topics, and toward the end of the meal, Garrett answered questions about his business. "I'm installing a satellite system for a trucking company in

Riverton, so they can manage and communicate with their fleet of tractor-trailer rigs," he explained. "My company is erecting a transmission tower tomorrow." Turning toward Lloyd, he said, "Acorn Hill could use a tower. I'd be happy to put together a bid for you, if you'd like."

"We're just a small town," Lloyd said. "I don't see the need for such high tech right now. Perhaps someday in the future."

Garrett nodded. "Sure. I'll leave my card with you, just in case." He took out a business card, which he handed to Lloyd. Then he placed his napkin on the table and stood.

"If you'll excuse me, I must get to work. Thank you for the wonderful dinner and the conversation. I enjoyed meeting you. I do get tired of my own company."

"We have dessert," Jane said. "I'm ready to serve it if you'd like some gingerbread with lemon sauce and whipped cream."

"Oh, no thank you." Garrett patted his stomach. "It sounds delicious, but I've overindulged this week at the Coffee Shop. I'm afraid I need to take a walk instead of eating dessert. In fact, I believe I will do just that. Otherwise, I might fall asleep at my computer."

"Nothing like a good Sunday-afternoon nap," Cyril said. "And I don't need to go to work, so I'll have some of that dessert, Jane. Then Lloyd can take me home, and I'll sit in my recliner and have that nap."

Lloyd laughed. "A man after my own heart," he said. "I believe I'll follow suit."

"Sleeping on a full stomach isn't good for you," Ethel piped up. "All that cholesterol just sits there and coagulates in your veins."

"All right, my dear. I'll take a little walk, then watch the football game. That will keep my blood pumping."

"I'll be happy to keep you company," Ethel said.

Lloyd graciously accepted Ethel's offer.

"What are you doing this afternoon?" Ethel asked, turning to Rev. Thompson and the sisters.

"I have some visits to make," the pastor said.

"A nap sounds appealing," Alice said.

"I believe I'll look through my music library for some suitable music for the camp I'm attending with Cynthia. I haven't played folk music since I was a student, but I should have some pieces I can practice to get into the mood. I don't want to go unprepared. How about you, Jane?"

"I plan to sort through my recipe books this afternoon. I want to do some experimenting."

"I hope you're not planning something too exotic," Louise said. "I love most of your creations, but sometimes..."

Jane laughed. "I'll try to control myself."

Chapter Three

Sunday afternoon, Jane stared at the computer screen in disbelief. The search engine listed 2,830,000 entries for children's cookbooks, only a fraction of the 19,700,000 general listings for cookbooks.

Jane's enthusiasm plummeted as she scrolled down the first few pages of entries. What could she offer in a cookbook that hadn't been done dozens of times? Most of the cookbooks seemed to specialize in one type of food, like snacks or desserts. To stand out from the rest, she would have to come up with something unique.

Jane went into the kitchen and sat at the table, twiddling her pencil against her cheek as she considered her extensive library of original recipes. As a professional chef, she carefully recorded her experiments, triumphs and failures.

As she thought about possibilities, Jane doodled on the light-green steno pad in front of her. A sketch took shape of a bouncy teenager in black and white saddle oxfords, a poodle skirt and an apron. The girl leaned over an open oven, removing a fully frosted and decorated layer cake. Too bad making a cake wasn't that simple. Cooking took work and concentration, but Jane loved it. Creating a beautiful cake gave her great satisfaction, especially when smiles blossomed on the faces of those who ate it.

Beneath the girl, Jane wrote, "Cooking is fun and fulfilling." She laughed and shook her head, sending her ponytail bobbing. Her sketch looked like something from the fifties, and the words were neither catchy nor title material, but at least she had a theme.

Alice came into the kitchen and filled the kettle with water. "Would you like a cup of tea?" she asked.

"No thanks."

While the water heated, Alice came to peer over Jane's shoulder.

"Cute picture. Even your scribbles are good, Jane. It's not fair that you and Louise got all the artistic talent in the family," she said, smiling. Jane knew Alice was not envious of her art or Louise's music. Alice bragged about her sisters and didn't have a jealous or unkind bone in her body.

"I don't know how you can say you're not talented. You've taught the ANGELs every imaginable craft."

Alice chuckled. "Yes, but I don't have to be good at that to teach it. I just read the directions and let them do the creating. The ANGELs are talented young ladies."

"You can claim some credit for that," Jane declared. Alice led the girls on Wednesday nights while the adults were at prayer meetings. In addition to their Bible lessons and crafts, the girls were involved in many charitable projects. They enjoyed helping others in Acorn Hill and had great fun keeping their good works secret, just as their name, ANGELs, was a hidden acronym that only they and Alice knew.

The tea kettle whistled. Alice poured boiling water into her tea cup and carried it to the table. "So what are you working on?"

She sat down and dunked her tea bag up and down several times, then set it on the saucer.

"I was just thinking about how I could inspire young girls to learn to cook."

"Really? Are you thinking of starting a cooking school?"

"Dear me, no!" Jane said, imagining a swarm of little girls climbing all over her kitchen. She shuddered, picturing white frosting smeared on her paprika-colored cabinets, and red gelatin all over the black and white checkerboard floor. She frowned. "I would love to interest young girls in cooking, though."

"How young?" Alice asked.

"I don't know. Younger than the ANGELs, I think. Young enough that they would need help from their parents, to encourage family time together in the kitchen."

"There are several young girls at church. I'm sure their mothers would love your giving them a cooking lesson."

Jane gently tapped the pencil against her chin for a moment before she looked at Alice. "I might do that. Thanks, Alice," she said, flipping the notebook shut. She rose and gathered up her pile of recipes and carried them to the shelf where she kept her volumes of recipe books and notes.

"Glad to help," Alice said, peering at her quizzically over the rim of her teacup.

A cooking school, indeed, Jane thought. She would have to be crazy to attempt something like that, but she did need some practical experience, some research for her cookbook.

"Maybe I'll join you for that cup of tea after all," she said, turning on the flame under the kettle. "Would you like a lemon poppy seed muffin?"

"That would be nice," Alice said. "I'll need another cup of tea to accompany it."

"Uh-huh," Jane said, nodding. Alice's response barely registered as Jane surveyed her kitchen, thinking about what she could teach the little girls to prepare that would make the least mess.

Just before noon Monday, Alice heard the vacuum cleaner shut off as she carried a load of neatly folded towels up the stairs to the second-floor guest rooms. Jane came down the hall from the closet.

"I'm finished. I think Louise is done too. How about some lunch?"

"Let's treat ourselves to the Coffee Shop for lunch. I think this is June's day to make stuffed pork chops."

June Carter owned the local restaurant, where she produced delicious home-style meals. "Good idea." Jane looked down at her baggy sweatpants. "I'll go change."

"And I'll put these in the bathrooms."

Jane went up the stairs to her third-floor bedroom, while Alice went through the Sunset Room to the bathroom. After she arranged the towel sets, she went through the Garden Room to the bathroom and hung fresh towels there. Louise was smoothing the bedspread and fluffing the pillows on the rosewood bed.

"Is this room booked tonight?" Alice asked Louise.

"No, not until Wednesday, but I wanted to have it ready." Louise stood straight and stretched. "I'm finished."

"Good. Jane and I thought a Coffee Shop lunch would be a treat. Does that appeal to you?"

"Sounds lovely. I'll meet you downstairs in five minutes."

Louise was waiting by the front door, holding her navy wool jacket, when Alice and Jane came downstairs.

The sun was shining and a slight breeze swirled fallen leaves in front of their feet as they walked down the hill to town.

Cheerful voices greeted the sisters as they entered the restaurant and made their way to a booth near the back. Hope Collins hurried over with a water pitcher and filled their glasses.

"Hey, Jane, Louise, Alice, it's good to see you." She smiled warmly as she handed them menus, then laid out silverware and napkins.

"Good crowd in here today," Jane said, looking around. "We're lucky we got a table."

Hope glanced around. "You should have seen it earlier. I think everyone in town knows that today is pork-chop day."

"That's what I want," Alice said.

"Me too," Jane said.

Louise ordered the meat loaf.

"I'll check and make sure we still have pork chops," Hope said. She stopped to leave a bill at a table, then hurried to the kitchen.

Two groups stood to leave, opening up the center of the room. Alice nodded at a table across the room. "Garrett Yeager looks like he's set up his office here," Alice said.

Jane and Louise followed her gaze. He sat in a booth with

his laptop computer open on the table. He was talking on his cell phone. Hope went over and refilled his coffee cup. He looked up and smiled and said something to her. Hope smiled back at him, then came over to their table.

"You're in luck. We have two pork chops left."

"Great, thanks," Jane said.

Hope went to wait on someone else, and Alice turned to her sisters. "What do you think about doing the scrapbooking retreat? I need to get back to Penny with our decision."

"I say let's do it," Jane said.

Louise looked at Jane, then at Alice. "You do realize the earliest weekend we have open is the weekend I'm gone with Cynthia."

"Yes, and I'm sorry you'll miss the scrapbooking. It should be a fun group," Alice said.

Louise smiled in response. "I'll survive. You know that I'm not much interested in crafts, and I already have my photos in albums."

"Yes, you are amazingly organized," Jane said.

Hope came over carrying two pots of coffee. She offered some to Jane.

"Yes, please. Thanks, Hope." Jane turned to Alice. "I'll probably not do an album. Cooking will keep me busy."

"Too busy, perhaps," Louise said. "You will need extra help."

"I don't think so," Jane said. "I talked to Pauline Sherman about this. She's been to several scrapbooking events in Potterston and Lancaster. On her advice, I plan to feed the attendees snacks and finger foods. I might even resort to paper plates. They want to work and spend time together, not eat."

Hope finished filling Jane's cup and reached for Louise's cup.

"We've never used paper plates for our guests," Louise said. "I'll have the decaf," she told Hope. "Thank you."

"We've never hosted an event like this either," Alice inserted gently. "I'll be there to help, and we can ask Penny to help. We'll be fine."

"If you need help with something, I'll be glad to pitch in," Hope said.

"Thanks for offering, Hope. We're having a scrapbooking weekend at the inn."

"Really? When? If I'm off, I'd be glad to help."

"Three weeks from now," Jane said. "That is, if we decide to do it." She looked at Louise.

"If you want to host this craft event, then of course you have my blessing," Louise said.

"Good. I'll tell Penny this afternoon. And we'd love to have you come join the fun, Hope," Alice said.

"I don't know. I never take photos, but I'll be happy to help you," she said, moving on. She offered coffee to the next table, but they declined and stood to leave.

By the time Hope brought the sisters their lunches, the restaurant was empty except for Garrett, who kept typing away on his laptop.

"Must be nice to have a portable office," Jane said.

"Why would you want a portable office?" Alice asked.

"Oh, not for me, but for someone like Garrett. He has the freedom to take his work anywhere."

Louise looked over at their guest. "He looks isolated to me. I can't imagine living that way. I wonder if he has family."

"He doesn't wear a wedding ring," Alice said. "I'd guess not."

Hope came over and picked up their empty plates. "How about dessert today? June made carrot cake."

"That sounds good. Bring us one piece and we'll split it," Jane said.

"In that case, I'll have a cup of tea," Alice said. Louise and Jane asked for refills.

While Hope went back to get their dessert, June came out with a piece of cake for Garrett. They talked for a moment, then June went back into the kitchen. Hope brought their cake with two extra plates and the tea.

"I'm going to take my lunch break now. Can I get anything else for you?"

"No thanks. Enjoy your lunch."

Hope disappeared into the kitchen, then carried a plate out and sat down across from Garrett. They were soon deep in conversation. Hope's laughter rang out, echoed by a low chuckle.

"I would assume that answers the question about his single status," Jane said. "I've never seen Hope get chummy with a stranger before."

"*Hmm.* Interesting," Louise said. "It's nice to hear Hope laughing, though it's a shame he isn't a local boy. He'll be leaving as soon as his job is finished."

"He's hardly a boy," Alice said with a laugh. "He must be close to Jane's age." Jane gave Alice a thanks-a-lot look, but Alice just continued. "I mean that Hope is a grown woman. She can take care of herself."

Chapter Four

I called Mary Jo Barton, the woman who gives the scrapbooking classes, and she confirmed that she can do the scrapbook weekend when you suggested," Penny Holwell said excitedly to Alice on the phone Monday afternoon. "Maybe we can make it an annual event."

"That would be nice, but first let's see how this year goes," Alice said. She didn't want to dampen Penny's spirits, but she found it hard to believe that women would enjoy an entire weekend pasting photos in a scrapbook.

"This'll be great, you'll see. Thanks, Alice."

After she hung up, Alice put on her green and yellow bulky-knit sweater.

"I'm going walking with Vera," she told Jane as she headed out the front door. She stood on the porch, stretching tall, taking in a deep breath and holding it for a moment before she let it out and took another deep breath. The whir of a leaf blower sounded nearby. The crisp air smelled of damp, decomposing leaves and of Jane's asters that bloomed profusely by the porch steps. Alice stretched, then descended the steps and walked briskly down the hill toward Vera Humbert's house.

Vera was waiting for Alice and fell into step beside her.

"I sure am glad the weather's holding for our walks. After a day in the classroom, I really need the fresh air and exercise," Vera said, matching Alice's rapid pace.

"I need it too. Wouldn't it be wonderful if the weather would stay mild, so we can walk all winter."

"I wish, but Fred's predicting a cold snap in the next week or so, and you know he's usually right. Moving to a more interesting topic, I heard you're holding a scrapbook retreat at the inn."

Alice glanced in astonishment at Vera. "How did you hear that? We just decided today at lunch."

Vera grinned. "Penny told me when she picked up Bart from school. She's so excited. It sounds like fun. I'd like to come."

"Good. I'll be glad to see you there."

"Are you going to make a scrapbook?" Vera asked.

"I don't think so. I'll be busy waiting on the guests."

"You won't be busy all the time. You should make one and keep me company."

"I don't have many photos, but I'll think about it."

Patsy Ley waved at them from her car as she drove up the street toward the rectory. As wife of Grace Chapel's assistant pastor, Henry Ley, Patsy was active in the church and community and was good friends with the Howard sisters. She stopped her car and rolled down her window. "Hi, Alice. Vera. I just heard you're having a scrapbooking retreat at the inn. I want to come. How do I sign up?"

Alice shrugged her shoulders and held up her hands. "I don't know. I think Penny Holwell is going to handle reservations. I'll tell her you're interested."

"Thanks." Patsy waved and proceeded up the street.

"My, my, word travels fast," Alice said, watching Patsy drive away. "Perhaps there's more interest in scrapbooking than I realized."

Vera laughed. "Scrapbooking is big right now. You'd better figure out how many people you can accommodate, because I predict you'll have to turn people away."

"Really? I never dreamed that the idea would be so popular. I better warn Jane. Perhaps we shouldn't tell Louise, though. She will be away that weekend, and she's already worrying that we'll be shorthanded."

"I'll be glad to help you serve meals or clean up. Lots of the ladies would be glad to pitch in."

"Thanks. We may need some help." Alice began to wonder if they were biting off more than they could chew. It was too late, though. They had committed to the event, and apparently, Penny was making sure everyone in town knew about it.

Tuesday morning after breakfast, Jane spread her jewelry-making tools and materials out on the kitchen table. Her jewelry making had become a lucrative hobby. Nellie Carter, who owned the local dress shop, carried Jane's creations locally and wanted to market the jewelry through her New York connections, but Jane didn't want the enterprise to take over her life. While she enjoyed creating beautiful things, Jane felt her purpose lay in running Grace Chapel Inn with her sisters, and she wanted to keep that focus.

"Well, I'm off to the hospital," Alice said, coming through the doorway from the hall. She was dressed in a white nursing pantsuit and carried a jacket. "It looks warm outside, but Vera told me that Fred is predicting a cold front soon."

"Then it's a sure thing," Jane said.

"I see you're going to be busy today."

"Yes. Nellie told me she's running low at the dress shop. I need to get a jump on the winter season if I can. If I wait until after the scrapbook retreat, it's almost too late."

"Why do you have your pasta press out? Are you making pasta too?"

"No. This isn't my kitchen pasta press. I have this other one to press the polymer clay for my beads and pendants. I also have special baking sheets and graters for jewelry."

"Oh." Alice shook her head. "I don't know how you come up with such clever ideas."

Jane laughed. "Alice, you always make me feel so good."

The phone rang, and Alice answered it. "Grace Chapel Inn. Alice speaking."

"Hi, Alice, this is Penny. I'd like to talk about the scrapbook weekend and make some arrangements."

"Hi, Penny. I'm just on my way out the door to work, but you probably should talk to Jane anyway. Just a moment." Alice handed the phone to Jane. "I'll see you later."

Jane took the phone as Alice went out the back door.

"Good morning, Penny. What can I do for you?"

"I wanted to touch base with you about the scrapbooking

retreat. I called Mary Jo, and she wants to stop in to see the inn, if that's okay."

"Sure. When does she want to come?"

"Today. This afternoon. Is that convenient for you?"

"Yes, it is. I'll be here."

"Great. I'll meet her there so we can talk about preparations. See you about one o'clock."

Jane said good-bye and hung up. It was nine thirty. That gave her about three hours to work on her jewelry and tidy up. Alice had gone to work, and Louise often fended for herself at lunchtime, so Jane didn't need to stop to prepare a meal. She'd hoped for the whole day, but she'd make the most of the time she had. She sat at the table, staring at the materials spread out before her. A vague idea formed in her head. When she'd stopped in at Nellie's, she was enchanted by a line of ruffled, sequined and rhinestone-studded clothing. Nellie called it *bling-bling*. Even the denim jeans were decorated with sparkles. Jane knew the ornate style had been growing over several years, and it seemed to have survived the fad stage and become a fashion standard. She loved the fun, feminine styles and decided to incorporate bling in her jewelry.

Jane fed several different shades of blue and violet polymer clay through the pasta press to make thin, wide noodles of clay. She cut and layered the different colors with sheets of gold leaf, alternating the two and pressing them together until she had a thick block of clay, which she grated into fine shavings with the cheese grater. She grated a block of translucent clay and mixed the shavings together, forming a new block, rolling and pressing it into a tight log. She was concentrating so hard, she barely heard Louise enter the kitchen.

"You've made some creative pasta dishes before, Jane, but blue noodles?" Louise peered over Jane's shoulder. "How ever will you cook those? I hate to say this, but it doesn't look very... appetizing."

"I could string you along and have you dreading dinner, but these aren't edible. This is jewelry clay. I'll just pinch off a bit and roll it through the pasta maker again," she said, feeding a wad through the machine, "and voilà!" She pulled out a flat piece of clay like a lasagna noodle and carefully laid it on a board on the table.

"It looks marbled. Very pretty. What are you making?"

"Shapes to hang on a necklace." She used a sharp blade to cut several ovals, then she punched round holes in the middle of each one. "I could use cookie cutters for even shapes, but I want something a little less structured. This doesn't look like much now, but it will bake up beautifully."

"I see shiny gold highlights in it."

"I used gold leaf. I'll make a whole tray of these, and then I'll bake them."

"That reminds me of the flour and salt clay Cynthia and I made into Christmas ornaments one year."

"Yes, it's a bit like that, only more delicate." She cut out a leaf shape freehand. "Penny called earlier. The scrapbook lady is coming here this afternoon to see the inn."

"I hope she comes before my piano students arrive."

"She'll be here at one. Penny's joining her."

"I'll be happy to show them around if you want to keep working," Louise offered.

Jane glanced at the work she had spread out over the table. "Thanks. I'll need to talk to her about meals. Perhaps I could leave this here and we can talk in the living room. Maybe we'll eat dinner in the dining room tonight for a change."

"Would you like me to fix dinner?"

"I thought I'd fix something simple, like pasta and Alfredo sauce," Jane said. "That won't take long, and I have yummy chicken and artichoke sausages to serve with it."

"As long as the pasta isn't blue..."

"Actually, it's going to be green."

Chapter Five

I don't know where Mary Jo is," Penny said, looking out the living room window of the inn Tuesday afternoon. "She said she'd be here at one o'clock, and it's now twenty after."

"I'm sure she'll be here soon," Jane said, not at all sure, since she did not know the scrapbooking lady. "Have you been to a scrapbook weekend?"

"No, but my cousin goes to one every year. She's asked me to go with her, but I'd have to drive up to Connecticut. I just haven't been able to take the time. That's why I'm so excited to have one here in Acorn Hill. Oh, she's here. She...has her children with her."

Jane looked out the window. A heavyset young woman was getting several children out of her minivan. She lifted out a little girl who appeared to be about five. The girl stood primly near the van, while two little boys, who looked a bit older than the girl, climbed out and began jumping up and down beside her. One boy pushed the other and he tumbled and rolled. Laughing, the culprit pounced on the one on the ground and they began rolling around. The mother turned to them and said something, but they ignored her. The little girl went over and began to tug on the boys. The woman pulled out an infant carrier and a large bag and shut the van door. Turning to the boys, she barked out, "Timmy! Jimmy! Stop this instant."

The boys slowly untangled and stood. Jane could see their petulant expressions, and the dry leaves and grass covering their T-shirts, jeans and even their hair.

"Oh dear," Penny said. "She told me she was leaving the children at day care."

The mother was attempting to brush off the leaves and dirt from her sons just as Louise came into the living room. She came over to the window and regarded the scene outside.

"Perhaps the children would like to play outside in the garden," she said.

Jane pictured the large mound of leaves she'd spent hours raking into a pile. A whirlwind couldn't wreak more havoc on the pile than these two little boys. She glanced toward the garden, then looked at Louise, resigned to the demolition of her work.

Louise gave her a sympathetic smile. "Remember when Father would rake the leaves and you would delight in jumping in the pile?" Louise said. "I can still remember your squeals of happiness."

Jane sighed. "You're right. In fact, I had an urge to jump in the leaves myself yesterday after I raked them." Jumping in leaves had been a favorite activity each fall. Her father raked the same leaves a dozen times for her and never once complained. "Let's put the children in the sunroom first, and I'll give them milk and cookies. Then they can go outside." Jane went to the front door to greet their guests.

Mary Jo answered Jane's greeting with a harried, apologetic smile. "Hi. I'm afraid the twins are too dirty to come inside. Perhaps we can talk out here on the porch?" She tugged on one of the boy's sleeves when he started to dash away. He stopped.

Jane stepped out on the porch. "Why don't you come with me? We have the perfect place for the children."

"A large padded room?" Mary Jo quipped. Jane suspected she was only half-joking.

"A sunny room." Jane led them around the side of the house and into the sunroom. The enclosed, windowed room with inviting wicker furniture and a profusion of potted plants brought a smile to Mary Jo's face.

"This is wonderful!" she exclaimed.

The twins spotted Wendell, the inn's large gray and black tabby, napping on a bright, floral chair cushion and ran to pet him, dropping and sliding on their knees on the floor without wincing. Wendell opened one eye, then slowly rolled onto his back to let the boys pet him. One of the boys scooped up the cat into his arms. Wendell dangled precariously but didn't protest.

"Timmy, put the cat down...carefully," Mary Jo commanded.

"Aw, Mom, I won't hurt him."

"Yeah, he won't hurt him," his twin echoed, grabbing for the cat.

Mary Jo set the baby carrier on the floor and pounced on her boys. "You will not fight over this poor cat. Timmy, you sit right there," she said, pointing to a chair. "Jimmy, you sit there," she said, pointing to a chair on the opposite side of the room. The girl, who wore a red sweater, a black and white checked skirt and white tights, sat in a chair at the wicker table, folded her arms and looked at the boys with a smug, superior look.

At the sound of her mother's stern voice, the baby started from sleep and let out a wail. Mary Jo sighed and picked up the baby, who ceased crying immediately.

"I'm so sorry," the young mother said. "I should have called and canceled when the day care stopped me at the door. They've had an outbreak of chicken pox. I don't need that right now."

Louise and Penny came through from the parlor carrying a tray of cookies, paper cups and a pitcher of milk, which they set on the table. The boys started to get up from their chairs, looked at their mother and sat back down.

Mary Jo pulled disposable wipes out of her large bag. "Here boys, wipe your hands before you touch anything, and behave yourselves." She gave each of the boys a warning look. They power walked to the table where their sister sat, each heading for the same chair.

"Jimmy, why don't you sit over here?" Jane said, not sure which child was Jimmy, but hoping one would take her suggestion and avoid a fight. The boys looked identical, though one wore a blue T-shirt and one wore a green T-shirt. The boy in green scooted into the chair and gave her a wide smile, showing the space where he'd lost a front tooth.

Louise put two cookies on a napkin in front of each child, and Penny poured a glass of milk for each of them. Straightening up to her full, piano-teacher height, Louise looked at each child.

"When your milk is gone and you've eaten your cookies, you may go outside in the backyard to play. Do *not* climb the fence."

Timmy's shoulders sagged. "Aw."

"Tell the ladies thank you," Mary Jo instructed her children.

The little girl smiled sweetly and said, "Thank you." The boys mumbled the same with their mouths full of cookies. Timmy took a swig of milk, dribbling it down his chin. He wiped his mouth with his shirt. Mary Jo groaned and shook her head.

"Come into the parlor," Louise invited her. "We can talk in there and you can still see the children."

"Thank you." She picked up the baby carrier and carried it inside. She glanced a bit nervously at the antique Eastlake chairs but took a seat, perching so her baby couldn't drool on the upholstery.

"My sister-in-law will watch the kids for the cropping weekend," she said. "She has a teenage son who helps her."

"That's good," Louise said. "They have a lot of energy, don't they?"

Mary Jo laughed. "That's an understatement."

"Cropping weekend?" Jane asked.

"That's what we call a scrapbook event," Mary Jo explained. "My invitations invite people to 'crop till you drop.' We spend much of the time cropping pictures for the scrapbook. I teach various cropping techniques."

"Ah." Jane nodded. "Would you like a cup of tea?"

"Oh, no thanks. I wanted to see your facilities and make sure there is room for the attendees to work. Have you ever been to a scrapbooking weekend?" she asked Jane and Louise.

"No, but we put on events here all the time," Jane said.

"I won't be here," Louise said. "Jane and Alice, our other sister, will be here to prepare meals. Is there anything else they must do?"

"We'll need tables set up as work areas, and I will have a display of materials that I use to demonstrate the techniques. I bring along merchandise that the ladies can purchase, or they can bring their own supplies."

"Would you like to see the other first-floor rooms?" Louise offered.

"You go ahead with the tour, and I'll take the children outside," Jane offered. "I'll be back in a moment."

Mary Jo and Penny followed Louise into the hallway, and Jane went out to the sunroom.

"Are you finished?"

"Yeah, can I have more cookies?" Timmy asked.

"It isn't polite to beg for food," the little girl admonished her brother, who glared at her.

"We don't want to spoil your dinner," Jane said.

"We won't," Jimmy said.

Timmy spotted Wendell's soft yellow and red ball. He dashed over, picked it up and threw it at his brother. "Come on, let's play ball," he said.

Jimmy grabbed the ball and raced outside with Timmy on his heels.

"Shall we join them?" Jane invited the little girl. "What is your name?"

"My daddy calls me Princess. You may call me Princess too."

"All right, Princess. Let's go see what your brothers are doing." Jane held out her hand, and the little girl stood, shook out her hair and daintily placed her hand in Jane's.

"If we must," she said.

The little girl's regal response caused Jane to laugh. They went out the door and found that the boys had already discovered the giant leaf pile. Jimmy was on top of it. From the little eruptions of leaves, it seemed Timmy was swimming through the middle of it.

"Boys, you shouldn't be doing that," Princess said in a stern voice that mimicked her mother.

"You can't tell me what to do," Jimmy said. Then he looked at Jane. "Can we play here?" he asked meekly.

Jane smiled. "Yes, you may play in the leaves. Perhaps you'd be kind enough to rake them back into the pile when you're finished. There are rakes by the shed."

A head burst through the leaves. "Yeah. Then we can knock 'em down again." He dived back under.

"Do you want to play in the leaves?" Jane asked Princess.

The little girl eyed the leaves, then her brothers. "No thank you," she said. "I'll just stay with you."

"Boys, promise you'll stay in the backyard?"

Both boys promised, so Jane took Princess around to the back porch and in through the kitchen door.

Princess went straight to the kitchen table, where Jane had her jewelry supplies spread out. The girl picked up a handful of the bright, shiny beads and silver and gold findings. "Oh, these are pretty!" she exclaimed.

Jane hurried to rescue her work. "Yes," she said, gently extricating the pieces from the child's hands. "Would you like to make a bracelet for yourself?"

Princess's eyes danced with delight as she looked up at Jane. "Oh, yes!" She clapped her hands gleefully and reached for a dish of pink beads. "I want pink. It's my very most *favoritist* color."

Jane rescued the dish. "First you need to wash your hands. Come over to the sink."

Jane scooted a stool up to the sink and helped Princess wash her hands, then set her at the table with a large blunt needle and nylon line to string the beads. While the child worked, Jane began gathering up her supplies and moving them to the counter. Just then, Louise, Penny and Mary Jo came through from the dining room.

"Oh dear. I hope Jasmine isn't bothering you," Mary Jo said, coming to the table.

"No. She's fine. She's making a bracelet," Jane said.

"See what I'm making, Mommy?" Jasmine said, holding up her string of beads proudly.

"It's beautiful, sweetheart. And your favorite color too." She turned to Jane. "Thank you so much. I'd better check on the boys. They can get into trouble faster than a speeding bullet."

Jane grinned. "I'll bet they can. Right now, I believe they're buried in a pile of leaves. Look out the window."

Mary Jo, Penny and Louise peered out the kitchen window.

"Oh no, they're making a mess of your yard!" Mary Jo said, moving toward the back door. "I'll make them clean it up."

"Wait. They're all right. I told them they could play there. I used to love jumping in the leaves when I was a child. They'll rake it back into a pile when they're finished," Jane said.

"Are you sure? I feel so bad that I've disrupted your day and brought chaos to your inn."

"The children are fine," Louise said. "Let's complete our business. This, of course, is the kitchen. Jane prepares the guest meals here, and we serve them in the dining room."

"If possible, we should reserve the dining-room table for scrapbooking for the entire weekend," Mary Jo said. "Besides that, we'll need enough tables for everyone to have at least three or four feet of workspace."

"I'll get folding tables," Penny said. "I believe that I can borrow some from the chapel."

"Good. It'd help if meals could be served cafeteria-style. The women will leave their scrapbooks and pictures at their places all weekend. Can they sit on chairs and couches to eat?"

"I can serve a buffet, but it is more comfortable to have tables to eat at," Jane said. "Perhaps we could set up card tables in the parlor and the sunroom during meals, plus a few folding trays. We can put a space heater in the sunroom if necessary."

Mary Jo nodded. "That would allow us to spread out with our albums and leave them out. We don't want to disturb them once we start. We'll need snacks between meals and coffee available all day long. Oh, and lots of desserts, especially chocolate."

"Do you have a set fee you charge for the weekend and the instruction?" Louise asked.

"Yes. I try to keep it at a minimum. It includes two classes, a few basics and door prizes," Mary Jo said. "I can provide you with brochures."

"I'll take care of advertising the weekend in Acorn Hill," Penny said.

"We'll figure out the cost of the food for local attendees and a weekend package for overnight guests," Louise said. "We only have three rooms available."

"I'll probably commute, so you will have more room for guests," Mary Jo said.

"I have a guest room if you'd like to stay with me," Penny said. "That way we can stay in the evening and be back for breakfast."

"Thank you. I'll check at home and see if my husband or my sister-in-law is willing to watch the children at night."

A heartrending cry sounded from the dining room.

"Oh dear, I left the baby sleeping in her carrier. I'd better round up my children and head for home. I barely have time to get dinner ready."

"Speaking of dinner, I'd better get busy myself," Jane said.

Louise was tossing a salad and Jane was preparing the rest of the meal when Alice arrived home from work. She carried in the mail and set it on the kitchen counter. "Here's a letter from Cynthia," she told Louise, handing her a thick envelope with the return address of her publisher on it. "Otherwise, it's just magazines and junk mail."

Jane picked up a kitchen catalog. "My catalogs aren't junk," she said.

Louise put the salad in the refrigerator and slipped on her reading glasses. She slit open the envelope with a kitchen knife and pulled out several pages of paper. Unfolding them, she read the contents.

"It's the schedule for the music camp and a picture of the ranch." She held up a color printout of a web page that showed a ranch house and barn surrounded by oak and pine trees. Other than a small patch of grass in front and a few flowering bushes against the lodge-style home, the yard seemed to be dirt. It made Louise think of a cowboy movie set—attractive but very rustic. "Here's another picture," she said, holding up a printout of a bright blue two-story house. Pink gingerbread decorated the eaves and the porch roof. The caption called it one of Northern California's finest painted ladies.

Looking over Louise's shoulder, Jane said, "I doubt that. San Francisco and Eureka have fabulous Victorian houses. But this is pretty."

"I can't say I care for the colors," Louise said. "They're so... bright."

Jane laughed. "That's the way they painted them. It looks as though you are going to rough it in luxury, Louie."

Chapter Six

*A*fter an early dinner, the sisters took a brisk walk down-town. Alice stopped at Time for Tea to buy some Earl Grey loose tea, then Jane picked up an order of raspberry and apricot Danish for breakfast from the Good Apple Bakery.

"Let's stop at the Coffee Shop for a warm-up," Alice suggested.

"Good idea," Jane said. "I should have brought my gloves."

Alice half-expected to find Garrett at the Coffee Shop, but he wasn't there. In fact, the restaurant was nearly deserted.

"Hi," Hope said when she came to take their order. "Getting chilly out, isn't it?"

"Sure is," Jane said. "Looks like the cold kept your custom-ers home."

Hope reached for the pencil behind her ear. "We had a rush earlier. Are you here for dinner?"

"No. Just something hot to drink," Alice said.

"I might want some dessert with my coffee," Jane said. "What did June make today?"

"She made a triple-layer coconut cake this afternoon. I had a piece. It's delicious," Hope said.

"I'll have a piece with a cup of coffee," Jane said. Louise and Alice ordered tea.

"I don't know how you keep your girlish figure," Louise said.

Jane laughed. "I intend to entice you to eat part of it," she said. "Hope, please bring two extra forks."

After Hope left to fill their orders, Alice asked, "Did the scrapbook lady come today? Are we still hosting the weekend?"

"She and Penny came. We'll have to do some rearranging to accommodate the crafters, but it can be done."

"That depends on how many ladies sign up," Louise said. "I'm still not convinced this is a good idea, but I suppose we're committed now."

"We'll get everyone in," Jane said. "I'm more concerned that Mary Jo has someone to take care of her children."

"Didn't she say her sister-in-law will take care of them?" Louise said.

"Yes, and I hope she's right. Can you see her bringing them along?" Jane shuddered in mock horror. She turned to Alice. "She brought all four of her children with her today. Her seven-year-old twin boys have the energy of a tornado."

"Oh my, is that what became of your leaf pile? I thought a strong wind had blown through the yard," Alice said.

Louise laughed. "It was a strong wind, all right."

"They tried to rake it back into a pile," Jane said. "They're good kids, just...active."

Hope came with their beverages. When she left, Louise said, "I don't know how Mary Jo gives scrapbook events and takes care of her family."

"To tell you the truth, I thought she looked a bit harried. Perhaps she needs the break scrapbooking gives her," Jane said.

"No doubt that's true," Louise agreed.

After Hope delivered the piece of cake, she pulled a chair over from an empty table, sat down and leaned forward.

"Tell me what you think of Garrett," she said in a low voice.

Alice glanced around, wondering why Hope was whispering. No one sat near them. In fact, the restaurant only had one other customer.

"He seems like a pleasant fellow," Louise said. "Why?"

"He asked me to go to the movies with him on my day off."

"Well, I can say that he's polite and agreeable and seems to be hardworking," Louise said. "Beyond that, we don't know much about him."

"Oh, I know all about him," Hope said. "He's told me his life history and about his family. He's a widower, you know."

"Really? I didn't know that. His wife must have died fairly young," Jane said.

"He seems lonely," Alice said.

"I like talking to him, but I'm not sure I should go out with him," Hope said. "After all, he's only here temporarily, you know."

"Perhaps he just enjoys your company and wants to be friends," Jane said.

Hope got up and pushed the chair over to the next table. "I like him a lot. I just don't want to get hurt."

The object of their conversation came through the front door. A broad smile appeared on his face when he saw Hope, leaving no doubt that he liked her a lot too. Then he spotted the sisters and came over to their table.

"Evening, ladies. How was your day?" His smile, though friendly, didn't have the warmth of the one he'd given Hope.

They exchanged pleasantries, and Garrett excused himself and went to a table across the room, the same table he'd occupied the last time they saw him at the restaurant. He took the chair facing the kitchen. His gaze followed Hope wherever she went. When she took him his coffee, she sat down across from him and talked for a few minutes before she took his order and returned to the kitchen.

"Well, well. Romance is in the air," Jane said, watching them. "How nice."

"Personally, I think Hope is right to be cautious," Alice said. "Maybe we should invite them both to Sunday dinner. You know, let them get to know each other better in neutral territory. Maybe I'll invite him to church too."

Late Wednesday morning, Louise sat at the piano, her fingers flying over the keys. Frowning, she stopped and began the run over again. She had the notes down, but the timing wasn't right. She was thankful that Alice had gone to work and Jane was bagging leaves, so they couldn't hear her practice.

She'd played much more challenging music than the "Bumble Bee Boogie." In fact, she'd played the original "Flight of the Bumblebee" by Rimsky-Korsakov in college and now taught it to her more advanced students, but the boogie had a different beat. She'd never cared for the style. As far as she was concerned, it lacked depth and form. Cynthia's music camp, however, encompassed the rhythm-and-blues style, and so she felt she should brush up on the genre. Ending the piece, Louise folded her hands in her lap and looked at the piano keys. Cynthia's letter held so much excitement and hope for this project. Louise wanted to make a success of the music camp for her daughter's sake, but she was a classical pianist, not a ragtime, boogie-woogie or country-western piano player.

Taking a deep breath and straightening her shoulders, Louise placed her hands on the keys and began again. This time, she slowed the tempo and counted carefully, playing the syncopated rhythm deliberately. She increased the tempo. Her left hand created the rumbling drone of the agitated hive while her right hand lightly tripped about like the frantic bee, darting to and fro, faster and faster. She could feel her adrenaline pumping. Yes, that was more like it. She might not play popular music often, but she could play anything that was written. With a flourish, she finished the score, then sat motionless, letting her heart rate return to normal.

"Wow!" Jane said, poking her head into the parlor. "You rock, Louie. That was awesome."

Louise laughed. "*Rock* and *awesome*? You sound like a teenager. I just hope I can give a creditable showing at this music camp. It means so much to Cynthia."

"You will. You haven't played anything quite so...upbeat in some time. You're going to wow them."

"I wish I had your confidence." Louise closed the music and set it aside.

"I was just going to have a cup of tea. Want to join me?"

"Yes. I'll be there in a minute." Louise stood and put the music away inside the piano bench. As she straightened the room, making it ready for after-school lessons, she thought about her students. Were any of them ready for something as intricate as the "Bumble Bee Boogie"? Perhaps a simplified version. Maybe she would find some fun, challenging pieces to bring back from the camp.

Jane once again had her jewelry production spread out on the kitchen table, so they carried a light lunch to the sunroom: thin sandwiches of Black Forest ham, scones, crème fraîche, lemon curd and tea.

"What a gorgeous day," Jane said. "I think Mary Jo's boys did me a favor. I could have stayed outside raking leaves all morning."

Louise chuckled. "Father used to say much the same thing about you when you destroyed his leaf piles. I love autumn. I almost hate to leave Acorn Hill this time of year, even though the leaves are nearly all gone."

"I think you'll be pleasantly surprised. Northern California has lovely fall seasons."

"I hope so. I'm wondering about what clothes to take along. The list Cynthia sent me calls for western wear. It suggests blue jeans and denim jackets for daytime. I don't have anything western in my wardrobe. I don't want to buy clothes that I'll never wear again."

"You can borrow my denim jacket. Since you're most comfortable in skirts and sweaters, take your normal clothes. You might need blouses for daytime. We'll check the forecast before you go. And the camp sounds casual, so you might leave your pearls behind."

Louise's hand went to her neck, to the pearls that she put on nearly every morning. The thought of leaving them behind unsettled Louise more than the concern over her clothes. Eliot had given her the pearls for their anniversary one year, and she'd worn them almost daily ever since. They had become her signature. "I don't see why I shouldn't wear my pearls. They're always proper. Perhaps I'll purchase a pair of casual slacks, though. I might wear them occasionally. I'll check at Nellie's."

"I have a pair of cowboy boots that should fit you. Want to try them on?"

Louise shuddered. "No, thank you. My shoes are fine."

Jane shrugged. "Suit yourself."

"The air is really getting nippy," Vera said, raising the collar of her turtleneck as she walked with Alice Thursday afternoon.

"Yes, I guess that should urge us to walk faster," Alice said, keeping in step with her friend. "Might be time to get out the winter gloves and hats, although I think we'll still have some warm days ahead."

"Fred thinks the warm weather will hang around for another week. After that, watch out, he says. He's been studying the almanac and weather patterns. He's predicting a hard winter. I'm mulching and wrapping my roses this weekend."

"Jane already started winterizing the garden," Alice said. They turned and started up Acorn Avenue past Sylvia's Buttons and the dry cleaners, walking briskly.

"I've been sorting through my photographs of the girls' high school years for the scrapbook retreat. I meant to do an album a long time ago, but I've procrastinated. What kind of scrapbook are you making?" Vera asked.

"I don't know. I've never taken many photos." Never having been married, Alice didn't have the kinds of photograph collections a mother would amass. "I suppose I could go through the old family pictures."

"Did you take pictures when you restored the house and turned it into an inn?"

"Jane has pictures. She put some on the inn website."

"What about old pictures of the house? You could do a history of the house and the family," Vera suggested.

"Oh yes! I like that idea. Don't tell Jane or Louise. Louise will be gone, and Jane will be busy with cooking, so she won't notice what I'm working on if I'm careful. I'll make it as a surprise."

They cut across to Chapel Road and began heading toward

the inn. "I'll have to make up an excuse to dig around in the basement and the attic for pictures," Alice said.

"Good luck."

They had reached the inn. Vera said good-bye and continued on. Alice entered through the back door. Jane was grating carrots for dinner.

"Need a hand?"

"I'm almost finished. How's Vera?"

"Fine."

"Is she coming to the scrapbook weekend?"

Alice gave Jane a startled look as if Jane had overheard their conversation. *Goodness,* Alice thought. *I already feel guilty about sneaking around gathering pictures, and I haven't even started yet.*

"Halloween falls on Wednesday this year. Are you planning something special for the ANGELs that night, Alice?" Jane asked as the three sisters cleaned up the dinner dishes.

"I should do something special for the girls, shouldn't I? Do you have an idea?"

"As a matter of fact, I do," Jane said.

"Of course you do," Louise said. "You always have an idea."

Alice laughed. "I'm open to suggestions," she said. "We only have a week, so nothing too elaborate."

"How about a little fall festival for the girls?" Jane suggested. "I could cook for them, and maybe the parents would provide candy for a piñata and apples for dunking."

"They could make individual piñatas to fill and take home," Alice said, catching the spirit of Jane's idea. "What kind of food do you have in mind? We don't have a budget for hot dogs and such."

"I've been experimenting with some new recipe ideas that I'd like to try out. I'll cook and foot the bill for the food. You take care of the rest."

"You are sweet. I'd better make myself a list of things to get." Alice finished drying the last pan, put it away and left the kitchen. Louise excused herself and went to the living room to read.

Gleefully, Jane dried her hands and took out her cookbooks. With a pad of paper, she began planning her fall festival menu. Hot dogs, of course, and macaroni and cheese. No, better yet, noodles that looked like worms. No, save that for a dessert idea—sweet noodles, er, worms, in chocolate dirt.

Chapter Seven

*F*riday evening, the front door opened and Louise heard voices in the hallway. Sitting on the couch in the living room, she looked up from her knitting. Garrett and Hope stood inside the front door talking. Garrett went upstairs. Hope watched him, then turned toward the living room and spotted Louise.

"Hi, Louise." She approached the doorway and saw Jane and Alice. "Hi," she said almost shyly. She looked lovely in trim gray wool slacks and a handsome, rose, cable-knit cashmere sweater. Her short hair was sleeked back, and she wore large free-form silver earrings.

"Good evening. Come in. I gather you're waiting for Garrett?" Louise said.

"Yes. We're going to the movies. He forgot his cell phone. He said he never goes anywhere without it. I can't imagine needing a phone all the time."

"I had one in San Francisco," Jane said. "I'm glad I don't need one here."

"Me too," Hope said.

"Come in and sit down while you're waiting," Louise invited.

"Oh, no thanks. Garrett said he'll be right back." She went over to see what Louise was making. "I've been wanting to take up knitting again," she said. "I used to make pot holders and socks, but I never tackled anything as complicated as a sweater. And speaking of crafts, Penny Holwell came in today. I heard her talking to a couple of ladies about your scrapbook weekend. They sounded excited about coming."

"Really?" Louise glanced at Jane, who just smiled. For the life of her, Louise couldn't understand why a bunch of women wanted to spend a weekend together, away from home, putting pictures in albums.

"Are you coming, Hope?" Jane asked.

"Oh no. I don't have any memories that I want to put in a scrapbook, but I'll help if I can."

"A scrapbook could be made up of things besides pictures, couldn't it?" Alice asked. "I have lots of memories but not many pictures. I saw a scrapbook filled with old Christmas cards in a museum once. It was beautiful."

Hope shifted as if she was uncomfortable and looked out the window. "I don't save cards," she said. Just then Garrett came down the stairs and into the room.

"There." He patted his side. The cell phone was clipped onto his belt. "Good evening, ladies. Are you ready, Hope?"

Hope said good-bye, and the couple went out. The car's interior lights came on when Garrett opened the door for Hope. A moment later, the car made a U-turn in the street and drove off down the hill.

"So Garrett is a gentleman," Jane observed.

"He held Ethel's chair at dinner last Sunday," Alice commented.

"That's admirable; however, he's a traveling man. Hope needs to find a nice, settled man," Louise said.

"They're going to the movies together, not committing to a relationship," Jane said. "Two nice, lonely people enjoying each other's company. Good for them."

"Hope needs to have some fun. She works hard and doesn't seem to have much of a social life," Alice said.

Louise held up one hand. "I agree. But she needs to guard her heart. That's what I mean."

Late Saturday morning, Jane added a quarter cup of sugar, a teaspoon of almond extract and several drops of yellow food coloring to the dough in a large stainless-steel bowl before she kneaded the dough into a smooth, elastic consistency. Using the pasta press reserved for food, Jane fed pieces of the dough through until she had an even sheet. She cut strips and rolled each one with her hands to form long, skinny worms, which she hung on dowels to dry. That task finished, she began cleaning out a large, barrel-shaped pumpkin that she'd brought in from the garden.

The sound of footsteps on the basement stairs startled Jane, and she spun to look at the basement door. It creaked open, and Alice stepped up into the kitchen.

"What—?" Jane hurried over to help Alice with the box she was carrying.

"I've got it," Alice said.

"I didn't know you were downstairs. When I heard your foot-steps you nearly scared me out of a year's growth—which might not be a bad thing if we're talking girth. What are you doing? What's in the box?"

"Sorry. I didn't mean to frighten you. I just remembered a box of old papers I wanted to look through. Probably nothing interesting, but you never know."

Alice clutched the box and made a beeline for the back stairs, which led to the second-floor staircase and their rooms on the third floor. Jane stood for a moment, listening to Alice's foot-steps. Alice rarely went to the basement. Jane wondered what was in the box that had attracted her sister's attention.

Garrett came to church with Hope Sunday morning. The pair scooted into a pew across from Jane and Alice just as Rev. Thomp-son asked the congregation to rise. Louise played the introduc-tion to the first hymn on the organ. On the second stanza, a rich, unfamiliar baritone voice sang out the bass part, clearly enunciat-ing the words as if he knew them by heart. Jane turned toward the singer, and then back to Alice, giving her a surprised look. Alice looked pleasantly surprised and went on singing the alto harmony, but she listened with appreciation to the pleasant male voice. She thought Garrett would make a great addition to the choir.

After the service, as the congregation filed out of church,

Alice caught up with Hope and Garrett, who were standing in the crowded aisle.

"Good morning," Alice said. "You have a wonderful voice, Garrett. Are you a member of a choir?"

"I was years ago. My wife and I belonged to our church choir before she passed away," he said.

"I'm sorry," Alice said. "I hope I didn't resurrect unhappy memories."

"Oh no. I just haven't attended church much the last few years, but singing the old hymns brings back fond memories."

"Well, it was nice hearing you sing them. Would you two like to join us for Sunday dinner? Jane always fixes enough for an army, and we eat early, so you'd still have the afternoon free."

Garrett looked at Hope, whose cheeks turned pink. She looked down, then up at Garrett. "If you'd like," she said. Alice hadn't ever seen Hope blush or at a loss for words. And Hope looked unusually attractive. When she smiled at Garrett, her brown eyes sparkled.

"We'd be glad to join you. Thanks," Garrett said. The crowd thinned, and Garrett stepped forward to shake hands with Rev. Thompson.

"Good sermon, Pastor."

"Thank you, Garrett. It's nice to see you again," Pastor Ken said. He greeted Hope, and then asked about Garrett's work. They spoke for a moment, then the couple moved on so that others could speak with the pastor.

While she waited for Louise and Jane, Alice watched Garrett

and Hope walk away together. Hope laughed at something Garrett said to her, and the pair seemed oblivious to people around them. Hope was always cheerful, but today she seemed younger and more carefree.

Jane and Louise joined Alice and looked in the direction of Alice's gaze. "Hope looks especially pretty today, don't you think?" Jane asked.

"Yes, she does. It's nice to see them attending church together, but in a few weeks he'll be gone," Louise said.

"Yes, but in those few weeks they can enjoy each other's company," Jane said.

"We'll enjoy their company this afternoon," Alice said. "I invited them to dinner."

"Then why are we standing here?" Jane asked. "We'd better get home so I can fix something for us to eat."

"As if you haven't already started something," Alice said, laughing.

"Well, yes, but now I need to dress it up a little."

"Everyone in town is talking about your scrapbook weekend," Ethel said, sitting ramrod straight in her chair at the inn's dining-room table. "Imagine how embarrassing it is for me that my own nieces neglected to tell me about it."

Next to her, Garrett held a platter of meat, waiting for her to take it.

"Ethel, please take some meat and then pass it," Lloyd said.

Ethel frowned at Lloyd, then took the platter from Garrett. "I'm sorry. Lloyd can be quite impatient," she said. Garrett nodded politely.

Taking a piece of pot roast, she passed the platter to Lloyd. "I had to hear about the weekend from Florence, of all people. I was mortified."

"I'm sorry, Aunt Ethel," Jane said. "We're still in the planning stages." There was nothing Ethel hated more than being upstaged, especially by Florence Simpson. The two ladies vied to be the queen of buzz when it came to the local social scene.

"Well, you'd better get on the ball. Someone has it planned," Ethel replied. "I saw a poster in the Nine Lives Bookstore window yesterday afternoon."

"Ethel, the potatoes, please," Lloyd said, eyeing the bowl Garrett was holding.

Ethel took the bowl and plopped a spoonful on her plate. "Is there something wrong with the potatoes?" she asked, looking at her plate, then at Jane.

"I mixed sweet and white potatoes," Jane said.

"And they look delicious," Hope said. "Penny came in and taped a poster in the Coffee Shop window yesterday. Nia Komonos and Carlene Moss were in having lunch. I heard her telling them about the scrapbook weekend."

"Did they say if they're coming?" Alice asked.

"I don't think so, but Penny was really talking it up."

"I'll be there," Ethel said. "I once made a beautiful scrapbook of my engagement to Bob. We had a lot of engagement parties, you know. We were quite popular."

"Would you like some coleslaw, Mrs. Buckley?" Garrett asked, holding another bowl for Ethel.

"No, thank you," she said.

"Well I would," Lloyd said. This time he reached across and took the bowl from Garrett. He glanced at Louise apologetically. She smiled and gave him a nod. Jane had to stifle a smile at Lloyd's annoyance. He was usually the soul of patience and indulgence with Ethel.

"I'm sorry you feel left out of the loop, Auntie," Alice said. "We wouldn't hurt your feelings for anything in the world. Thank you for letting us know. We had no idea Penny was already advertising the event."

"I do try to be helpful, you know. I'm happy to assist you when I can. Meanwhile, you'd better find out what Penny's advertising. You only have two weeks."

"Will you need my room for that weekend?" Garrett wanted to know.

"Oh no, your room is reserved for you. We don't know yet if anyone will book the other rooms. I do hope the ladies won't disturb your stay, though," Louise said.

"I'm sure they won't," he said. "What do ladies do at a scrapbook weekend?"

"They make decorative albums filled with photographs and mementos," Jane said.

"I'm afraid it might be a bit confusing around here," Louise said. "But most of the women will return to their homes at night, so your sleep won't be disrupted. You may want to take your breakfast in your room or in the kitchen."

"I could always go to the Coffee Shop," Garrett offered.

"No, don't do that. Everything will be fine," Jane reassured him.

After dinner, Jane served coffee in the living room. Lloyd had promised to put up a whatnot shelf for Ethel, so they left. Garrett sat next to Hope on the couch.

"I've saved pictures of my family on my computer," he said. "My mother turns ninety this year. I've been racking my brain trying to think of something unique to give her, but she has everything she needs. Do you suppose she would like a scrapbook?"

"I'm sure she would," Louise said.

"That's a great idea," Hope said. "I'll be glad to help you."

"Would you?" Garrett gave her a grateful smile. "That's wonderful. Thank you. Let me get my laptop, and I'll show you what I have, if you'll excuse me for a moment." He rose and went upstairs to his room.

"Now why did I offer to do that? I don't even like crafts," Hope said, shaking her head. "I suppose I'll have to attend the weekend after all." She sighed, then brightened. "It might be fun to see customers outside the Coffee Shop environment. That doesn't happen often."

"I suspect the scrapbooking will turn into one big party. You might as well join in," Jane said.

Hope grinned. "Yes, I might as well, but I'll also help you. I'll wash dishes or something."

"We're using paper plates and cups, but I appreciate your offer," Jane said. "I can holler if I need anything."

"Just be sure you do. I'm not very artistic. Maybe the scrapbook lady has some albums ready, where all we have to do is slip in the pictures."

"I hope you're right. I'm not artistic either," Alice said.

⌒

Garrett returned to the living room, carrying his computer. He sat next to Hope, opened his laptop and booted it up.

As the computer whirred to life, he pointed to the screen. "That's my son and daughter when they were little," he said. "I keep their picture on my desktop."

"Cute children," Hope commented, leaning close to Garrett so she could see the screen.

"Here's another one. We went camping that weekend." As Garrett brought up more pictures and explained them to Hope, Alice noticed the genuine interest in her eyes. Even as she exclaimed over Garrett's pictures and stories, however, Hope's brow crinkled when he told how his travels had caused him to miss a lot of his children's lives. Was Hope feeling sorry for him or for his children?

Alice knew a little about Hope's background. Her parents had moved often, uprooting their daughter from school and her friends. The moves had been the result of financial woes rather than opportunities for a better life. Hope had never known the security of a stable home. Now she hated to travel. She'd told

Alice once that she never belonged anywhere until she moved to Acorn Hill. Even in their small town she'd felt like a stranger until Alice's father made a point to befriend the young waitress. Hope had adored the elderly preacher who'd visit the Coffee Shop during the afternoon lull. He always invited Hope to join him while he ate. Soon after Daniel's death, Hope had joined Grace Chapel and attended the services regularly.

"That's all of them," Garrett said.

"You have a great family," Hope said. "No wonder you're proud of them."

Garrett turned off his computer. "I wish I had more pictures. I missed so much time with them as they grew up. If I'd only known..." He ran his fingers through his hair. "I don't know, maybe I'd have taken a different job that didn't require so much travel. I looked around once, but I couldn't find anything that paid as well or gave me the benefits. My wife did a good job of keeping things running smoothly at home, so I kept traveling."

Hope nodded, but she didn't comment.

"I'm sure your children appreciate your sacrifice," Alice said.

"Actually, they don't. My son is too busy to spend time with me, and my daughter...well, she sends me birthday cards, but we're not close."

"Wouldn't it be great if your daughter could help you make a scrapbook for her grandmother?" Alice suggested.

"Oh, I don't think that she'd have the time. She's newly married and trying to build a career. I wonder if she kept the pictures my wife took when the kids were growing up. Maybe I'll call her later."

"I'm sure she'd love to hear from you," Hope said. "It's been a lovely afternoon. I'm afraid I need to get home to get ready for another workweek."

"I'll put my computer away and give you a ride home," Garrett said. He closed the lid and went upstairs.

Hope got her coat. "Thank you for dinner. I love June's cooking, but this was a real treat," she said.

Chapter Eight

After Garrett and Hope left, Louise picked up her knitting and started a new row on the sleeve of a soft coral sweater that she was knitting for Cynthia. "I can't imagine how lonely I'd feel if Cynthia and I weren't close," she said.

Jane looked up from the newspaper she was reading. "You two have a special relationship. I always wished I'd known our mother, but with Father here every day and two older sisters to mother me, I never felt neglected."

Alice lowered the novel she was reading. "Not only did Father try to be both father and mother to us, but he was always there for the people at church. When I returned home from college, I realized how much the people depended on him to listen to their problems and give them advice and sympathy. But after Mother died, Father had no one on earth to lean on or to share his problems."

"Perhaps that's why he spent so much time reading his Bible and praying," Louise said.

"I always thought he was preparing his sermons," Jane said.

"Father worked on his sermons for days," Alice said, "but he drew his strength from the Word and talking with God. And he was so patient listening to people pour out their problems, sometimes for hours."

"Pastor Ken spends a great deal of time interacting with the church members and people in town," Jane said. "But he has no special confidante. Imagine how much he misses his wife. Whenever he speaks of her, you can tell she was his inspiration and support."

"As Eliot was for me," Louise said. "We sisters are fortunate to have one another."

"Amen to that," Jane said, making Alice and Louise chuckle.

Garrett came in the front door, letting a blast of cold air into the room, which stopped as the door shut.

"*Brrr.* Winter is nearly upon us," Jane said. "Looks like Fred's cold front has arrived."

Garrett appeared in the doorway. "Thank you for the wonderful dinner," he said. "Do you still have a room available for the weekend of your scrapbook event?"

"Your room is secure," Louise said.

Garrett nodded. "Yes. I mean an additional room. I called my daughter, and she wants to come and help me make a scrapbook for my mother."

"That's fabulous!" Jane said.

Louise set her knitting aside and stood. "You may have first pick of the rooms," she said. "Would you like to see them all?"

"Any room would be fine," Garrett said, but Louise went into the hall and started up the staircase, so he followed her.

"What an excellent turn of events," Alice said, watching them leave. "There's nothing like reminiscing over old pictures to stir up happy memories."

Alice sat on a cushion on the yellow, green and violet braided rug in the middle of her bedroom floor and looked at the piles of yellowed, faded photographs strewn around her. She picked up a picture of her parents at their wedding. Standing in front of Grace Chapel, her mother, Madeleine Berry Howard, looked like an angel in her white wedding gown, with her brown hair piled high upon her head and her voluminous veil flipped back. Her flashing smile, which Alice remembered so well, was aimed at her handsome young husband. Alice had forgotten how thin her father had once been. In his latter years, Daniel Howard had grown somewhat stout.

Alice uncovered a beautiful hand-colored picture of Madeleine as a teenager with her parents. She was standing in the living room of their Victorian home, in front of the fireplace. Her parents were seated on chairs in front of her, and Madeleine had a hand on each of her parents' shoulders. An ache tightened Alice's chest as she gazed at her mother's beautiful, youthful image and then at the photograph of her parents, beginning their lives together. Now their lives were together forever with the Lord they had loved and served so faithfully. That thought eased her ache, for Alice knew they were happy. Someday she would see them again and share that happiness forever.

What a legacy Madeleine and Daniel Howard had left their three daughters. Alice remembered her early childhood playing with Louise around the church while their father repaired something that needed attention. Then there were hushed times while he worked on his sermons or counseled someone. On those occasions, their mother would take them outdoors for a tea party or for a walk to town. Sometimes they helped their mother prepare a basket of goodies or a meal for someone who was sick or hurt or just needed encouragement. Seeing Madeleine and her daughters always seemed to bring joy and comfort to those they visited.

How fortunate she was that her parents had served the Lord. Of course, any album of their family history would have to include the purpose that drove Daniel Howard and his helpmate, who loved Grace Chapel and its members as much as her minister husband. Alice thought her mother's compassion had played a role in her own career choice to become a nurse.

"I can do that." Josie Gilmore tied an apron around her waist Wednesday after school. She shook her head, making her blond curls bounce in the loose ponytail she wore. She pushed up the sleeves of her long-sleeved T-shirt and washed her hands at the inn's soapstone kitchen sink.

Jane handed the eight-year-old a chunk of cheddar cheese and the grater. Jane had befriended Josie and her mother Justine, a young single mom, when they had moved to town. When Jane conceived the idea of putting together a cookbook with activities for mothers and their children, she'd immediately thought of Josie. If her methods worked with her young friend, she'd include them in the book.

Josie stood on tiptoe, reaching to get leverage on the cheese as she pushed it against the stainless-steel grater, creating a pile of shredded cheese.

Jane made a mental sketch of Josie's pose. It would make a perfect illustration for her cookbook. Jane filled a large pot with water and set it on the stove to boil. "Do you think some of your friends would like to learn to cook?" Jane asked.

"Oh yeah." Josie's cornflower-blue eyes lit up as she smiled. "Meghan and Bree would love it. And I could help you teach them, 'cause I know lots."

Jane smiled back at her young protégée, marveling at the uncomplicated confidence of youth. She hoped her little friend would keep her self-assurance as she grew older. Although she didn't know the girls well, Jane knew who Josie's friends were. She made a mental note to call the girls' mothers to see if they'd be interested in a cooking lesson for their daughters. That should give Jane the experience she needed to put her cookbook together.

"What are we making?" Josie asked.

"Macaroni and cheese," Jane said.

"Oh, yum. That's my favorite. Except for spaghetti and pizza. Mom doesn't make it this way, though. She cooks the macaroni and lets me mix the cheese in. Sometimes it doesn't mix very good."

"I'll teach you to make it a different way," Jane said. "Here's another kind of cheese to grate." She handed Josie a chunk of Monterey Jack cheese. "I'll grate the others so we'll get done faster."

While the macaroni boiled, Jane grated cheese: first a cup of Colby and then a cup of soft, white farmer's cheese.

"Okay, I'm done. What's next?" Josie asked, setting the grater in the sink.

"Now we make the sauce." Jane put a stool at the stove so Josie could reach to stir the liquid. She took out a large stainless-steel saucepan with a heavy bottom, measuring cups, a wire whisk and the ingredients.

Josie climbed up on the stool and picked up the whisk.

"You won't need that yet. First turn the heat on to medium and put a stick of butter in to melt. When it's melted, you add one half cup of flour and then use the whisk to stir it really well until the mixture is like a thick paste."

Josie followed Jane's instructions and stirred the mixture. "It's getting too thick, Jane." Josie's forehead wrinkled in concentration as she worked at her task.

"Let's turn the heat down a bit, so it doesn't cook too fast. Now you add three cups of milk, but only a little at a time while you keep stirring. I'll help you," Jane said. She slowly poured one cup of milk into the pan while Josie stirred.

"Oh, that's better," Josie said as the mixture turned into a velvety sauce. She stopped stirring for a moment, and lumps began to form.

"Keep stirring. It doesn't have to be fast, just steady," Jane said. "As it comes to a boil, it will get thicker again. I'll keep adding milk, so it won't get too thick." Jane slowly poured more milk into the pan.

"This is too hard," Josie said.

Jane knew the most difficult part for children would be making a smooth, creamy, lump-free white sauce. Since the sauce and the process formed the basis for many recipes, Jane thought it should be taught as a basic cooking skill, so she refused to take any shortcuts, like using a canned sauce. "I know, but it's worth the effort. Let me stir for a minute while you measure the rest of the ingredients." Jane switched places with Josie.

"Measure out one teaspoon of dry mustard. There. It's all right if it's a little over. Then measure out one-half teaspoon of salt. Now add that to the sauce while I keep stirring."

Josie dumped the seasonings into the pan, then peered in while Jane stirred. "The lumps are going away," she said.

"Yes. The trick is in stirring it until it's smooth. Now let's add the cheese. We'll stir it with a wooden spoon now, instead of the whisk."

Josie added the four kinds of grated cheese, a little at a time. The sauce turned a pale orange.

"Ooh, it's too pale. It doesn't look very good, Jane."

Jane smiled. "Then we'll have to add the secret ingredient. You stir while I get it." She handed the wooden spoon over to Josie.

"Now watch this." Jane added drops of red and yellow food coloring to the sauce. The bright color swirled around with each circle of the spoon, creating a spiral in the sauce.

"Cool," Josie said. "Oh, look. It's all changing color. But isn't that like cheating?" she asked, wide-eyed.

"No. They put it in the macaroni and cheese you buy in the

store. Most store-bought food contains food coloring. That's so food will look good as well as taste good."

"Oh. I get it," Josie said, nodding sagely.

"When we eat, we use all of our senses. The texture of the food is important. When there's something gritty in your food, your sense of touch finds it. This sauce will feel smooth on our tongues. The way it looks involves the sense of sight. If we put green food color in it instead of red, it would look gross, and we wouldn't want to eat it."

"That'd be funny. We should do that since it's Halloween. We could pretend it's green slime."

"Yuck! You have a morbid imagination, Josie. We will *not* add green food coloring."

"Phooey!" Josie said, pouting. The upward twitch of her lips gave away her teasing.

Chapter Nine

While Jane packed the food for the ANGELs' party, Alice carried a large basket of individually wrapped candies to the front door.

"Are those for trick-or-treaters?" Garrett asked from the living room. He was sitting on the couch, working on his laptop.

"Yes. I'm going to leave them on the porch so the children can help themselves. We'll be at church. I lead a group of preteen girls on Wednesday nights. The girls will be at church, instead of out trick-or-treating, so Jane and I are putting on a little festival for them."

"I still have some work to do here tonight, but I'd be happy to pass out the treats."

"That's not necessary. I don't want to interrupt your work. I'll leave a note for the parents on the basket."

"Really, I'd like to. I missed a lot of holidays with my kids, but I remember the fun of those Halloweens I did make," he said.

"Okay. I'll leave the basket by the door. I must admit, I love seeing the children in their costumes," she said.

"Christmas was my magic time," he said. "I never missed that holiday. My wife always bought the kids new red-plaid pajamas, and they'd wear them downstairs first thing Christmas morning to see what Santa had left them. Of course, I loved the frosted sugar cookies and chocolate milk they set out for Santa." He chuckled. "I miss those times." He sighed. "Maybe someday I'll share those things with my grandkids."

"I hope you do," Alice said. Although she never had children of her own, she'd been blessed many times over by the children she nursed and those she nurtured at Grace Chapel. "Help yourself to a treat in the dining room. Jane set out a bowl of goodies. Her popcorn balls defy comparison. There's fresh cider in the refrigerator too," Alice said before she left.

Jane had loaded the backseat of her car. Although they usually walked to the church, they had too many dishes and platters to carry.

When they arrived at Grace Chapel, they carted the food downstairs to the Assembly Room. When Alice reached the bottom of the stairs, Jenny Snyder came up to her.

"I'll take that, Miss Howard." She took the platter of cupcakes and set them on a table.

"Thank you. I'll go get another dish." Alice turned to go back upstairs when another of the ANGELs, Sarah Roberts, stopped her.

"I'll do it." Sarah bounded up the stairs.

Alice looked around. The room had been transformed into a harvest scene. Corn stalks, pumpkins, colorful gourds, and orange, green and red streamers decorated the room. "This looks great."

"Thanks, Miss Howard," Sissy Matthews said. "Ashley and Sarah and I did it. Jenny and Briana brought games."

"Wow!" Jane said, stopping at the foot of the stairs. She was holding a Crock-Pot. She went into the kitchen. "I'll plug this in and get everything ready."

A few minutes later, Josie Gilmore came rushing down the stairs. "Hey, cool!" she said when she saw the room.

Jane was pouring ginger ale into a bowl of orange punch. She saw Josie and called her over. With Alice's permission, Jane had invited Josie to help her serve the older girls, since she'd helped Jane prepare the food.

Fifteen girls crowded around the punch-bowl table to see what was floating in the punch.

"Oh wow!"

"Cool!"

"Awesome!"

Alice knew Jane had made some kind of ice sculpture, but she hadn't seen it. Now she was really curious. "Okay, girls, everyone take a seat," Alice said.

While the girls hurried to the tables with a scrape of chairs and excited chatter, Alice went to look at the punch. Jane grinned at her.

A large, green ice frog floated in the punch. It even had bumpy skin, and its big eyes stared at Alice. She half expected it to raise its head and let out a *ribbit* or to jump out of the punch bowl.

"Yuck," Alice said, and Jane laughed.

Jane went into the kitchen, and Alice turned to the girls. "I know you're excited about the party, but first I thought we could find out about fall festivals from the Bible." The girls gave

Alice their attention, but she knew she'd better get her lesson underway, as she wouldn't be able to hold their interest for long with all the goodies awaiting them.

"Did you know that God loves parties?" Alice asked. "Near the beginning of the Bible, after God brought the Israelites out of Egypt to the Promised Land, God gave Moses instructions for the people to celebrate festivals and feasts. In Exodus 23:14–16, God told them, 'Three times a year you are to celebrate a festival to me. Celebrate the Feast of Unleavened Bread.... Celebrate the Feast of Harvest with the first fruits of the crops you sow in your field. Celebrate the Feast of Ingathering at the end of the year, when you gather in your crops from the field.' Then, in the book of Leviticus, chapter 23, God gave specific instructions to the Israelites on how and when to have their festivals. Why do you suppose God wanted the Israelites to have festivals?"

Several of the girls raised their hands.

"Sarah. What do you think?"

"Is it like at Christmas and Easter when we celebrate Jesus being born and Jesus going to the cross?"

"Yes. The festivals are much like those celebrations. What do we do on those holidays, besides exchange gifts?"

"We have feasts?" Josie said, making it a question.

"Yes, we have feasts," Alice agreed. "Food is a blessing from God. He took care of the Israelites in the desert, sending them manna and meat to eat and water to drink. Then they settled in the Promised Land, they grew crops, and God blessed them. The Israelites celebrated the Feast of Harvest and the Feast of

Ingathering. In America, we have Thanksgiving. We give thanks to God for the food and blessings He has provided."

"My mom has a really big garden, and we got tons of zucchini this year," Sarah said. "She gave lots of it away and put a bunch of bags of it in the freezer." Sarah giggled. "Mom said it was coming out her ears."

Alice smiled. "It sounds like she's been abundantly blessed." Alice paused, then continued the lesson. "We pray before meals so we can thank God for our food. God told the Israelites to have festivals because He wants us to remember that He loves us and takes care of us and gives us gifts, like food and sunshine and beautiful flowers and animals. So, in keeping with the Festival of Ingathering, let's thank God for our blessings. Each of you tell us one thing you thank God for."

"I'll start," Jenny said. "I'm thankful for my family."

"I'm thankful for my friends," Sissy Matthews said, looking around the room and smiling at her friends.

"I'm thankful that my dad brought home a puppy," Kate Waller said.

One by one, the girls each expressed thanks for their blessings.

"Let's thank the Lord for the feast we're going to have," Alice said. The girls bowed their heads. Jane came out of the kitchen and stood against the wall, her head bowed

When the grace was finished, Alice raised her head. "Now we can begin our party, if Ms. Howard is ready." She looked over at Jane

"I'm ready. The girls can line up and take what they'd like."

Chairs scraped back, and the girls rose and rushed to the serving table.

Josie went to stand beside Jane as the girls took helpings of macaroni and cheese, pickles and cream cheese wrapped in salami, orange and green layered Jell-O salad, and deviled eggs. Jane put a hand on Josie's shoulder and smiled down at her. Watching them, Alice wondered if Jane had a young chef in the making.

Jane tried to gauge the girls' reactions to the food. The Blue Fish Grille, where she'd worked in San Francisco, catered to adults. The clientele at the trendy restaurant liked sophisticated cuisine. Jane didn't have much experience cooking for children. At the inn, the younger guests usually found something they loved on the breakfast menus. Pancakes or French toast or sweet rolls and fruit had intergenerational appeal.

Josie frowned as she watched the other girls eat. Jane had gained confidence in her own cooking from years of experience and success. This was Josie's first time. How well Jane remembered the first meal cooked for restaurant patrons, as well as her nervousness and deep relief when they liked the food.

"What are the curly things in the macaroni and cheese?" Kate asked, hesitantly poking at one. "They look like worms."

"That's hot dogs," Josie said. "We cut them in long pieces, and they curl while they cook."

"Cool!" Briana said.

"*Um*. Good," Sarah mumbled, swallowing a mouthful of macaroni and cheese. "It tastes different." She took a gulp of punch. Jane wasn't sure if she was being polite, then washing the food down quickly, or if she was just thirsty. Josie's frown deepened.

"Could I have some ketchup, please?" another girl asked.

Jane hadn't brought ketchup, but she went into the kitchen and found a half-empty bottle in the refrigerator. "Here," she said, handing it to the girl, who upended the bottle and drowned the macaroni and cheese in the red sauce.

"Thank you," she said.

"Please pass the ketchup," Sissy requested. Then she liberally spread the sauce over her food.

"Josie, shall we bring in the pizza?" Jane said. Josie got up and followed her to the kitchen, where Jane took a baking sheet out of the oven.

"Hold the pan with pot holders," Jane said. "You can take them out."

"Okay. I don't know if they like the macaroni and cheese," Josie said quietly. "It is different, you know. Maybe we should have used a package."

"I'm sure they like it," Jane said as she put the hot pizzas on a tray.

"I hope you're right." Josie took the tray to the girls. It was covered with small English muffin pizzas. Each one had a curved slice of bell pepper for a mouth and ripe olive slices with a caper in the middle for eyes. Each girl took at least one, except for Briana, who put her hands in her lap and said, "No thank you."

When everyone had been served, Josie took a piece and sat down. She took a bite. Then she looked at Jane, gave her an exaggerated smile and nodded. Several girls removed the garnish, then ate the pizza.

When they finished eating, Jane watched the girls throw their paper plates away. The eggs and the pizzas were gone, but most of the pizza toppings, some of the Jell-O, the salami wraps and a little of the macaroni and cheese were left on plates. She wanted to ask the girls what they liked and didn't like, but she didn't want to interrupt as they moved on to their craft session.

Tonight they were making individual pumpkin-shaped piñatas. The girls formed the gourds by wrapping strips of cardboard over inflated balloons, gluing them in place and leaving a small opening at the top. They created stems from sections of paper-towel rolls. They taped these over the opening in each ball. Over the forms, the girls glued fringed strips of orange crepe paper in rows to cover the gourds. Then they covered the stems in green crepe paper and drew faces on the pumpkin piñatas with colored markers. Wire attached at the top allowed for hanging.

Jane loved the imaginative variety of pumpkin faces. The girls used a pin to pop the balloons inside their creations and then put small wrapped candies and trinkets in each piñata. Carefully setting aside their crafts to take home, they cleaned up the mess and then dunked for apples, laughing and cheering one another on. Jane hoped their noise wasn't disturbing the service upstairs. At least they were making a joyful noise.

Saturday afternoon, Louise surveyed the clothes spread out on her bed, looking for inspiration. What exactly should she pack to take to music camp? Cynthia would be arriving in a few hours. They planned to leave in the morning.

"Here's my denim jacket, all clean," Jane said, entering Louise's bedroom. "Oh my. Where are you planning to sleep tonight?"

"Very funny," Louise said. "I'm trying to decide what to pack. This camp sounds so casual. I don't want to appear overdressed. I'd feel more comfortable going as an observer, like Cynthia. Then it wouldn't matter what I wore."

Jane shrugged. "Look on the bright side, Louie. This should be a cakewalk for you. You could teach the teachers."

Louise sighed. "As a general rule, I don't teach their style of music, although I include an occasional rhythm-and-blues or bluegrass piece for an advanced student." She picked up a stack of undergarments and pantyhose and tucked them into the pocket of her suitcase. "I know I need those," she said.

"You'll be gone eight days, so just plan an outfit a day."

"I wish it were that simple. We have activities in the evenings, too, and they specified western wear for those." She picked up a pair of lightweight denim pants that looked more like casual slacks than jeans. "These will have to do."

"You should go shopping for something western when you get there."

"And buy something I'll never wear again? That would be

wasteful." She took three skirts out of her closet. "I'd much rather wear these than pants. I'll take skirts and sweaters. At least I'll be comfortable." She folded the skirts and placed them in the suitcase.

"The week will fly by, and you'll be back home unpacking. You'll probably never see any of those people again."

Louise straightened and looked at Jane. "You're right." Then she frowned, wrinkling her brow. "I don't want to disappoint Cynthia, though."

"You won't," Jane assured her. "I'll leave you to pack. If the camp is really western, the food might be a little heavy for you. Maybe you should pack antacids, just in case you need them."

"That's a good idea. And I need a small bottle of shampoo. I'll have to make a trip to the General Store."

"Alice is going to the store for me in a few minutes. Tell me what you need and I'll add it to my list."

"Thanks. I've already made a list of a few items I need," Louise said, taking it out of her pocket.

Jane took the list and looked it over. "Vitamins, breath mints, antiseptic hand wipes," she read out loud. "Looks like you've thought of everything."

Chapter Ten

Cynthia pulled her car into the Grace Chapel Inn driveway behind Alice, who was just returning from running errands. Cynthia parked, jumped out of her car and came around to open Alice's car door.

"Hey, Aunt Alice!" Cynthia enveloped her in a big hug, which Alice enthusiastically returned. "It's soooo good to see you."

"Hey yourself. I'm glad you're here. Your mother has been counting the minutes until your arrival. May I help you with your luggage?"

"I'll leave most of it in the car. I just need my overnight bag," Cynthia said, opening the trunk. She took out a small bag, shut the trunk, then carried one of Alice's sacks as they walked to the house.

Cynthia stood several inches taller than Alice, causing her aunt to look up at her. "You look wonderful. Are you ready for your grand adventure?" Alice asked.

"Oh yes!" Cynthia's eyes sparkled. "I can't believe I'm getting an all-expenses paid week away from the office and Boston. Of course, I'll be working, but it will feel like a vacation, especially since Mother is going along. We're going to have such a great time."

"I'm sure you will." Her aunt didn't tell Cynthia that her mother had doubts. Alice suspected Louise would lose her misgivings as soon as she saw her daughter.

"Mother!" Cynthia cried, dropping her bag just inside the kitchen door. Cynthia wrapped her mother in a hug, blocking the doorway.

The two were the same height and equally slender, so Alice managed to get inside and close the door against the chill. Jane stood at the sink drying a pan and smiling at their niece.

"You're next," Alice said.

Jane set the pan on the counter and dried her hands just before Cynthia broke away from her mother and turned to Jane.

After a hearty hug, Jane said, "You got here in time for dinner."

Cynthia laughed. "Of course. I planned it that way." She turned to her mother. "Am I bunking with you tonight, Mother?"

"We put you in the Garden Room, dear. I'll walk up with you. We have so much to talk about."

"And we have a whole week to catch up," Cynthia said.

"Tell me about your new imprint," Louise said as they went out to the hallway.

The door closed behind them. Alice turned to Jane. "Is it just my impression," she said with a laugh, "or is Cynthia excited? I feel like I've just survived a hurricane."

Jane laughed. "And doesn't she look wonderful? I hope this camp lives up to her expectations."

~

"This is delicious, Aunt Jane," Cynthia said after sampling a bite of cranberry chicken. "My taste buds have been celebrating, knowing I'd be eating your cooking tonight. *Mmm.*" She popped another bite into her mouth.

"I'm glad you like it," Jane said, pleased. She had debated what to fix in honor of Cynthia's visit. She wondered if children would like the fruity dish. It had a sweet but also tart flavor. Perhaps if she used dried cranberries instead of fresh, and less vinegar.

"Did you finish packing, Louise?" Alice asked.

"I hope so. I had to sit on my suitcase to latch it. If they go through it at the airport, they might not get it closed again."

"They'll manage. Some two-hundred-pound man will sit on it," Cynthia said cheerfully.

At Louise's look of mock horror, Jane hooted with laughter. "Never fear, sister dear, you will arrive at your destination with your luggage intact—maybe even on the same plane."

Louise groaned. "You're not helping, *sister dear.* You did say they have pianos available, didn't you?" she asked her daughter.

"They rent keyboards to the students for the piano classes. I've already ordered a really nice one for you. I think you'll like it."

"I packed some music. I'm sure they have music available, but I want to be prepared."

"They assured me that they provide everything you'll need." Cynthia turned to Alice. "So I hear you're doing a scrapbooking weekend while we're gone. I'd love to attend if we weren't going to be in California. Maybe you could do another weekend later, when I'm free. Hint, hint." Cynthia winked at Jane.

"Too bad you can't be here. We could have put you to work," Jane said. "I didn't know you liked to scrapbook."

"Oh, I've just been to one cropping party, but it was fun."

"What is a cropping party?" Alice wanted to know.

With a twinkle in her eyes, Cynthia preened a bit before she imparted her superior knowledge. "A cropping party is where you cut up your pictures." She laughed. "At first I was horrified that they would cut up perfectly good photographs. After all, once it's chopped up, you can't paste it back together. I didn't know you could turn photo-album pages into works of art. You should see them. I guess you will see them."

Jane noticed Alice's frown. She seemed disturbed by Cynthia's description, but she didn't say anything.

"When I make a montage, or collage, I cut pictures and bits of various objects, then arrange them onto a board, overlapping them to fill the entire board," Jane said. "A scrapbook page would be similar, only not so crowded."

"Couldn't you leave the pictures whole?" Alice asked.

"You could, but it wouldn't have the same visual effect of highlighting the object of the picture. If you don't want to cut up your photographs, you could make copies and keep the originals," Jane said.

"That's a good suggestion," Alice said, nodding.

Jane wondered what pictures Alice planned to use for her scrapbook. She thought about offering to scan the pictures and make copies for her, but Alice seemed unusually quiet, as if reluctant to talk about her project. Jane decided to wait and see. She had all next week to talk to Alice about the scrapbook weekend. She rose from the table.

"Anyone for dessert? I fixed your favorite caramel-apple bread pudding, Cynthia."

"Oh, yum! Do you have hot caramel sauce and whipped cream?"

"I do. Just the way you like it."

Louise groaned. "I'm going to gain five pounds before we get on the airplane."

Cynthia laughed. "We'll wear it off dragging our luggage around."

Sissy Matthews sat very straight, hands clenched in her lap, at the piano near the altar of Grace Chapel. Alice said a silent prayer for her. Louise had arranged for Sissy, one of her best students, to accompany the choir and the congregational singing in her absence. She and Cynthia had to leave for the airport just after the service began in order to check in for their 1:00 a.m. flight. Alice had heard Sissy practicing the songs during her piano lesson and knew the teenager could handle the job, but she understood the girl's nervousness. The choir filed in, and the director turned to the congregation.

"Please stand and join us in singing 'Just a Closer Walk with Thee,'" the director announced, then nodded to Sissy.

Sissy raised her hands over the keys, then brought them down and played the last part of the chorus flawlessly. After a second's hesitation, she launched into the verse. The choir and congregation began singing. After the first verse, Sissy seemed to relax.

Alice didn't realize she'd been holding her breath, praying for Sissy as the girl played. Alice felt a great deal of pride in Sissy, one of her ANGELs. She imagined God smiling down on the girl, who was concentrating on the music as the congregation sang praises to Him.

Alice loved seeing the young people participate in the church services and activities. Louise had several students capable of playing piano specials, and Alice hoped more of them would play in the future. For now, she was glad Sissy had accepted the opportunity.

After the service, as they were leaving the church, Penny Holwell stopped Alice and Jane.

"So far we have six ladies, counting myself, coming to the scrapbook weekend," she told them. "Two others are maybes. Do you have any out-of-town people coming?"

"Just one," Jane said.

"Really? I'm sorry there aren't more so far. I hope this works out for you or for Mary Jo," Penny said.

"That will make about a dozen including Mary Jo. That's a good group, don't you think?" Alice said.

"I'm sure it'll be fine," Jane said. "Let me know your final count by Wednesday morning, so I can do my grocery shopping."

"Okay. I'll call you. I'll see if I can round up some more women. See you later," Penny said. She went back inside the church.

Alice looked at Jane, who shrugged. "One or two more can't hurt," she said.

"We're not talking a couple of hours for a tea party," Alice said.

"That's true, but we won't have to entertain them. Just feed them, and that I can do," Jane said. "No problem."

Dry heat hit Louise as she stepped through the automatic doors to the sidewalk outside of the Sacramento airport. California was having a heat wave with temperatures considerably above normal. Wheeling her suitcase, with her carry-on bag attached, she shifted her shoulder to keep her tote bag and purse from slipping off as she followed Cynthia across several lanes to the rental car parking area.

"Are you all right, Mother?" Cynthia asked, glancing back at her. "I could take your suitcase."

"I'm fine, dear. Just getting a better grip on my bag. Keep going. I'm right behind you." Louise felt a little strange trailing her grown daughter out of the airport. She was used to taking charge of travel. Eliot had always relied on her to make their arrangements. As she pulled her rolling suitcase up over a curb, Louise thought about the trip so far. Cynthia had driven them to the Philadelphia airport, gotten them checked in, through security and to the right gates in Philadelphia and in Denver, where they changed planes and had a two-hour layover. She'd helped stow Louise's carry-on bag in the overhead bin and even given her a bottle of water and a new erasable pen and crossword-puzzle book for the long flight.

Cynthia had grown into a lovely, intelligent, sensible and capable adult. Louise knew this, but today's events brought the realization home in a new way. Louise's heart filled to nearly bursting with pride and thankfulness. How fortunate she was to have Cynthia in her life. How blessed she was that her daughter cared so much about her. How pampered she felt to let her daughter take care of her and lead the way. And truth be known, she was a bit tired. She'd forgotten how hard traveling could be on a body. She supposed age might be a contributing factor.

"Here we are. It's not fancy, but it will get us where we need to go," Cynthia said, stopping beside a small, new, red compact car. She unlocked the trunk.

"As long as it has air conditioning," Louise said, relinquishing her bags to Cynthia, who stowed them in the trunk.

"It's a lot warmer than I expected at this time of year," Cynthia said, removing her linen blazer and laying it on top of her suitcase. "Do you want to put your sweater in the trunk?"

"Aren't we going into the mountains? Perhaps it will be cooler there."

"It's in the foothills. It might be cooler, but it feels like it's ninety degrees here."

"I'll keep it up front," Louise said. She removed her sweater and draped it over her arm.

Cynthia took a sheet of paper out of her briefcase, then shut the trunk.

"I have a map," Cynthia said as they got into the car. She studied the paper for a moment. "Okay. I know where we're going. It's about an hour and a half from here. Are you hungry? We can eat here or wait until we reach Nevada City."

"That sandwich at the Denver airport was filling. Unless you're hungry, let's wait. I have an apple in my purse if you'd like."

"I'm fine too. And I found a cute restaurant online that we can try after we settle in and unpack. It's not too far from the bed-and-breakfast." Cynthia left the airport parking lot and headed out of the city. Before long, they were driving up the interstate through suburbia.

"Well, Dorothy," Louise said, looking out at a sea of shopping centers, fast-food restaurants and new housing developments, "we're not in Kansas anymore."

⟳

Perched on a slope overlooking pine- and oak-covered hills, the three-story Victorian bed-and-breakfast was such a bright royal blue, it seemed to shine in the afternoon sun. Pink gingerbread trim dripped off its eaves and porches. At least it looked well kept, Louise thought as they took their luggage out of the trunk. The day was still warm, but not as hot as in the city.

A ramp led to the front porch, an addition that catered to guests. That suited Louise. She rolled her suitcase up the ramp. A white picket railing and white trim bordered the screened-in patio. She saw lace curtains in the windows. An overstuffed couch and several rocking chairs were arranged invitingly on the porch, which was shaded by tall pine trees.

The front door swung open. "Hello, come in, come in," a

cheery voice beckoned them from the shadowed hall. As Louise followed Cynthia inside, the interior became visible. Dark hardwood floors framed a thick floral carpet runner in the hallway. The stairway to the upper floor ran up the right side, exactly as the stairs in Grace Chapel Inn, except these stairs were painted white and gold.

As her eyes adjusted to the dim light, Louise noticed the wallpaper in the hallway. The cream background held green and gold Greek statues and colonnades with frolicking maidens in flowing gowns. A large, ornate crystal chandelier hung from the high gold-and-white molded tin ceiling. Next to a curved glass china cabinet filled with cut-crystal dishes and delicate china teacups, a tall Chinese vase held plumes of dried ornamental grasses and peacock feathers. The effect was very elegant and very Victorian.

Louise loved antiques; however, living with Jane and her eclectic mix of styles had worked a subtle change in Louise's tastes. This house was done exclusively in Victorian decor, which seemed authentic but was a bit overwhelming. Still, the owners had good taste and had amassed an impressive collection of artifacts.

"I'm Earlene Eldenburg," the lady said. "Welcome to the Blue Peacock Inn."

Louise turned her attention to their hostess. She was short and plump, with a pleasant smile and the most riotous, untamed black curls Louise had ever seen.

"I'm Cynthia Smith, and this is my mother, Louise Smith. We're so glad to be here. Your home is lovely."

"Thank you. Come into the parlor. Our reception desk is in

here," she said, leading the way. "You did reserve just one room to share, didn't you? I gave you our largest room, with two queen-size beds."

"Yes. That will be wonderful. You have my company information for billing, I believe." Cynthia checked them in while Louise stood by, letting her daughter take charge. The parlor had an ornately carved fireplace with a cast-iron insert. Above it, a long mantel held a collection of bisque, china and brass bells. Each bell rested on its own lace doily. In fact, lace doilies seemed to dot every surface. A curved red-velvet Victorian sofa faced matching chairs around a claw-footed coffee table with a tray top. A side window looked out at a small garden with a fountain in the center. Water bubbled out of a ewer held by a marble Grecian maiden.

"If you'll follow me, I'll take you to your room. Just leave your suitcases here. My husband will carry them up. Charley," she called.

"Coming, my dear." A round-faced middle-aged man with a receding hairline and a jolly smile came into the parlor.

"Welcome, ladies," he said. "I'll take those." He reached for their bags and bid them precede him. He followed the procession up the stairs.

After their host and hostess departed, Cynthia sat carefully on the edge of one of the blue satin bedspreads. A lacy bed skirt peeked out beneath the spread. Stacks of pillows in various shades of blue and in different patterns were propped at the head of the identical beds. Lace and ruffles covered the top pillows. Prints lined the walls.

"This is lovely, but I'm afraid to touch anything," Cynthia said.

"I suspect these satins are washable. I can't imagine running an inn with anything you couldn't throw in a washing machine," Louise said. "Meanwhile, we might as well enjoy the luxury." Louise peeked into the closet. "There are plenty of hangers. Shall we unpack?"

"Yes, then let's go eat. I'm starving."

"Is the town nearby?" Louise asked.

"About a mile, but the restaurant isn't actually in Nevada City. It's not far from here, though. It's in a town called Rough and Ready."

"Oh." Louise tried not to look horrified. Rough and Ready? What kind of a name was that for a town? She pictured eating on splintery tables in a converted shack, and prayed that her vision was wrong.

Chapter Eleven

*I*n the darkness, without the glimmer of a street or house light, Louise wondered if they'd taken a wrong turn into the wilderness. The road wound downhill with so many twists and turns, she was glad for her empty stomach. That didn't bode well for the return trip, however.

"Are you sure we're on the right road?" she asked, hanging on to the door's armrest.

"We should arrive at the restaurant any minute," Cynthia said, apparently unconcerned.

They rounded a curve, and magically the lights of Rough and Ready came into view. Soon they arrived at the restaurant and Cynthia slowed, then turned into a parking lot. "We're here."

Cars lined the parking area. That was a good sign, Louise thought.

THE ROUGH AND READY GRILL, the sign declared. At the front of the cedar-sided building was a covered porch supported by posts, and a square, false front that made Louise think of a livery stable or a saloon. She wondered what Cynthia had seen online that attracted her to the restaurant. She was quite certain it wasn't the name.

A hostess led them to a table that looked like an old wagon wheel with a glass top. Each table had a bouquet of fresh flowers. She handed them bound menus.

"There are two specials tonight," she said. "We have a fresh mesquite-grilled swordfish topped with mango, fig and pineapple salsa, served on a bed of rice pilaf, and we have smoked prime rib served with horseradish mashed potatoes. Frank will be your waiter."

She left, and a woman brought them water with lemon slices, served in glass mugs shaped like cowboy boots.

"Thank you," Louise said. She looked at Cynthia, who was smiling. When the woman left, Cynthia leaned forward.

"So far, it lives up to its website."

"The specials sound delicious. I think I'll try the swordfish."

Cynthia opened her menu. "You might want to look at what else they have before you decide. I hope their chef does justice to these entrees. They sound wonderful."

Louise looked at the menu. The variety of choices surprised her. "This could be an upscale restaurant in Philadelphia," she said. "Yet we seem to be in the middle of nowhere."

Cynthia laughed softly. "This is a rural area, but people commute to the city from here. Many of them work for high-tech companies."

After their waiter took their orders, Louise looked around, admiring the beautiful original landscape paintings on the walls. This was not at all what she'd expected. She looked forward to seeing the surrounding area in daylight.

Early Monday morning, Louise sat at the bed-and-breakfast's oval, oak dining-room table, sipping her coffee. Cynthia stood looking at one of many display racks of small sterling silver spoons that decorated the walls of the dining room. Their hostess came carrying a platter of thick slices of French toast. A little note card at each place listed sourdough French toast and peach sauce on the day's menu.

"Good morning, ladies," Earlene said, smiling cheerfully as she passed the platter to Louise. "Did you enjoy your dinner last night?"

"Very much. The food was fabulous," Cynthia said. "Thank you for giving me directions. Without them, I'm afraid I'd have gotten lost."

Earlene chuckled. "Our winding roads can be intimidating in the dark. Nevada City is closer and the drive much easier, but then you'll probably be eating dinners at the ranch."

"Are we your only guests right now?" Louise asked.

"We have a couple with one child at the other end of the house. They're attending the music camp too," she said. "They left early to eat breakfast at the ranch. The camp includes the meals, you know, but breakfast here is a little more relaxing. Just depends what you're looking for. Many of the families come to the camp as much for socializing as for the music lessons. We're expecting another couple tonight. We usually have two or three rooms reserved for the camp week."

"So we're not the only ones staying outside the ranch," Cynthia said.

"Oh no. Several local inns and motels book students from the camp. I think the ranch appeals to the teenagers and younger families," Earlene said.

"I'm glad Cynthia found your inn," Louise said. "It's lovely and quiet here. I might find it difficult to face the activity of a ranch for a week."

"Anytime it gets to be too much, you just come back here and rest," Earlene said. "I believe they break in the afternoon for a couple of hours before dinner."

"I might do that," Louise said, thinking it sounded like an excellent suggestion. "I'd like to hear about your inn too. My sisters and I run a bed-and-breakfast in Pennsylvania. It might be interesting to compare notes."

"Really? Let's do. I love hearing what other inns do," Earlene said, and she seemed genuinely enthusiastic. "Now I'll leave you to eat your breakfast before it gets cold. I'll bring out more coffee." She disappeared into the kitchen.

Cynthia took two pieces of French toast and drizzled peach sauce over them. "This looks delicious. I'm developing a real taste for sourdough bread, West Coast–style. Aunt Jane makes great sourdough bread too."

"Yes, but she complains that hers isn't the same as San Francisco sourdough," Louise said, taking a bite. "This does have a different flavor and texture than Jane's bread. She says it has something to do with the climate."

"Fascinating. Especially considering the pioneers brought sourdough starter with them from New England," Cynthia said. "I'll have to taste Aunt Jane's bread when we get home and compare it with this."

"Wow, would you look at that," Cynthia said later in the morning as she drove beneath a tall ranch gate topped with wrought-iron cowboys on horses. A hanging sign announced Rock Creek Ranch. She drove down the long, oak-lined gravel driveway. "That must be the ranch house. It's larger than I expected."

The two-story, rambling log house dominated the scene. At the end of the trees, the ranch yard opened onto a large, graveled field with the house beyond. Cars were parked off to the right of the driveway. An assortment of motor homes, trailers, trucks with camper shells and even an old converted school bus were parked in a makeshift campground to the left. Beyond that, a long, two-story barn-red building bordered the left side of the yard. Evenly spaced windows lined both stories. Several teenagers were standing out front. Louise guessed it must be the bunkhouse, where some of the students were staying. Across the yard from it, another long red building had several large barn doors trimmed in white. Three cupolas with horse-topped weather vanes sat above a green metal roof.

A man in jeans and cowboy boots, wearing a cowboy hat, came toward them. He held a clipboard in his hands. Cynthia rolled down her window.

"Welcome to Rock Creek Ranch." His smile created deep dimples in his cheeks. "Are you here for the music camp?"

"Yes. We're Cynthia and Louise Smith," Cynthia said.

"I'm Tobias Luken," he said. He checked the list. "Here you are." He checked them off. "You can park over there," he said, pointing to the field. "Registration is in the dining hall, which is in the old stables."

He chuckled at Louise's surprised look. "The stable's been converted. We have new stables and a corral out back," he explained.

Cynthia followed his instructions, and they were soon standing in a line to register. Louise looked around. The stables had a concrete floor imprinted to look like natural sandstone. The rough cedar-paneled walls were decorated with colorful striped saddle blankets, ancient guitars and fiddles, spurs, hats and horse tack. Behind the registration table, rows of redwood picnic tables were arranged perpendicular to a raised stage. A cowboy boot filled with daisies decorated each table. Louise wondered if they were real boots.

A group of young people stood in one corner, playing a lively hoedown tune on guitars and violins.

"There's coffee and tea over there," Cynthia said. "Want a cup while we wait?"

"No thanks. I had enough coffee at the inn. I suppose that's the kitchen," Louise said, looking in the direction Cynthia had indicated. Large sheets of wood, painted with X's across the middle to look like the stable windows, covered what Louise suspected were kitchen pass-throughs. Cafeteria-style counters ran along the bottom of each window.

On the stage, a circle of keyboards surrounded an upright piano. Louise wondered if the keyboards were set up for her class, and if so, which keyboard was hers. The line moved up and Cynthia gave the lady their names.

When they reached the front of the line, a woman, whose name tag read BONNIE DALTON, MUSIC CAMP COORDINATOR, greeted them. "We're glad you could join us," she said. "This is your first time here, isn't it?"

"Yes," Cynthia replied. "It looks as if you have a lot of families here. Are they all students?"

"Not all, but most of them take classes—even the parents. Some of the teenagers and husbands come with their families, then take off during the day to go hiking or participate in other activities in the area. Now, here are your name tags." She handed Louise's tag to Cynthia. "You need to wear your name tag every day. It's your meal ticket and entry to all events," she said.

"Actually, I'm the guest. My mother is the student," Cynthia said.

"Oh." Bonnie looked at them. "I'm sorry, I should have asked. Usually the parent is the guest, and the child is the student. I guess you're not a child, though, are you?" She blushed. "I'd better stop before I embarrass myself more." She handed each of them a folder. "You'll find the class and meal schedules and a map of the ranch buildings inside, and also a list of the concert events. I'm always here, so please let me know if you have any questions or concerns. We don't have an assembly before classes begin, so just find your class. Instruction begins at ten o'clock this morning. I hope you have a wonderful week." She smiled at them, then looked at the next person in line.

"Let's sit down and look these over," Cynthia said.

They took their folders to the end of one of the tables. Sitting next to each other, they opened them.

"My class meets in here, on the stage, all week," Louise said, studying the schedule. She glanced at her watch. "I have an hour before my first class starts."

"Besides your class, there are three other piano classes, from beginner to intermediate and advanced. There are also four fiddle classes, three guitar classes and a bass class. I'll spend my time visiting the different classes and interviewing people. Shall we look around?" Cynthia asked. "I'd like to get my bearings."

"Lead the way."

Louise followed Cynthia through double doors at the back of the dining room. The first thing they found were the men's and ladies' bathrooms at the head of two long hallways, one on each side. Classrooms lined both the halls. Peeking inside the rooms, they found one filled with keyboards and other spaces set up with chairs in rows. At the end of the hallways was a small corridor between them with a set of double doors leading outside.

Cynthia pushed through the doors. They stepped out onto an area with picnic tables. Several families with young children had congregated in the grassy area. Half a dozen elementary-age children were playing tag. Beyond the tables, an old-fashioned white clapboard chapel, complete with steeple, stood between the stable and the ranch house.

Louise thought it odd that a ranch would have its own chapel. She went over to get a better look. Cynthia followed her. At first glance, the freshly painted building looked new, but the wooden steps showed deep wear from years of foot traffic. The large oak door arced to a point at the top.

Louise opened the door and stepped into a cool, softly lit room. Although everything looked clean, she smelled the slightly musty scent of age and something else she recognized but couldn't identify.

White eyelet curtains covered two windows on both sides of the one-room chapel. At the head of the chapel, the sun streamed through a tall stained-glass window, sending shafts of colored light through a large cross entwined with roses, casting a rainbow over the rows of golden oak pews facing the oak pulpit.

"What a lovely room," Cynthia whispered.

Louise walked down the center aisle. At the front of the room, the fragrance got stronger. Then she looked at the altar and recognized it. On the table were two hand-rolled beeswax candles in candleholders. Off to one side, she spotted an old pump organ. She walked over to it.

"I wonder if it works," Cynthia said.

"The cabinet has been restored. Perhaps the organ is in working order too." Louise smoothed her hand over the satiny walnut cabinet. Intricate carved curlicues created grillwork on either side of the music rack and beneath the keyboard. The legs were carved to depict lions' heads and feet.

"I'd love to hear you play it, Mother."

Louise touched one of the celluloid keys. "I'd love to play it. I'll ask about it." She turned. "If we're going to see the rest of the ranch before the classes begin, we'd better go." She cast a longing look at the organ, then led the way down the aisle and out into the warmth of the morning sun.

Chapter Twelve

Seated at a keyboard on the dining-hall stage, Louise looked in fascination at the man at the piano. He had a toothpick stuck in the side of his mouth, which he chewed on as he played a honky-tonk tune with more speed and movement than she'd ever heard or seen before. He practically bounced on the piano seat. As he played, he looked at his students and grinned. He finished with a flourish, then sat back, took the toothpick out of his mouth and looked around.

"I'm gonna teach y'all to play that way this week," Farley Blackthorn drawled in a thick western accent. "Turn on your keyboards and let's get started."

Eight keyboards came to life as the students turned on their instruments and began playing scales and arpeggios and any number of songs. The cacophony increased as Louise looked around, astonished. The players ranged from children no older than Louise's students to several adults. She appeared to be the oldest student.

By lunchtime, Louise was ready to quit. Chaos had reigned in the Master Piano class.

Cynthia found her amid the crowd assembling in the dining room for lunch. "Let's get in the lunch line. How's it going?"

"It's too early to tell," Louise said, getting into what looked like a line behind Cynthia. She had to speak loudly to be heard over the din. "Where did all these people come from?"

"They have a full complement of students and their families," Cynthia said, looking around, clearly excited.

Louise frowned. "Why aren't these children in school?"

"I asked Bonnie about that. Many of these families home-school their children, so this is part of their education."

"They should enroll their children in real music classes. If the other classes teach similar methods, they won't learn anything this week. I don't know how they can call this a music camp."

Cynthia's eyes widened. "They've been doing this for ten years, and the camp has a good reputation, Mother."

Louise stopped looking around and looked at her daughter. "I'm sorry, but so far I haven't heard any teaching. Just noise."

Cynthia frowned. "The other classes were disorganized too. I hope I haven't wasted the company's money on a wild venture. I was so sure this would be a great experience."

Louise looked around and saw that people were cheerful and excited. Could she be wrong about the camp? "Maybe we should reserve judgment until tomorrow," she suggested. "Let's give it a chance. It is the first day, after all."

On her way home from work Monday afternoon, Alice parked in front of the office of the *Acorn Nutshell*, the local newspaper. She took a box out of the backseat and carried it inside.

Carlene Moss looked up from behind the counter. Her dimples showed when she smiled. "Hello, Alice. Good to see you. What can I do for you today?"

Alice set the box on the counter. "I have a box of old photographs that I need to copy. I was hoping you might know where I can get that done. Some of them need touching up."

"Let's see what you have." Carlene lifted the lid. "Oh, there are some oldies here. Good idea to copy them. Is this for your scrapbook weekend?"

"Yes. I want to surprise Louise and Jane with a history of the house."

"That's a fabulous idea." Carlene looked through the stack of pictures. "You know, this would make a great feature article. I could do a series on old homes in the area. I don't normally do copies, but I'd love to have some of these for a future project, with your permission, of course. I could scan them onto my computer and enhance them a little. That will help with the ones that are faded. I can make a disc for you, if you'd like. That preserves them and you'll have them to duplicate again."

"I'm sure Louise and Jane would be happy to have you do a feature on our house. And we'd love to have the pictures on a CD."

"I'll make a couple for you. Maybe Cynthia would like one. This might take a few days. Is that all right?"

Alice hesitated. She knew Carlene had a tight schedule with getting the newspaper out. "I need them by this weekend. I could have copies made in Potterston if you'd recommend the best place to have them done. Then I could let you have a set so you could take your time."

Carlene glanced at her desk. "If I start today, I'll have enough time. I don't have anything that I must do this week other than the paper, and I have this week's issue just about ready to print. I can do it."

"If you're sure. I don't want to impose."

"You're not. I heard that Louise is out of town."

"Yes. She went to California with Cynthia to attend a music camp."

"Is she teaching?"

"No. She went as a student, if you can imagine."

"Louise? This must be some music camp for her to go as a student," Carlene said.

"I suppose so. Cynthia is researching a book series on family activities. She asked Louise to go along to help her gather information and to have some time together. I think Cynthia is relying on her mother's music expertise."

"Well, I hope they have a great time. Maybe I'll interview Louise when she gets home. I've never reported on a music camp. My readers might be interested in how one works." Carlene picked up the box of photographs. "I'd better put these on my desk where they'll be safe. You may remember that we did a series on Grace Chapel and your father ten or fifteen years ago. I have all that in the archives. I'm sure I have lots of pictures and news articles. People brought in old photographs then. I think some of them were of your father in his house. I'll see what I can find. You might try the historical society too. As you know, your mother came from one of the town's most prominent families."

"I suppose she did. Thanks, Carlene." Alice hurried back to her car, which she'd parked across the street in front of the library. The chilled wind cut right through her bulky-knit cardigan sweater. *Time to get out the winter coats*, she thought, pulling her sweater closed.

Alice looked across the street and saw Nia Komonos, the librarian, at the door of the library. She quickly crossed to the foot of the steps. "Hi, Nia. Are you opening the library on Mondays now?"

"Oh, hi, Alice. No, I just decided to come in for a few hours and get ahead on some paperwork. Is there something you need from the library?"

"I don't want to bother you. I am interested in information on Acorn Hill in the eighteen hundreds. Perhaps you can just tell me if you have a book on that time. If so, I can come back tomorrow to borrow it."

"You're in luck. I just received a brand-new book compiled by the historical society. It covers the entire county. There's a fairly extensive section on Acorn Hill. Would you like to check it out? It's no problem for me to do that now."

"Oh yes. Thank you."

"Are you looking for anything in particular?" Nia asked once they were inside. "I'd be happy to do research for you. I can find almost anything on the library's computers."

"I'm looking for the history of our house," Alice said. "I'm working on a surprise for my sisters. I'll look in that book and see if there's anything helpful. If not, I may take you up on your offer."

They moved to the front desk, where Nia brought a large book out of the back room. "Here it is." She scanned the library card Alice gave her, then scanned the book's barcode. Suddenly the front door opened. Nia looked up and quickly snatched the book. "Let me put this in a sack for you to carry."

"There you are, Alice," Ethel said. "I saw your car out front. I looked in the post office, but of course you weren't there. As I was coming out, I saw you going in here. I didn't know the library was open." Ethel barely glanced at the plastic bag Nia handed to Alice.

"Hello, Auntie. Actually, it's not open. Nia and I were just chatting. She's here to do some paperwork. Are you walking? I'll be happy to give you a ride home."

"Bless you, Alice. I rode to town with Jane and told her to drop me off. I planned to have Lloyd take me home, but he is tied up in a meeting. You don't mind stopping at the General Store on the way, do you? I need a few groceries. You are such a comfort to me." She turned and waved to Nia as she headed for the door. Alice followed and hurried to open the car door for Ethel.

Ethel talked nonstop about the scrapbook event. She'd been sorting through photographs for some sort of theme. "I just can't decide what kind of scrapbook to make," she said. "What do you think? I can't come unprepared. Florence plans to make a scrapbook of her dinner parties. Viola will make an album of her cats, no doubt. I was thinking of making a family album, but my darling daughter Francine sent me a number of albums of my grandsons as they were growing up. Of course I could go back and put together an album of when Francine was a little girl, but that doesn't really appeal to me. I don't know what to do," Ethel said, waving her hands for emphasis.

Alice smiled.

"What are you making?"

"Making? For what?" Alice responded, temporarily losing the conversation's track.

"Why, your album. What kind of scrapbook are you making?" Ethel turned questioning eyes on Alice.

"I'm...just going to put together some old pictures. Nothing fancy."

"I know Jane could make something artistic, but she tells me she isn't making one at all." Ethel perked up. "That's it. I'll get Jane to help me."

"Jane will be busy cooking for all those ladies," Alice said.

"That's all right. She'll find time to help me. She simply must." Ethel crossed her arms and sat back against the seat, determined, and finished with the conversation.

Monday evening, Jane said, "It's awfully quiet around here without Louise. Not that she's noisy." She laughed at the idea as she cleared the remains of a tuna-noodle casserole, fancied up with toasted slivered almonds, from the table. "I'm so used to hearing the piano every afternoon, I felt lonely today."

"I suppose it would feel lonely to be here by yourself," Alice said. "Before you and Louise moved home, I had Father here. Besides, I wasn't home that often during the day. Doesn't Garrett work here?"

"No. He's either in Riverton at the company site or he's working elsewhere. I think he's set up office at the Coffee Shop. By the way, I took reservations for three women from Harrisburg today. They heard about the scrapbook weekend through an Internet newsletter. I began to think Garrett and his daughter would be our only overnight guests. The Harrisburg ladies asked to stay together in one room, so I told them one of them would have to sleep on a rollaway. They said that's fine. I put them in the Sunset Room."

Alice shook her head. "I hope the one on the rollaway will be able to rest."

"I don't think they're coming to sleep. It sounds more like a slumber party to me, which is fine as long as they don't keep the rest of us awake."

The phone rang as Jane was tidying up the kitchen. She picked it up. "Grace Chapel Inn, this is Jane speaking."

"Hi, Ms. Howard, this is Meghan Quinlan. My mom says you invited me to come cook with you and Bree tomorrow. I can come. What are we going to make?" the girl asked.

"I haven't decided yet, but it will be fun," Jane replied, smiling at Meghan's abruptness. After a long silence, Jane said, "I'll see you after school then?"

"Okay. Bye." The phone clicked and went silent.

Almost laughing, Jane hung up the receiver. *That's two for tomorrow*, she thought. *Too bad Josie can't come again tomorrow.* Bree and Meghan were two of Josie's elementary-school friends. Jane put away the last pan from dinner and removed her apron. She put on water for tea, then pulled her notebook off the shelf and set it on the kitchen table.

Alice had gone upstairs with some laundry, so Jane opened to her list for the scrapbook weekend. Under Friday night, she had *baked spaghetti, antipasto salad* and *focaccia bread* for dipping. Mary Jo had suggested stocking up on sodas. She added *soft drinks* to her grocery list below *candy* and *pretzels*. She had to be careful to plan snacks that would not leave oil on the scrapbookers' fingers. For dessert, she planned on chocolate caramel brownies and ice cream.

She wrote *Italian olives, pepperoncini, Italian salami, cherry tomatoes* and *marinated mushrooms* on her grocery list. She'd order bread from the Good Apple Bakery for Friday night and Saturday and Sunday morning. As she made a note to remind herself, the telephone rang again. She started to get up, but it cut off in the middle of the second ring. *Alice must have picked it up*, she thought and went back to her menus. Saturday: baked French toast for breakfast; chicken-and-Swiss-cheese grilled panini sandwiches for lunch. The kitchen door opened, and Alice looked in. "Do we still have a room open for next weekend? I didn't see any more reservations in the book," Alice said.

"Yes. The Garden Room is available. Did you tell them we have a scrapbook event going on? It might be a bit noisy."

"They want to come for the scrapbooking. Two ladies from Baltimore. I left the caller on hold. I'll be right back." The door shut.

Jane started listing names. They now had seven overnight guests. The three ladies from Harrisburg and two ladies from Baltimore, plus Garrett and his daughter. Jane wasn't sure if the other scrapbookers would be eating breakfast and dinner at the inn. She knew Penny and Mary Jo, Ethel, Florence, Vera and Viola, Hope and Patsy were planning to share those meals. That made at least fifteen plus Alice and her.

"We now have a full house," Alice said, coming into the kitchen. The water in the kettle was boiling, so she removed the kettle from the burner, put two tea bags into the teapot and poured the hot water over them. She opened the cupboard and got cups out, then set the tea things on a tray and brought it to the table. She sat across from Jane. "Working on the weekend meals?"

"Yes. We'll have a good-sized group. Penny is supposed to call me tomorrow with a final number. We'll have to push back the furniture to get the craft tables set up."

"I think it's going to get noisy around here. Perhaps it's a good thing Louise is gone this week. I wonder how she's doing."

Chapter Thirteen

I don't know, Cynthia. So far, I'd have to call this camp organized chaos. At least the meals are ready on time, and there's a system in place," Louise said Monday evening as they stood in line for dinner. "My class spent half the day trying to get keyboards working properly and playing unrecognizable renditions of whatever anyone wanted to plunk out. One little girl played 'Twinkle, Twinkle Little Star' over and over and over while a teenager played some honky-tonk country-western piece and a woman tried to jazz up a hymn. I couldn't even tell you which one, I was so confused. My head is ringing. I'll hear that cacophony in my sleep tonight."

"Attention, everyone," said someone over the audio system. "May I have your attention, please?" A tall, good-looking young man stood on stage holding a microphone. He waited a few seconds. "Thank you. I'm Jacob Luken and I want to invite you to stay this evening for our first jam session. Tonight you'll be the audience as the instructors play, and I promise, you're in for a treat."

He gave a few announcements and instructions for those staying in the bunkhouse. "Now if you'll bow your heads, my dad, Jake, will ask a blessing on the food." He handed the microphone to his father, who stood almost a head shorter than his son.

All the men in the room removed their hats and held them over their hearts. Little boys, mimicking their fathers, removed their cowboy hats and baseball caps. "Thank You, Lord, for bringing this wonderful group of people together to enjoy this week of music. I ask Your blessing on this camp and on this meal. In Jesus' name. Amen."

The line moved steadily forward. Louise held her tray while a teenager plopped a large spoonful of mashed potatoes on a plate and handed it to the next server for roast beef. A third server added a helping of corn. All the servers wore head coverings and plastic gloves.

"Would you like gravy?" a fourth young woman asked Louise.

"Yes, please...but not too much." The girl began pouring gravy over the meat and potatoes but stopped before she dumped the entire ladle of liquid over Louise's food. Another worker added a roll, then handed Louise the plate.

Cynthia stood next to her with a similar plate of food. "Let's find a table," she said. "Then I'll get our drinks." She headed for the middle of the room, winding her way between tables that were already filled with diners. She stopped at the end of a table with a family of eight. There was just room for two more people.

"May we join you?" she asked.

"Please do," the mother said. She instructed her children to scoot over and make room, although there was plenty of space.

Louise sat across from Cynthia, who set her plate down and collected their trays. "Coffee, iced tea or fruit punch, Mother?"

"Iced tea would be fine. Thank you."

After Cynthia walked away, the mother leaned toward Louise.

"Hi. I'm Melinda Perry," she said, smiling. "Is this your first camp?" she asked.

"Yes." Louise introduced herself. "I came with my daughter," she added, smiling.

"What instrument is she taking?" the woman asked.

"Actually, I'm the student. I'm taking Master Piano. Cynthia is an editor. She's researching a book about music camps."

"Really? How interesting." Melinda turned to her children. "Don't argue. Leave your sister's plate alone." Then she turned back to Louise and smiled. "We've been coming for five years," Melinda said. "My youngest was an infant the first year. Now she's in the intermediate fiddle class. The others are in advanced classes, three in fiddle, two in guitar and two in piano, except for Tyler, who accompanies the Fiddle Two class on the guitar." She looked at her children. "Nathan, use your napkin." She sighed and shook her head.

Louise looked over at the children. They were eating and chatting and seemed to be enjoying themselves. Six children sat at the table, but Melinda had mentioned nine children. She recognized Nathan from the piano class. She thought he might be about ten years old.

"My three oldest are helping in the kitchen. We get a scholarship for the camp if they work. My husband helps with the sound system and I help with breakfast. That's the only way we can bring everyone," she explained. "Where are you from?"

"I'm from Pennsylvania. My daughter is from Boston."

"You've come a long ways. We're from Oregon. Are you staying at the ranch?"

"No. We're at a bed-and-breakfast."

"That's too bad. You miss a lot of the activity. So many of these people come every year, it's like a big reunion. We brought our travel trailer, but the older children are staying in the dorm. They tend to stay up half the night jamming or playing games and talking."

Cynthia returned with their drinks, and Louise introduced her.

The food was very good. Louise and Cynthia chatted with Melinda while they ate. Louise began to suspect that the week served more as a family vacation than a musical learning experience. If so, Cynthia was in for a big disappointment.

As they rose to take their plates to the dish receptacles, Melinda said, "I hope you're staying for the jam session tonight. The instructors play for us. It's well worth hearing."

Cynthia glanced at Louise, seeking a reaction. Louise nodded. She was tired, but this was Cynthia's party. She wouldn't put a damper on the experience.

"Today probably seemed a bit disorganized," Melinda commented, as if reading her mind. "Tomorrow will be better."

"It's only seven o'clock. We'll stay for a bit," Cynthia said. "Is that all right, Mother?"

"Perfectly fine," Louise said. "Perhaps I'll have dessert."

Louise and Cynthia were still eating their carrot cake when the men and teenagers began moving the tables and stacking them one on top of the other in the back of the room.

Louise looked up as two men took the table next to them.

"That's okay," a strapping teenage boy said as he wiped off the table on the other side. "They'll wait until you're finished."

"Thank you," Louise told him. She ate a little faster.

"I'll take our trash," Cynthia said, rising. Dinner had been served on regular plates, but they served dessert on paper plates. "I'll be right back," she said as she went off toward the large trash cans.

Louise stood. The teen finished wiping their table, and instantly two men lifted and carted it away. Louise looked around. The chairs were arranged in rows facing the stage. She took Cynthia's notebook and sweater and went to find seats. The teenagers gravitated to the back rows. Families with small children congregated near the front, some reserving whole rows or sections for their large families.

"Come sit by us," Melinda said. "There's plenty of room."

"Thank you," Louise said, sitting next to the woman. A screechy scraping noise drew her attention to the stage. Two men were testing microphones while two others moved the keyboards to the back of the stage. The upright piano was rolled forward.

Cynthia slid onto the seat beside Louise. "I talked to Doris Luken, the ranch owner. She's in charge of the kitchen crew. She told me they always start the camp with the instructors giving a concert, so everyone can see what they can do. She has six children, and they're all instructors. Several of them are married and live in other states, so the camp brings them home at least once a year."

"I saw a brochure about their chuckwagon dinners," Louise said. "They serve barbecued-beef and bean dinners all summer long, and three of their boys entertain. They call themselves The Rock Creek Wranglers."

"The Luken family gives a concert the last night of camp. It's a benefit concert for camp scholarships. They hold it at the county fairgrounds. Evidently, their facilities aren't large enough to hold the crowd that comes from Sacramento and surrounding towns. I got tickets for us."

"Howdy, campers. Welcome to Rock Creek Ranch and the Luken Family Music Camp."

The room got quiet. A tall, good-looking man stood on-stage, holding a microphone. "I'm Micah Luken, and that good-looking fellow over there by the bass fiddle is my twin, Matthew. We'll be doing most of the announcements this week. I want to introduce the rest of the crew."

Matthew looked up from arranging instruments and waved. The audience applauded wildly. Obviously the handsome young men were popular.

"Aren't they cute," Cynthia said in a low voice, leaning toward her mother. "They're the only Lukens who are still single. I saw a group of girls following them around earlier." She chuckled. "If I were a few years younger, I might join them."

Louise looked at her daughter. "You don't strike me as the cowgirl type."

Cynthia smiled and wiggled her eyebrows. "Western wear is in vogue right now."

"You can wear the style, but you don't have to adopt the life-style. Boston is far enough away from Acorn Hill as it is."

"You're right. But I'm determined to go shopping and get a western hat. Maybe we can sneak away some afternoon and go into town."

"I'd love to see the town while we're here." Louise thought she might want to skip several afternoons if the class didn't improve, but she kept those thoughts to herself.

Micah introduced his sister Bethany and his brothers Abraham, Tobias and Jacob, then had their families stand. Before he moved on, he introduced his mother, who was standing by the kitchen still wearing her apron. Her golden-blond hair was held back by large silver-and-turquoise barrettes, then hung to her shoulders in a pageboy. She looked too young to have such a grown-up family.

The audience cheered for the Luken family. When they settled down, Micah introduced the instructors one by one. As he said their names, they came onstage. The Blackthorn Boys were last. When they went up, the other instructors left the stage and Farley, Louise's instructor, sat at the piano. Sheldon picked up a guitar and Hurley picked up a fiddle. After a couple of warm-up bows and plucks, they launched into "When the Saints Go Marching In."

Farley's hands flew over the keys as he bounced along the piano bench. Louise got caught up in the energy of the music and began clapping along with the audience. The faster he played, the faster the guitar and fiddle followed. After a couple of verses, Farley sat back and played a left-hand cadence, while the fiddle took off on a tune of its own. Listening closely, Louise could pick out the melody in his run, but he could have been playing a counterpart to any song in the same key.

Sheldon banged out the rhythm on his guitar, hitting the strings instead of plucking them. Several filaments broke on the fiddle bow and bounced around as Hurley finished with a long double bow. The guitar jumped into the fray, double and triple strumming, then picking a fast countertune. Farley continued to play a bass cadence, gradually getting louder and louder until the guitar solo resolved and Farley jumped to his feet and wildly ran his hands up and down the keyboard.

Abraham Luken jumped up on the stage and began banging out a bass duet on the piano. Farley moved to the right and let Abe take over for a few moments, then moved down to the bass and started playing again. The two began dueling piano pieces, each faster and more complicated than the other.

Louise realized she was holding her breath. How could he keep up such a frenzied pace? She exhaled and forced herself to sit back and relax, but the music pounded through her veins.

Finally, the trio ended with a flourish that gained them a standing ovation.

Micah picked up the microphone, thanked the Blackthorn Brothers and announced that their CDs and the instructors' albums were for sale at the registration desk.

"Now wouldn't you like to play like that?" Micah asked. "Farley, Sheldon, Hurley and the rest of us are going to teach you these techniques this week, so pay attention. You'll have a chance to perform on Friday night."

"I don't have the energy to play like that," Louise said.

"Maybe you need a cowboy hat, to put you in the mood," Cynthia said. "You're every bit as good as Farley. Just different."

"I'm a bit rusty when it comes to the swing-style music," Louise answered.

"Is that what they play? Swing?"

"It's a form of swing that was popular in the jazz era of the twenties and thirties, but that was closer to a boogie-woogie, I think."

"Next we have the Afton sisters, who teach beginning and intermediate piano, and Nainsi Donovan on the fiddle. They'll play some Celtic songs for us."

The sisters shared the piano bench. One began playing a lilting Irish song, and the other picked it up and began a different tune. Louise relaxed back in her chair and smiled as she kept time with her foot to toe-tapping Celtic rhythms.

After a two-part reel, Nainsi raised her fiddle and joined in playing a Scottish lament. The haunting minor key told a story of aching sorrow that ended on an unresolved note. As Louise sighed from the emotion of the music, Nainsi bowed a ta-dum beat to signal a new song, and fiddle and piano began a happy folk dance. They segued into a lively tune that escalated into a rousing reel. Next to her, Cynthia began tapping out the beat with her hands against her jeans. Louise glanced over, and Cynthia smiled.

"Wow," she mouthed.

"She's good," Louise said, nodding agreement with her daughter's assessment. They shared a smile. After a confusing day, the music lessened Louise's dissatisfaction. The school might be disorganized, but the instructors played beautifully.

The evening rounded out with several songs by the Luken family. Each instrument took a short solo in a medley of well-known hymns. Louise had never before heard "In the Garden" and "Because He Lives" played with guitars, fiddles, bass fiddle, piano and banjo. The three younger boys and their sister sang along. Louise knew the words by heart and sang the verses in her head. The combined instruments lacked the grandeur of a pipe organ, but the hymns still told a story of trust and God's faithfulness and love.

Chapter Fourteen

"Good morning, ladies. How did you sleep?" Earlene asked Tuesday as she poured coffee for Louise and Cynthia.

"Very well, thank you," Louise said.

"Are you enjoying the camp?"

Louise glanced across the table at Cynthia. "It's interesting," Louise said.

"The instructors treated us to a wonderful concert last night," Cynthia added.

"The Lukens bring in fabulous talent," Earlene said. "We always attend the benefit concert at the end. It's so popular, it draws people all the way from San Francisco. The inn will be full for the weekend. We try to attend Friday night too. That's when the students play. We like to encourage our guests, you know."

"I didn't realize we would play for the public," Louise said. Based on the previous day's session, she thought, a public performance might cast a negative light on the school. Louise couldn't imagine pulling together a performance out of Monday's chaos. Her students practiced their recital pieces for over a month.

"Just a few of the locals, and it's always a treat," Earlene said.

"I can't wait to hear it," Cynthia said.

Louise looked at her daughter. Cynthia had the audacity to grin at her.

⤶

On the stage at the far end of the dining hall, Farley Blackthorn sat at the piano, facing a semicircle of keyboards. The stage was plain, with no curtain or backstage area, and only one strip of spotlights overhead illuminated it.

"Mornin'," Farley said. He was dressed casually in blue jeans and a T-shirt. "Yesterday was set-up day, and we were pretty disorganized. Today we need to get down to work. In this class, we'll use the Nashville number system and the twelve-bar blues form. Each number represents a chord. On the C scale, a Roman numeral I chord is a C-major chord." He explained the chords and root notes. Everyone around her seemed to understand, so Louise assumed the students knew some music theory, although the use of numbers for chords was new to her. Since her music education was extensive, she was surprised that she had never before encountered Farley's system.

"There are seven chords, or some people call them *scale degrees*, on the piano white notes. That's what we'll be using. Is that clear as mud?" he asked.

Several people nodded their heads. Louise looked at Farley, perplexed and a bit disturbed. His system made her think of a paint-by-numbers picture. Playing the piano involved notes and rhythms and sequences. Real music was a science as well as an art form. She taught her students notes and scales and eventually, when they mastered the basics, how to read scores that had been developed by musical masters. This man intended to reduce music to a few numbers. *If you play the numbers right, you'll get a tune.* She shook her head. Cynthia would be disappointed, but this was not material for a children's book. Children needed to learn the correct way. Not some shortcut.

Farley played a quick, short run on the keys. Louise recognized the blues format. The first four bars set the melody and the second four bars repeated it, then the third four bars resolved the tune.

"For some of you, I'm asking you to set aside your musical training and go along with what we're doing here," Farley told the group of eight. "We're going to learn the blues format in several keys, as well as the peculiar chord combinations that mimic tones that lie somewhere between our notes, sort of like sharps and flats, only not quite semitones. This is basic music with a tonal quality that doesn't fit the piano keys, so we resort to dissonant chords to achieve the sounds."

Louise wasn't a fan of blues and the subsequent pop music that came out of the blues movement, but she had a basic knowledge of the styles. The blues had risen to popularity in Chicago, Kansas City and New Orleans when musicians increased the tempo for dancing and developed the boogie-woogie. From those roots, the big-band era softened the music to swing style for ballroom dancing. Louise loved some of the swing classics from Benny Goodman, Glenn Miller and Duke Ellington. She remembered her mother putting records on the phonograph and dancing around the living room with Alice and her.

"Everyone in this class should be proficient on the piano," Farley said, drawing Louise back to the present. "If you can play along with a blues or folk or early rock-and-roll song, or play a jazz standard or a Bach two-part invention or an equivalent classical piece, you're in the right class. I'm not teaching you traditional music, though. I want you to have fun with this camp, so if you feel stressed out by what we're doing, you might want to go to the Piano Three Class. And don't feel bad if you decide to do that."

Louise could play the pieces he'd mentioned, but that didn't mean she wanted to participate. She wondered if the other class taught a traditional style and method.

Farley demonstrated the basic blues scale, playing slowly. "I want you to copy the scale that I just played. It's in the key of F. I'll repeat it, then you play it," he told the class. He played it again.

Louise played the scale, which varied slightly from a standard major scale. Most of the class played the notes together, although they weren't in perfect time.

"Good. Now let's add a blues note. In the F scale, it will be the B-natural between the B-flat and C. This doesn't duplicate the blues note exactly, but it is as close as we can get on the piano." He played the revised scale and the class repeated his scale.

"I know this seems elementary, but we want to get the basics right before we proceed. Now we'll play chords. I'm in the key of C, playing a I, IV, V, I progression." Farley played a twelve-bar sequence with chords.

"For the next couple of days, this will seem repetitive, but bear with me. I'll play the chords again, and I want you to play them back to me."

Louise easily repeated Farley's chords.

"Very good. Now play the chords, only play the root with your left hand and do not play it with your right hand." He demonstrated, and the class responded, sounding rather sloppy.

"Now we'll play a few blues chords, including some of those extra notes I mentioned. You'll notice they are slightly discordant. These chords are not set in stone. Learn these, but if you feel a note combo that you like better, use it." He demonstrated. This time, when the class played the chords, the notes were all over the place.

The rest of the class time, Farley had the group play the blues chords in every key. After a couple of hesitations, the exercise became simple for Louise. She wondered if her students got bored with practicing the various scales. Reminding herself that mastering the scales and chords were basic prerequisites to playing the piano, Louise applied herself with as much enthusiasm as she could muster.

Bonnie Dalton, the music-camp coordinator, set her lunch tray next to Cynthia and climbed over the bench to sit down. Her jeans were tucked into the top of brown and gray tooled-leather cowboy boots. Her western shirt had fringe along the front yoke and sleeves. "Mind if I join you?"

"Please do," Cynthia said. "I've wanted to talk to you."

"That's what Doris told me. She said you're a writer. I don't know much about the actual classes, but I can tell you about the clerical part of running the camp. How can I help you?"

"Actually, I'm an editor researching a book idea for my publishing house, and I'd like to ask you some questions." Cynthia handed Bonnie a business card. "We do children's books, and I'm trying to put together an educational series about activities families can enjoy together. Your camp was recommended by a former student."

"How neat! I'll be glad to help if I can."

Cynthia got out a notepad and set her lunch aside while she launched into a list of questions for the music-camp coordinator.

Louise listened to their conversation for a time, but her mind wandered back to the piano class, mulling over Farley's instruction. She wondered about the rest of the classes. The camp tuition was modest compared with those of the music festivals where Eliot had taught, but these people had come to learn to play their instruments. Some were taking beginner classes. What kind of instruction were they getting?

Tuesday afternoon, nine-year-old Meghan Quinlan and ten-year-old Bree Brubaker stood on stools by the stove in Grace Chapel Inn's kitchen, watching Jane demonstrate turning milk and flour into a thickened sauce.

"Before we start, it's important to follow safety rules in the kitchen, and most of them are common sense," Jane said. "Don't lean or reach across a hot stove or burners. Keep pan handles off to the side, so you can reach them without getting burned or knocking them off the stove. Use pot holders to pick up hot dishes and pans. And as we did just a minute ago, always wash your hands before you touch food. Now, for our sauce. We start with just enough of the milk to dissolve the flour over a medium heat," Jane said as she stirred. "We use a wire whisk and keep it moving, stirring constantly. Bree, do you want to stir?"

"Sure." Jane handed Bree the whisk and stepped aside.

"Keep stirring, but you don't have to do it fast," Jane said. "Meghan, pour a little more milk into the pan, please. Come at it from the side so you're not reaching across the burner."

Meghan poured half of the contents of the glass measuring cup into the flour mixture, while Bree continued to stir.

Jane explained the basics of a cream sauce to the girls, just as she'd taught Josie. Although this was a different recipe, the process was the same.

Meghan looked at Jane, listening intently. Bree turned to look at Jane for a moment, then started stirring vigorously. "Eek. It's getting lumpy," she said.

"That's not a problem. Keep stirring. It's getting thick, so, Meghan, you can slowly add the rest of the milk."

After Meghan poured the remaining milk into the pan and Bree stirred it in, Jane said, "There, that looks done." She turned off the burner and took the pan.

"This will be the basis of our frosting. I'm going to put the sauce in a bowl and put it in the freezer for a few minutes to get it cold quickly while we make the cake. Usually, I just put it in the refrigerator."

After Jane emptied the pan, Bree put her finger in it and got a bit of the mixture from the pan's side. She put the sauce in her mouth, wrinkled her nose and leaned over to Meghan. "It's not sweet," she whispered.

Jane heard and smiled. "We haven't added the sugar yet. It will be sweet, I promise. Being a cook is a little like being a magician. You mix things together and when you get done, you have something completely different from what you started with. That frosting is called Crazy Frosting, and it goes on a Crazy Cake."

Bree and Meghan exchanged glances and giggles. Then they shrugged and turned to see what Jane would do next.

"Here's the recipe," she said, setting a recipe card in front of them. They looked at the card.

Crazy Mocha Cake

frosting P. 141

Before starting cake, make first part of frosting and refrigerate.
Mix cake by hand.

3/4 cup unsweetened baking cocoa

3 cups flour

2 cups sugar

1 teaspoon salt

1 teaspoon baking soda

10 tablespoons cooking oil   *5/8 cup (1/2 c + 2 TBL)*

2 tablespoons white or cider vinegar

2 teaspoons vanilla

2 cups brewed coffee, chilled, regular, decaf
  or espresso

Mix dry ingredients together in large bowl. Make three 3
wells in the dry ingredients. Pour cooking oil in one
well. Pour vinegar in the second well and vanilla in the
third. Pour coffee over top. Mix well by hand. ''
  Pour into greased nine-by-thirteen-inch pan. 9 X 13
  Bake at 350 degrees thirty-five to forty minutes or
until cake springs back when lightly touched in center.

Jane placed a large stainless-steel bowl on the kitchen table. "I think we'll work here, since it's lower. Bree, I want you to measure the baking cocoa into the bowl."

Bree measured, and Jane showed her how to level it off. Then she showed the girls how to measure out a level cup of flour. To the flour and cocoa, they added and mixed in the rest of the dry ingredients.

Following Jane's instructions, Bree and Meghan made wells and added the oil, vinegar and vanilla. The girls stared into the bowl, as if expecting something magic to happen.

"Vinegar?" Bree asked, making a sour face. "I don't think this will taste good, Miss Howard."

"I don't see anything happening," Meghan said.

Jane smiled. "I promise you won't taste the vinegar, and the crazy part is the vinegar. That's not a usual cake ingredient, but it activates the baking soda to make the cake lighter. Now pour the coffee over the whole thing and stir it by hand." Jane had picked the recipe for its simplicity.

"My mother doesn't let me drink coffee yet," Bree said.

"I've tasted it. I don't like it," Meghan said. "Maybe we should add something else, like..." Meghan scratched her head. "Maybe milk, so it would be like cocoa."

Jane brought out a pitcher of cold coffee. "Not to worry: This is decaffeinated. Once it's mixed in, you won't taste the distinct coffee flavor."

The girls took turns stirring the cake mix with a large wooden spoon, scraping the sides and getting some of the ingredients on the table.

"My mom lets me help make cakes. She doesn't make them like this. She uses a cake mix and a mixer. It's faster, you know, and a lot easier," Bree said, as if Jane was out of touch with modern technology.

"Me too," Meghan said. "We made brownies last week. They were re-e-e-ally good, and I licked the bowl."

Jane couldn't suppress a smile. "With this cake, we don't use an electric mixer, because the vinegar and baking soda set up a chemical reaction that raises the cake. If we mix it too much, it would go flat when it cooks. Some packaged mixes are really good, but it's nice to be able to make something from scratch too. Once you learn to make a basic cake, you can vary the ingredients to create different flavors."

"From scratch?" Bree said. "What's *scratch*?"

"Well, it means starting from the beginning," Jane said.

"That's funny," Meghan said. "My mom tells me not to scratch." She giggled.

"Maybe we're supposed to scratch the flour," Bree said, joining Meghan in the giggles.

"*Hmm*," Jane said, purposely scratching her chin. "That would be scratching the surface."

The girls giggled. In truth, she had no idea where the term *from scratch* came from. Jane turned on the burner under a large pot of water.

"I think that's mixed enough," Jane said. She asked Meghan to grease a glass baking dish, then had Bree spread the cake mix into the pan.

Bree licked a bit of the cake that was stuck to the bowl. She looked at Meghan and nodded. "It's sweet," she whispered.

Jane had the girls put the cake in the preheated oven. Then she set the timer for thirty-five minutes. For a few seconds, the girls watched the cake through the glass in the oven door.

Jane smiled. "Okay, on to the next thing. Don't worry, the buzzer will tell us when it's done." She steered the girls to the sink.

The girls washed their hands while Jane took the cooled frosting base out of the freezer.

This time, she got out the electric hand mixer. She set the recipe in front of them.

Crazy Frosting

¼ *cup flour*
1 *cup milk*

Crazy Frosting

¼ cup flour   1 cup milk

½ cup shortening

½ cup butter

1 cup granulated sugar

1 teaspoon vanilla

Mix flour and milk and cook on stove until thick and smooth, stirring constantly. Remove from heat. Refrigerate until chilled.

Cream together shortening and butter. Add sugar. Mix well.

Add creamed mixture to chilled sauce. Then add

vanilla. Whip with electric mixer until fluffy.

The girls took turns adding the ingredients and whipping the frosting to a light, fluffy confection. They were licking the beaters when the oven timer buzzed.

Jane demonstrated testing the cake and had each girl try it. Then she removed the cake from the oven and placed it on a wire rack to cool. She washed the bowls, measuring cups and spoons, then had the girls dry them to occupy their time while they waited.

Later, as they frosted the cooled cake, Bree kept accidentally getting frosting on her fingertip, which she had to lick off. She nodded her head. "This is pretty good," she declared. "Could use some chocolate, but it's sweet."

"I know it's tempting to lick the frosting," Jane said, "but it's important for health reasons to keep your hands clean and out of your mouth, and not to lick the spatulas until the cake is completely finished. That way we don't spread germs."

"Can we have a piece when we're done?" Bree asked.

"A small piece," Jane said. "You can take some home to your family."

"Oh goodie," Meghan said. "I hope it's yummy."

Jane laughed. "It will be."

She poured three glasses of milk and cut a small piece of cake for each of them.

Bree finished hers in three bites and gulped down her milk. Meghan savored her piece. Bree set her glass down and pronounced, "That's really good. But you know, I think it would be even better with chocolate chips in it."

"Perhaps we could crumble a candy bar on top, like toffee candy," Jane suggested.

"Yeah, that might be good. I mean, the frosting's good, but I like chocolate. That's my favorite," Meghan said. Bree agreed.

"Great ideas, girls. I'll make a note of your suggestions." She could list several alternatives to suit the tastes of the bakers. Based on the reactions to the macaroni and cheese and the pizza faces that she had made for the ANGELs, she knew she could count on a variety of opinions.

Chapter Fifteen

oung Nathan Perry seemed oblivious to the people around him as the class gathered for the Tuesday afternoon session. Louise thought that he was playing "I've Been Working on the Railroad," but he was trying to improvise a counterpart, and the results rendered the song nearly unrecognizable. She was about to offer to help him when Farley walked up the steps.

"Good job," Farley said. "Let's try a different key."

Farley sat next to the boy, who beamed with the attention. He played a couple of bars for the boy, then got up and patted his shoulder. "Keep at it," he said.

Louise had to press her lips together to keep from saying something. The boy needed written music and proper instruction before he could improvise.

"This afternoon we're going to play a song," Farley said. "I'm hoping you know 'Swing Low, Sweet Chariot.' We'll play it in twelve-bar blues format. Once we get the chords down, we'll improvise. Ready?" He sat at the piano and looked around. All eyes were on him. He played a simple rendition once through. Then he paused for a dramatic moment and dived into a jazzed-up version, pounding a fast succession of chords with his left hand and a series of runs, trills, arpeggios and counterchords with his right hand.

Louise listened, amazed. She'd never heard the old spiritual played with such energy, such gusto, such...such passion. Farley was smiling as he played. It was the first time she'd seen him smile. He was enjoying himself. Louise looked over at Nathan, who was watching Farley with rapt attention. Farley finished with a flourish, then stood. The change in his demeanor was disconcerting. Suddenly he was once again the laid-back cowboy, chewing on his toothpick.

"We'll start with the simplified version, but you can see how it can be jazzed up with improvisation."

Louise was amazed that Farley didn't pass out any music to the students. She thought he must have forgotten. Without music, Louise wasn't sure she could play a rendition like Farley had just played, and she doubted the other students could either.

When Farley still had not handed out music at the end of the class, Louise went up to ask him.

"Excuse me, Farley. You didn't pass out the score for this arrangement," she said.

"The score?" he responded, giving her a blank look.

"Yes. The music. Could I have the written music, please," she said politely.

He rubbed his chin and gave her a perplexed look. "We don't use written music in this class," he said. "I thought everyone understood that."

"You're not serious, are you? Students need to read the arrangement as interpreted by the composer, the timing, the phrase notations, the accidentals, all of the things that go into a score, in order to play a piece. You can't expect us to play without guidance."

"But I am guiding you," he said, giving her a kind smile.

The man must be self-taught. He just didn't get it. "I don't mean to be uncompromising. You're a wonderful musician, and I know different people have different methods of teaching, but I don't believe this is the way to teach piano," she said.

Farley looked at her, then turned around, shaking his head. She thought he was being terribly rude, but then he turned back to her.

"Do you have written music with you? Show me what you mean. Play something. Anything," he said. "I will play it with you, without music."

Louise looked through the music in her tote bag. She'd packed some Gershwin and a few jazz and ragtime pieces. He would know most of them. Luckily, stuck in between two jazz pieces, she found Bach's Fugue, no. 9 in E Minor. She doubted he'd know it.

She opened the music on her keyboard. He turned on Dan's keyboard and sat down on the bench. She began to play. He listened. After a few bars, he began playing a leisurely walking bass sequence that closely matched the bass part of the fugue. He took off on a descant over the top of her melody. It had nothing to do with the fugue, but it fit beautifully. She couldn't believe it. She forced herself to keep playing, following the written music precisely. He played for a couple of minutes, then descended and joined her, playing almost note for note the written part. She glanced over. He was not watching her. He had no music. He was looking up, his head slightly cocked, so that he appeared to be listening to her. They ended on the same note. Louise turned toward him.

"Do you happen to have Bach's fugue memorized?"

"Is that what we were playing?" he responded, giving her an innocent look.

"Yes. How did you do that?"

He shook his head. "I can't give you a simple answer. I've been playing for many years. The Nashville notation system that many bands use and that I teach makes it possible for any instrument to transpose music, but the short answer is that I hear the music and feel it, and it comes out in my fingers. I'm sure you can listen to music and know where it's likely going next. You can harmonize to songs you don't know. The music isn't on the written page, Louise, it's in here and here," he said, pointing to his heart and his ear. "I know this goes against everything you believe, but suspend your disbelief and give this a try."

Louise sighed deeply, raising her shoulders, then letting them drop. "You have an unusual ability, and to be honest with you, I doubt it can be taught. But it's your class. I'll try to keep an open mind."

Farley gave her a broad smile. "I look forward to changing your mind, Louise."

"Want to go walking with me?" Alice asked, poking her head into the kitchen. "Vera has to prepare for a teacher's meeting this evening, so she can't go."

Jane looked up from the sketch she'd drawn in her notebook. "Love to. I need a break." She stood and reached high, stretching first one arm, then the other. "Goodness, it's five o'clock already. I haven't thought about dinner." She laughed. "I spent the afternoon baking but made nothing for dinner. Let's eat at the Coffee Shop after our walk. We can come back here for cake. I saved a couple of pieces and sent the rest home with the girls."

"Sounds like a good plan to me. So what's with all this baking with the girls? It's not as if you don't have enough to do."

"Ah, you found me out. I was thinking about Cynthia's book imprint. A cookbook for families might be something she could use, but I don't want to suggest it until I have some firm ideas and recipes. So far, the girls are great pupils, but their tastes aren't developed. They'd rather have a mix out of a box than something homemade."

Alice nodded. "That may be, but your book is a good idea. They need to learn the basics, and it would be a great activity for the whole family."

"That's what I thought. I'm glad you think the idea has merit," Jane said. "Now if I could just come up with some kid-friendly recipes."

"I thought your macaroni and cheese with hot dogs, er, worms, was excellent," Alice said.

"I think the girls preferred macaroni and ketchup," Jane said.

Alice laughed. "They did seem to like that combination."

"You won't say anything until I'm ready?" Jane asked.

"My lips are sealed. Now, let's get going. You'd better bundle up. It's cold out."

Jane took her jacket and a scarf off the hook by the back door. She pulled gloves out of the coat pocket. When she was ready, they went outside through the kitchen door.

"Yoo-hoo. Oh, Jane. Alice."

Ethel waved at them from the dim light of the carriage-house porch. They veered across the lawn and went over to see what she wanted. Ethel wore a rose chenille bathrobe and fluffy pink slippers. Her bright-red hair was flat on one side and stuck up on top as if she'd been lying on it.

"Hi, Aunt Ethel. Have you been sleeping?" Alice asked.

Ethel raised a tissue to her nose. "Yes. I'm afraid I'm coming down with a cold. Are you going to town?"

"We'll end up there. Can we get something for you?" Jane offered.

"Please bring back some of that cold medicine I use and cherry cough drops. I simply must get a decent night's sleep if I'm going to fight this off." She sneezed into her tissue.

"Excuse me. What a terrible time to get a cold," she said. "I don't want to miss the scrapbook party this weekend."

"That would be too bad. We'll bring your medicine. It won't be right away, though. We're stopping at the Coffee Shop for dinner," Alice said.

Ethel placed the back of her hand against her forehead, striking a pose like the tragic heroine of an old-time movie. "I'll manage until you return. Just hurry." She sniffed and went back inside, shutting the door as they watched.

"I'll make some chicken soup after we get back. I hope she isn't terribly sick," Jane said. They started walking down the driveway.

"If I recall correctly, Aunt Ethel gets the sniffles every fall when the weather changes," Alice said. "Perhaps she really has an allergy. We can still treat it like a cold, just in case. Besides, a little coddling will make her feel better, and that helps too. Please make enough soup for us too. I love your chicken soup."

"I will. I have a whole chicken in the freezer. I'll boil it up."

"Good. That gets the good marrow out of the bones, which is what really does the trick with colds," Alice said. "At least that's my theory."

Jane laughed. "Something about it works."

After a brisk walk around town and a stop at the General Store for Ethel's cold remedies, they entered the Coffee Shop. Alice removed her gloves and stuffed them in her pocket, then took off her coat and put it on the faux red-leather seat of a booth. Jane removed her coat and slid in across from her.

"Hi, ladies. It must be cold outside. Your cheeks are red," Hope said, bringing them glasses of water. "Would you like some tea, Alice?" When Alice nodded, Hope turned to Jane. "Jane, do you want coffee?"

"I'll have tea too. Why don't you bring us a pot. We've been walking, and it *is* nippy out there."

"Will do. Are you here for dinner? June made chicken cacciatore. It's very good."

"Sounds like the perfect thing for this cold night," Alice said.

"I agree," Jane said. "Make that two."

While they waited, Alice looked around the room. Lloyd Tynan and Fred Humbert were eating dinner at one table. Nellie Carter shared a table with Sylvia Songer. They waved at Alice and Jane. At another table, Pastor Thompson sat across from Garrett Yeager.

"The chamber of commerce meeting must be tonight," Jane said.

Alice nodded. "It's nice to see Garrett has made friends. He must get lonely being away from home so much on business. I'd hate living that way."

"I suppose you'd get used to it. We should invite him to eat with us more often. I wonder if he likes chicken soup," Jane said.

"Everyone loves chicken soup. Especially yours. It might even cure loneliness."

"Now there's a thought. Maybe I should patent it. Then we'll become independently wealthy and we can retire."

"No, thank you. Then I'd need a cure for boredom."

"Chicken soup?"

When they both started laughing, several people turned around to see what was so funny.

"What are you doing, Mother?" Cynthia asked, taking a seat across from Louise in the dining hall Tuesday evening.

Louise looked up from her task. "Hello, dear. I was concentrating so hard I didn't notice you come in. I'm writing the score for the piece we worked on this afternoon. The song is simple, but Farley played it in the blues configuration and he embellished it a great deal. He insists we learn this without music, but I don't see how that's possible. I know if I can put the notes on paper, I can play it."

Cynthia shook her head. "None of the classes use music."

Louise saw that her daughter was looking at her as if she were cheating. "No music? I thought it was just Farley. Why?"

"I've learned from my interviews that the camp is based on auditory learning. They want you to play by ear."

"That fits with what Farley told me. But your father never taught that way. Cynthia, I'm concerned about your project. Perhaps your book should focus on a traditional music festival."

"Most traditional camps aren't geared to families, Mother." Cynthia sighed. "We're here. Why don't we wait until the end of the week before making a judgment on the camp's method? Can you stick it out?"

"Yes, of course, but I'm not the concern. I'm worried about the children. Nathan, for example, looks at Farley as if he's the greatest pianist on earth. I admit Farley plays the boogie style brilliantly, but musicians aren't always great teachers."

"Good evening, ladies and gents and little cowboys and cowgirls," Micah Luken said into a microphone. Louise noticed the teenage girls were sitting up near the stage tonight. The Luken twins were friendly and good-looking in a western way with their cowboy hats and boots and big silver belt buckles. Louise suspected most of the young women had crushes on them. The older Perry boys hung out with the Luken twins, which doubled the number of eligible young men.

"We've got a special treat," Micah said. "Get ready to clap your hands and stomp your feet. This is family night at Rock Creek Ranch, and we've got talent. We'll start out with the Perry family. Y'all come on up," Micah said.

He handed the microphone to Noelle, one of the older girls, who also was taking Farley's piano class. She introduced her eight siblings. They arranged themselves on stage with the tallest in the back. "We're going to play 'The Red Haired Boy,' then we'll finish with 'Jesus Really Cares,'" Noelle announced. She sat at the piano. The guitars started, then the three fiddles came in. Finally the piano, bass fiddle, a mandolin and a banjo joined in, and the audience began clapping and tapping their feet in time.

The players took turns, spotlighting the different instruments. Nathan played a mandolin. The youngest, a little girl of about six, played a miniature fiddle. She played a short refrain by herself and the crowd whistled and cheered. Louise wasn't used to such an enthusiastic audience, but their spirit made her smile. The crowd participated as much as the musicians.

Another family took the stage. The mother played the piano. The oldest child, a boy of about eight, played a cello. Louise couldn't believe the tone he pulled from the instrument. Two other boys, who looked like twins, played small fiddles. The youngest two, little girls in Sunday dresses with lacy socks and black patent-leather shoes, shared a microphone.

The mother played "Come, Thou Fount of Every Blessing." The girls sang, their angelic little voices ringing out to an appreciative audience, sending their pure notes right into Louise's heart. The performances lacked polish, but the musical talent was staggering, and Louise understood that these families came together for the sheer joy of playing and singing.

The last family to perform took the stage. Micah introduced them as three families, all related. There must have been fifteen people on the stage. One of the teenage girls, accompanied by the fiddles and guitars, sang a hilarious folk-ditty called "Railroad Bill," about a cantankerous railroad man who refused to behave, and so the songwriter wrote him right into disaster, and ol' Railroad Bill was done in by a lightning bolt.

As the rest of the audience roared with laughter, Louise and Cynthia laughed with them. After a rousing Celtic jig with three of the teenage girls do-si-doing with three little boys in the group, they finished their performance with a hymn. The whole group sang. Louise imagined Jesus looking down, laughing with delight at the three little boys in the front row who were yawning and singing in equal parts for all they were worth.

Chapter Sixteen

*B*ack at the bed-and-breakfast, Louise went though her nighttime rituals, climbed into one of the matching walnut beds, pulled the soft blue blanket over her and leaned back against a bank of fluffy pillows. While she waited for Cynthia to finish getting ready, she put on her glasses and opened her small travel Bible to the bookmark in the Psalms. She'd left off at Psalm 33, which she began reading.

> *Sing joyfully to the LORD, you righteous;*
>   *it is fitting for the upright to praise him.*
> *Praise the LORD with the harp;*
>   *make music to him on the ten-stringed lyre.*
> *Sing to him a new song;*
>   *play skillfully, and shout for joy* (1–3).

The playing and singing she'd heard tonight certainly praised the Lord with joy, with song and with skillful playing.

"Wasn't that something tonight?" Cynthia said, combing her hair as she came out of the bathroom.

"I was just thinking that," Louise said. "I loved the hymns, especially the last one sung by those little boys."

"Weren't they precious? They're taking Piano Two." Cynthia chuckled. "They expend so much energy all day long, they were running out of batteries."

"They made me think of some very active twin boys who visited the inn recently. Which reminds me, I wonder how things are going at home. I felt guilty about being gone during the scrapbook weekend, but they insisted they'd be fine."

Cynthia laughed. "They will. Not that they don't need you, but this week I needed you more. I'm so glad you came. How did it go today? Was it better? The classes I observed went much better."

Oh dear, Louise thought. *How do I answer without discouraging Cynthia?* She looked at her daughter, who was sitting on the side of the other bed, removing her slippers. Cynthia swung up her legs under the covers and turned toward her expectantly.

Louise closed her Bible and set it on the bedside table. "Much better organized today," she said. "Farley taught his method, and we worked on a song together. It's different from anything I've done before."

Cynthia nodded. "My friend warned me that they don't use the standard method here. If I'd paid more attention to you when I was a kid, maybe I'd understand what they're teaching. It's like a strange language to me."

Louise laughed. "It's foreign to me too. It doesn't fit any music theory that I know. I don't know what your father would think."

"Father loved classical music and modern classics, but he liked Gershwin, too, remember, and Gershwin composed and played jazz."

"Yes, but Gershwin was classically trained, and his music was heavily influenced by French composers. He studied in France, you know. His jazz was real music."

"Real music, Mother? It's all real music. I didn't know about Gershwin's training, though. I interviewed Doris Luken today. Her family sings and plays traditional western music, not the country-western music that's popular today. During the summer at their chuckwagon suppers, they perform cowboy songs and waltzes and western swing. During the winter, the family used to play in Texas and elsewhere in the South. Now the Luken children have struck out on their own, but there's so much interest in their music, they get together every fall to have a reunion and put on the music camp."

"I don't know much about cowboy music, but I remember the Sons of the Pioneers, and I loved watching Roy Rogers and Dale Evans movies when I was a child," Louise said.

"I researched cowboy music, and I was surprised that it's not old," Cynthia said. "I had imagined cowboys sitting around campfires on cattle drives singing to the cows, but the genre actually became popular when Hollywood started making western movies. You mentioned the Sons of the Pioneers." Cynthia laughed. "Did you know that one of their most popular songs, 'Tumbling Tumbleweed,' started out as 'Tumbling Leaves'?"

"Really? It's a good thing they changed the name," Louise said.

"I checked out the origins of the other music they teach at the camp," Cynthia said. "I want to include a bit of history in my book. The blues, jazz, bluegrass, swing and boogie-woogie developed from a mixture of the blues music that came to America from African culture and from old Scottish, Irish and European folk music that immigrants brought. Their cultures used music to pass down history and traditions."

Louise looked at Cynthia. "You've really done your homework, haven't you?"

"Yes. I want the books to give a full flavor of each subject. In this case, families sharing, learning and enjoying traditional music. I especially like that this camp is run by a family who wants to share the value of their faith in their music. They mix popular music with old hymns and spirituals. Too often, some people play down the importance of family values and the role faith plays. I don't want to do that, and my boss agrees. That's why I'm so excited about developing my own imprint. How often do we get a chance to do something we love while sharing our personal values? It's a chance of a lifetime, Mother."

"Yes, I *do* see. You're going to create a wonderful series, and I'm glad I'm able to help."

"You have some younger children in your class, don't you?"

"Yes. Nathan Perry is the youngest. There's another child about twelve years old, and a couple teenagers and some young adults."

"Perfect. I want to get your impressions of them and how the different ages interact. The camp culminates in the class performances Friday night. I've spent a little time in every class. I'll go back through each one tomorrow and Thursday. I can't wait to see how everyone improves."

Louise hoped Cynthia wouldn't be disappointed by the camp. More than that, *she* didn't want to disappoint her daughter. Somehow, Louise had to grasp the concepts and pull off a good performance, for Cynthia's sake.

"By the way, Mother. I almost forgot. Doris said you could play the pump organ in the chapel any time you want to."

"Wonderful! I will." At least *that* she would be certain to enjoy.

"I have nine confirmed registrations, plus Mary Jo," Penny told Jane on the phone Wednesday morning.

"All our rooms are full. In fact, they're overflowing," Jane said. "We have six ladies plus Garrett Yeager, who'll have meals with us, since his daughter is coming. That's quite a crowd. Do you think we have enough work space?"

"We'll make it work. I'll ask Zeke to come over on Friday morning with folding tables and chairs, if that's all right."

"That's fine. I hope he'll be willing to help us move furniture," Jane said.

"Oh, you know my husband: He'll be glad to help. I'm so excited. Thanks for doing this, Jane."

"You're welcome. I think it's going to be fun." Jane hung up the phone and turned to her menus. She had two days to get ready for the weekend. She suddenly realized how much she relied on Louise. Normally Jane handled the food and helped clean the inn, and Louise and Alice managed everything else. This time she had five meals plus snacks to prepare and had to help Alice run the inn.

Speaking of Alice, it was time for her to leave for work, Jane thought, looking at the clock. But her sister hadn't come downstairs yet. *That's* odd, Jane thought. She said a quick prayer that Alice hadn't caught a cold from Ethel.

Jane poured a cup of coffee and carried it to the table, where she opened her notebook to the scrapbook weekend. She'd planned Friday night and Saturday breakfast and lunch, but that left Saturday dinner and Sunday brunch. Taking a sip of coffee, she glanced out the window. The bare trees danced in the wind, their limbs waving and bowing, lashed by cold rain. The weather called for comfort food. Turkey came to mind, but a traditional turkey dinner would be too difficult for people to eat buffet style.

She wrote *turkey*, *ham* and *scalloped potatoes* on her list. Dressing would work, but not gravy. She twiddled her pencil between her fingers as she thought.

"Good morning," Alice said, entering the kitchen. "I can't believe I slept so late. I'm sorry I wasn't here to help with breakfast." Alice was dressed in corduroy pants and a sweatshirt with a birdhouse and bluebird on the front.

"I'm glad you got some needed rest," Jane said. "Garrett only wanted hot cereal and toast. There's some cereal left if you want it."

"That sounds fine."

"Let me get it for you," Jane said, rising.

"No, no. I'll heat it and make my tea." Alice opened the refrigerator and took out the container of cereal and a carton of half-and-half. She warmed the cereal in the microwave oven.

"You're not ill, are you?" Jane asked.

"No. Just lazy. I took today through Monday off so I can help with the weekend and cleaning up afterward."

"Bless you! I suddenly realized we only have two days to get ready. Zeke will bring tables on Friday morning. Then our guests and Mary Jo will arrive and we'll be off and running."

Alice made a cup of tea. She poured cream on the chopped pecans, dried cranberries and brown sugar that topped her hot wheat cereal. She set them on a tray and carried it to the table.

"How may I help?" she asked.

"Eat your cereal while it's hot, then we can plan our day."

Alice bowed her head and said a silent prayer.

As she watched Alice take a spoonful of cereal, Jane felt a bit guilty. She'd been so busy this morning, she'd forgotten to pray. Alice and Louise were so faithful. She silently thanked God for her sisters and added her own request that she would honor Him with her meals and her attitude this weekend.

Louise made a point to arrive at the ranch before the classes started Wednesday morning. Taking out the music she'd written, she turned on her keyboard to the lowest sound setting and practiced the song. The noise in the dining hall made it hard for her to hear herself play, but no one else could hear her at all.

Ten minutes before class, Nathan came up and turned on his keyboard. Louise put away her music.

"Hey, Mrs. Smith. Are you practicing our song?"

"Good morning, Nathan. I thought I'd run through it a couple of times. I enjoyed your mandolin playing last night. You're very good."

Nathan beamed. "Thanks. I'm better on the guitar, but I like the mandolin. If you need any help on the keyboard, I can help you."

Louise managed to hide her surprise at his offer. She had thought that perhaps she could help him.

⌒

"I can't believe the difference in the pictures," Alice said, standing in the newspaper office, looking through the copies of her photographs. "You did this on your computer?"

"Yes. Neat, isn't it?" Carlene said. "I have a program that enhances prints. It can even make them look like paintings or caricatures. You like them?"

"Very much. Thanks for the articles and photos from the newspaper's files. Jane and Louise will be so surprised. Now if I can just make the scrapbook attractive," Alice said.

"You'll do a beautiful job. I'd love to see it when you're finished."

"Come for tea next week. That is, if I finish the scrapbook over the weekend," Alice said. She picked up the large envelope and the box of old pictures.

Carlene came around the corner of the counter. "I'll get the door," she said. "You've got your hands full. Have fun making the scrapbook."

"I'll try."

Alice went out into the chilly afternoon air. The sun appeared as a gray ball behind the layer of clouds. It wouldn't break through today.

Alice stopped at Time for Tea. As she entered the shop, she stood for a moment, breathing in the tantalizing aromas of rich tea blends and exotic spices.

Laurie Lopez turned from dusting a shelf of china teapots. She was a young woman in her early twenties who worked part time in the shop. "Hi, Alice. What can I get for you today?"

Alice glanced at her list. "I need some ginger-peach and some blackberry-sage tea. We're having a group in for the weekend. I'd better get some more double bergamot Earl Grey also. I noticed we're low on it."

"I heard about the scrapbook retreat. My sister goes to scrapbook retreats and parties all the time in Louisville. She took my mom to a place about an hour and a half from her home. Mom had a blast. Now she makes scrapbooks all the time. In fact, she's visiting my sister now, otherwise she'd probably join your group."

"I'm discovering a lot of people love scrapbooking. How about you?"

"No way. I'm not into crafts. Maybe when I get married and have kids, like my sister, I'll do scrapbooks, but I'd rather go bowling or skating, you know...active things."

Alice did know. She'd always preferred outdoor, physical activities to crafts. "I'm making a scrapbook," Alice admitted, "but it's not my cup of tea either." She smiled as she gestured toward the offerings around her. Being in the tea shop gave her an idea, though. Grace Chapel Inn, formerly the Howard home, and before that the Berry home, had hosted many tea parties in its hundred-plus years. Her scrapbook must include a page or two dedicated to tea. She looked around the shop for something she could include. She spotted a stack of advertising brochures Jane had put together for tea parties. The brochures had a picture of the inn and another of the living room during one of their tea events. Alice picked up a brochure and put it with the teas Laurie had put in the bag. She could use a fancy tea napkin as a background. Jane was sure to have other things she could use to decorate the scrapbook pages.

"When does Wilhelm get home from his trip?" Alice asked.

"He should get home next week. He wants to get ready for the Christmas buying season, he said. I can't wait to see what new merchandise he's ordered."

"I'll have to come in and see," Alice said. Wilhelm Wood, the proprietor, loved to travel and often brought back unusual teas and tea accessories.

Alice took her purchases and said good-bye. The enticing aromas in the shop whetted Alice's appetite. She couldn't wait to get home and have one of the cranberry-nut bars that Jane was making today and a good, hot cup of tea.

Chapter Seventeen

The next class session won't start for almost an hour," Louise told Cynthia as they finished their lunches Wednesday. "Maybe I'll try out that pump organ."

"You go ahead. I'm going to talk to Bethany Luken. She's been toying with a children's book idea and wanted to discuss it with me. I'll take our trays up," Cynthia said, standing and picking up her mother's empty lunch tray.

Louise took her tote bag and went out the back of the stables to the ranch yard. As she walked toward the chapel, she heard music coming from it. She hesitated at the door, then curiosity won out and she entered the old building. She stood just inside the door, waiting for her eyes to adjust to the dim lighting, listening to the music.

The old bellows wheezed and snorted loudly in steady rhythm beneath the undulating sounds of "The Old Rugged Cross." Whoever was playing the organ had stamina as well as expertise.

The midday sun streamed through the stained-glass window, lighting the dust motes that danced in the air, disturbed by the air from the organ. As Louise's eyes adjusted, the organist turned toward her. She looked in disbelief. Farley Blackthorn rose from the bench.

"Come in, Louise," he said. "Did you come to hear me or to play?" he asked. "Of course, you could be here to pray. If that's the case, I will leave you to have some solitude."

"I'm sorry," she said. "I didn't mean to interrupt you. I did come to try out the organ. I haven't played a reed organ in quite a while. You play beautifully."

"Surprised? Yes, I can see that you are." He grinned. "I play ragtime and swing by choice, but I have a varied musical background," he said. "My mother dreamed of raising her own chamber orchestra. I'm afraid we were a great disappointment to her."

"I doubt that," Louise said. "You're very talented. Please, play something else." Louise sat on the front pew, just in front of the organ.

"Only if you will play a song for me," Farley said.

"I'm afraid I'm rusty."

"As am I," he said. "It isn't every day one has an opportunity to play an antique reed organ. Doris Luken takes excellent care of this one." He sat at the organ and began pumping, filling the bellows with air. "Sheep May Safely Graze," by Johann Sebastian Bach filled the room. When he finished, he swiveled around to face her. "Your turn," he said, making a sweeping gesture toward the bench as he rose and stepped aside.

Louise stood and picked up her tote bag. She reached inside for sheet music. "I'm afraid I'm not as accomplished as you. I need music," she said, although she had a large repertoire of memorized pieces. Sheet music gave her an extra measure of confidence.

Besides, she wanted to make a point: Students need the music. She selected a piece and propped it on the music stand, then sat at the bench.

She expected stiff foot pedals, but the bellows pumped easily. Still, it took an effort, like riding a bicycle. She picked a familiar hymn, "Blest Be the Tie That Binds." Matching the notes to her feet, the song dragged. She stopped after one verse.

"Play something from memory," Farley said. "That way you can concentrate on the song, not the notes."

Louise's mind drew a blank. What did she know from memory?

"How about 'Count Your Blessings'?" Farley suggested.

His choice surprised Louise. She turned to look at him over her shoulder. He smiled.

"My grandmother's favorite," he said. "She had a big influence on my music. Know it?"

"Yes, if I can remember how it starts."

"Try the key of E flat." He hummed a few bars.

Louise hit the E flat key on the organ. She listened and thought about it a moment, letting the tune go through her head. She pumped the pedals and hit a chord, then corrected a note and started to play. At first her chords kept time with her feet, dragging out the song as she had before. She felt a bit embarrassed under Farley's scrutiny, but she persisted, increasing the melody double time. The tune sounded better, but the pedals resisted her push. She concentrated on her feet, letting her hands play automatically. She couldn't believe how out of shape she was. At home, she went up and down stairs all day long. She played the song twice through, then quit as her legs felt like lead weights.

Farley applauded behind her.

"Phew! What a workout. That's harder than it looks," she said.

"You're right, but you played well."

"Thank you. I'd play better with practice."

"True, but you played without the music," he said.

"Yes, but I've played the song before, although not for some time. I have to admit, I play the organ at our church and I teach piano lessons."

"I can tell," Farley said. "You play with confidence and you have an ear for music."

"Thank you," she said. Louise hadn't felt confident since she arrived, but she supposed a certain amount of assuredness came from her years at the piano keys.

"I looked at your CDs at the registration desk. You must be popular. I'm sorry, but I don't follow country music or bluegrass, so I'm not familiar with your playing," she said. "Do you teach piano, other than here at the camp?"

"I've been on staff at a few music festivals, mainly bluegrass, as you guessed. This is my only annual teaching gig. To tell the truth," he said, lowering his voice and leaning forward as if telling her a secret, "I come so I can play this organ. Doris knows, but don't tell her son Abe. He thinks I come because of him. We've played a lot of gigs together over the years. He hauled me off stage and delivered me to the emergency room when my appendix burst. Then he covered my tour, so he figures I owe him."

Louise laughed, relaxing in front of this man for the first time. "He's right. You do owe him. But I won't tell." She ran her hand over the smooth, rich patina of the console. "Doris must love this old organ too."

"She's learning to play it. She wanted Abe to teach her, but he's so busy, he can't seem to find the time. Well..." Farley stood, hooked his fingers in his belt loops and hiked up his jeans. "Time for class." He strode toward the door, then turned. "See you there in a few."

As Jane dropped a spoonful of date-nut cookie dough on the baking sheet, the back door opened and Alice entered with a gust of wind.

"*Brrr.*" Alice set a sack and a box on the counter and removed her jacket, which she hung on a hook by the door. "I'll be down to help you in a few minutes," she said, then picked up the box and hurried out of the kitchen.

A moment later, Jane heard Alice going up the stairs. Jane finished filling the pan and slid it into the oven. Knowing Alice would want tea, she put the kettle on to boil.

The kettle had just started to whistle when Alice reappeared. "Oh good. Between the wonderful smells at Time for Tea and the wind, I'm ready for a cup of tea. Are you saving the cranberry bars?"

"I think we can sample a couple," Jane said. "I'll have hot cookies in a minute."

"Wonderful." Alice prepared the teapot and got out two cups. When the kettle shrieked, Alice removed it from the burner and poured boiling water into the pot. She covered the teapot with a cozy and carried it to the table.

"I see you've been busy," Alice said, looking around the kitchen. Cookies, loaves of fruit bread and a large bowl of crispy, spicy snack mix covered the counters.

"I wish I could make more ahead of time, but this will help," Jane said. "Bree, Josie and Meghan are coming to help tomorrow after school. I'll do the grocery shopping in the morning."

"I'd be happy to shop for you," Alice offered.

"Thanks, but I know exactly what I need and how much."

"I'll run the vacuum and dust tomorrow. It should hold through the weekend. I miss Louise. I hope she's having fun."

"She called this morning, using Cynthia's cell phone." Jane laughed. "She kept yelling into it, as if I couldn't hear her."

"Those phones take some getting used to," Alice said.

"I suppose so. She said the camp is going fine, but she didn't sound enthusiastic." Jane carried a plate of fresh, hot cookies to the table. "She said something about getting away from the ranch and going shopping this afternoon if Cynthia's willing. Then she wanted to know how we're doing. I didn't tell her how many are coming to the scrapbook party. I didn't want her to worry."

Alice poured two cups of tea. "I imagine she'll worry anyway." Alice stirred a lump of sugar into her tea and reached for a cookie.

⌒

"How was your afternoon session?" Cynthia asked Louise when they met in the dining hall.

"Don't ask," Louise said. After transposing the song Farley had played for them the day before onto staff paper, she'd practiced and felt confident with the song. "The Guitar Four class joined us this afternoon. They're going to play with us on Friday, it seems. Naturally, they couldn't just play the song the way we learned it. We had to transpose it to another key for the guitars. Why didn't he have us learn it in that key from the beginning?" She sighed.

"Were you able to play it?" Cynthia asked.

"Well yes, after a bit of trial and error. Actually, I felt good about transposing in my head. Then he told us he doesn't want us to think about it. 'Just play it,' he said." Louise let out a frustrated sigh. "That might work for someone who plays by ear, but not for a trained musician."

"I noticed that in other classes too. Doesn't it seem odd that an amateur can play so easily, while a trained musician struggles with this method?" Cynthia observed.

"Strange indeed. According to Farley, classical training hinders playing forms of folk music. 'It creates fundamental misconceptions about how music is learned.' His words exactly. I'm sure I gave him a look of complete disbelief. He had the audacity to raise his eyebrows at me. His entire diatribe was aimed at me. I tell you, Cynthia, perhaps I was just tired, but I was tempted to get up and leave the class."

Cynthia pressed her lips together. Louise couldn't miss the mirth in her daughter's eyes. "I wonder where he picked up the raised-eyebrow reaction, Mother. I haven't seen him do that."

"Yes, well, I suppose he mimicked me. I'm quite sure I've raised mine a time or two this week. How could I not? This is just so...so ridiculous."

Cynthia sobered and her brows knit. "I'm sorry, Mother. I didn't realize I would put you in such a disagreeable situation here when I asked you to come. I want you to enjoy a vacation. You don't have to continue the class. I need to spend part of the remaining time here at the ranch gathering information and taking pictures, but you could relax at the inn during the mornings. Then we could go sightseeing. I need a little information about the area too."

Louise's irritation waned as she realized she'd allowed her frustration to hamper Cynthia's project. "I'm overreacting. I've started, and I intend to see it through. I'm not so egotistical that I believe mine is the only teaching method." She smiled. "Who knows? Maybe I'll learn something."

"Mother, you're a peach." Cynthia hugged her. "Maybe Farley will learn something from you."

Louise's smile turned into a chuckle. "Now *that* would be something."

"Let's skip the rest of the day and go shopping," Cynthia said, her eyes brightening. "I've been dying to go shopping in Nevada City. It seems such a quaint town. Come on, let's do it. We can eat out."

"You don't even have to twist my arm. I'm ready for a break." She linked her arm through Cynthia's. "Let's go right now."

Chapter Eighteen

I love this town," Cynthia said an hour later, looking around at the restored, old clapboard and brick buildings of Nevada City Wednesday afternoon. The eclectic mix of Victorian, Colonial, Greek Revival and Gothic architecture fit the western ambiance of a town that had grown quickly with gold fortunes to fund the buildings. Brightly painted wood structures with ornate spindles, fancy gingerbread trim and tall cupolas rubbed shoulders with austere brick buildings that were sparsely decorated with tall, round-topped windows and wooden or wrought-iron shutters. False fronts hid flat roofs. One ornate building turned out to be an old firehouse. Old buckets, barrels and ore carts filled with bright geraniums, marigolds, snapdragons and pansies decorated storefronts and porches. Gas lamps lined the sidewalks. On the residential side streets, old oaks and maples spread their limbs over lawns, sidewalks and streets in front of lovely two-and three-story homes.

Walking along Broad Street, they passed the National Hotel, a stately building with a fresh coat of forest-green paint, with posts, porches, balconies and window frames painted in pristine white. The hotel, listed on the National Register of Historic Places, was also designated a California Historical Landmark as the oldest continuously operating hotel west of the Rocky Mountains.

They browsed through a gallery and a store that sold locally made jewelry. Louise bought a pair of dangling turquoise earrings for Jane. She looked for something for Alice, but nothing seemed right.

Cynthia spotted a store that sold western clothing. "Let's go in there. I'd like to find something special for Friday night. Everyone I've talked to is dressing up western."

Louise looked down at her tweed skirt and blue sweater set. Maybe she'd find something, a scarf perhaps, to help her get into the spirit of the camp.

At first glance, the store didn't appeal to Louise. It carried lots of denim clothing, cowboy hats and boots.

"Look at this, Mother," Cynthia said, holding up a blue fitted blouse with a deep scarlet, scalloped yoke adorned with embroidered flowers and light blue piping. "What do you think?" She held the hanger just under her chin.

"Very attractive," Louise said. "The color is good on you."

"I'm going to try it on. Have you found anything?"

"I think I'll buy this orange and navy plaid flannel shirt for Alice. She'd look good in that with her jeans, but this clothing isn't my style. Why buy something I'd only wear once?"

"Because you'll only have the opportunity once?" Cynthia asked in response.

"I have Jane's denim jacket."

"*Hmm*. I don't see that fitting with your wool skirts and sweaters. Let me look around."

A saleslady took Cynthia's choices to a dressing room while she wandered among the clothing racks.

"Ah. Here's a clearance rack," Cynthia said, heading to the back corner of the store. "Come look, Mother."

Louise followed Cynthia, knowing she wouldn't find anything that would appeal enough to make a purchase, but wanting to please her daughter.

Cynthia sorted through the rack.

"Oh, look," she said, holding up a white eyelet piece of clothing. "It's pantaloons." She pulled out a matching camisole. "Imagine wearing these under your skirts and sweaters," she said, her eyes twinkling with amusement.

Louise raised her eyebrow and tsk-tsked. "If you like them, you wear them," she told her daughter.

Cynthia laughed. "Not exactly my style either," she said, replacing them on the rack. She pulled out another hanger and held up an A-line denim skirt that flared at the bottom and had slash pockets. "This is your size," she said. She kept rifling through the clothes, then pulled out a blouse. "You'd look good wearing this style."

The plain, pale blue long-sleeved blouse had a traditional collar and a bib front held in place by pearl buttons. The collar and bib were piped in the same pale blue. The blouse had a Victorian look that could have been eastern as well as western. Louise imagined it with her wool skirts. She could wear it anywhere.

"I'll try that on," she said, holding out her hand. Cynthia gave her both pieces of clothing.

"You have to model them for me," she said.

Louise sighed. Cynthia was bound and determined her

mother would dress western. At least the clothes weren't what Louise thought of as cowboy western.

Louise was surprised by how well the clothing fit. She stepped out of the dressing room and stood in front of a three-sided, full-length mirror, turning from side to side to get the full effect. The denim made it western. Together with the midcalf-length skirt, the blouse looked western, although Louise could picture it paired with her usual skirts, and the skirt paired with her sweater sets.

"You look terrific, Mother. You have to get those. And look what I found." Cynthia held up a pair of light-brown lace-up granny boots.

"Oh no," Louise said, shaking her head emphatically. "My black flats look fine with this outfit, and they're much more comfortable than those contraptions."

"I bet these are comfortable," Cynthia said. "In fact, maybe I'll buy them myself."

"You do that." Louise turned and went back in the dressing room. *Granny boots, indeed.* She took one last look at herself in the dressing room mirror and smiled. Wouldn't Jane and Alice be surprised to see her in this getup? Perhaps the proper clothing would put her in the mood to play the western music.

"Would you like some more hash?" Alice asked Garrett Thursday morning.

"No thank you." He patted his stomach. "Tempting, but I

had plenty. That was delicious. I haven't had corned-beef hash and eggs in years. Is there anything I can do to help you get set up for your scrapbook weekend?" he asked.

"Nothing I can think of right now, but thanks for offering," Jane said. "Zeke Holwell is bringing tables tomorrow morning."

"I'll stick around then, in case I can help. In fact, I'm not working tomorrow or this afternoon. I moved my things into the back room already. Is it all right if my daughter arrives a day early? She got a ride from a friend who's dropping her off in Potterston today."

Garrett had volunteered to move to a room that shared a bathroom with his daughter and leave the rooms with private baths for the other guests.

"We'd love to have her come early. Her room is ready. Would you two like to join us for dinner tonight?"

"Thanks, but I want to take her to the Coffee Shop to meet Hope and June." He wiped his mouth and put down his napkin. "I'd better get moving. I need to put in a few hours' work before I pick her up. If you'll excuse me." He left the dining room and went upstairs.

"I'll tidy the kitchen and then go grocery shopping," Jane said.

"And I'll start on the Sunset Room, since Garrett has moved out. Then I'll make sure the other rooms are ready," Alice said, rising from the table and picking up her dishes.

Louise suggested to Cynthia that they should experience at least one breakfast at the ranch. Once there, Louise ate, then excused herself to go practice on her keyboard, leaving Cynthia to visit with Bethany Luken, the youngest child and only girl among the Luken children.

Setting her keyboard's volume on low, Louise played a progression of blues scales, then played from memory the piece she'd transcribed onto staff paper from Farley's example. Bent over the keyboard, running through the chords with her left hand, she frowned as she tried to play the right-hand runs. She couldn't remember exactly how the piece went. Frustrated, she fought the desire to quit. She kept the left-hand rhythm going while she toyed with a simple blues scale, adding triplets and tremolos. After a couple of minutes of repeating the patterns over and over, she began to feel the rhythm in what Farley called *licks* or *riffs*.

Falling into the rhythm, Louise added arpeggios and runs. Although it sounded entirely different, she had a sense of playing the "Bumble Bee Boogie," except she wasn't following a musical score. Gaining confidence, getting caught up in the sound, she played a little faster. Her fingers tripped over the notes. She'd certainly win no competition, but the discordant harmony and offbeat rhythm worked. She played a descending set of scales in triplets, ending on a tremolo.

Applause burst out right behind her head. Startled, she turned and looked up. Farley was smiling down at her.

"Good job, Louise. You caught it just right."

Embarrassed, Louise blushed. "I was just experimenting," she explained.

"Yes. That's what jazz is all about."

Farley walked to his piano. Louise realized that other class members were standing by their keyboards watching her. She blushed again, certain that she'd made a spectacle of herself and that Farley was being kind, hoping to encourage her playing.

With furtive glances at the clock, Alice rifled through a drawer full of odds and ends. She should have paid more attention to Jane's organization. Jane was particular about each utensil and pan and bowl going into its spot. Alice dried dishes often enough to know where everything went, but trying to find a noncooking or nonserving item in Jane's kitchen was a challenge. Where did she put the little decorative items she used for special occasions?

Jane would be home any minute. The girls would be arriving from school to get a cooking lesson. Alice thought it was wonderful that Jane wanted to teach the girls and develop an idea for Cynthia, but her timing could have been better. They had a scrapbook event in two days.

Giving up, Alice went into the storage room.

Perusing the shelves, Alice spotted several square storage baskets. Glancing back into the kitchen to make sure she was alone, she pulled one off the shelf. Packages of decorative paper napkins with bright flowers, stars, Christmas holly and Easter lilies filled the bin. Leafing through the packages, she found hand-painted place cards. Jane must have made them to match the napkins. *They'd be perfect*, she thought. Alice put several in her pocket. Packages of paper lace doilies rested on the bottom of the basket. She took a couple of pieces in various sizes and shapes. Underneath the doilies, she found a padded paper teapot about three inches in diameter. She couldn't imagine what it might be, but one wouldn't do Jane any good. Alice slipped it in her pocket. She heard a car door slam. Peeking out the window, she saw Jane take two grocery bags from the trunk. Alice intended to help her sister, but first she had to hide her treasures. She hurried upstairs and put her stash in a drawer. She suddenly appreciated what spies must go through, keeping their actions secret, having an excuse for anything they're discovered doing. Laughing to herself, she decided she was glad that spying was not in her future. Then she went down to help Jane.

Bags of groceries covered the counters. Jane was setting a large pot of water on the stove and turned the burner on high when Alice came into the kitchen from the back stairs.

"Are there more groceries?" Alice asked.

"Nope. I got them all."

"I'm sorry I didn't get down to help you. What can I do?" Alice asked.

"Would you mind taking the flowers up to the Sunrise Room? I set them in the hall."

"I'll do it right now. Be back in a moment." Alice disappeared out the kitchen door and returned a few minutes later.

"What do we need to do before the weekend?" she asked Jane. "I started a list. I think the rooms are ready except for the flowers and truffles. I'll do that in the morning and help Mary Jo and Penny get everything set up. Then I can take care of checking the guests in and showing them to their rooms."

"It sounds like you're planning to do all the work," Jane said.

"You're doing the cooking. That's the hard part."

"The girls are helping me make tomorrow's dinner. They should be here any minute. There's nothing else to make ahead of time, so we're in good shape."

She heard a knock on the door. "There they are now." Jane put the vegetables in the refrigerator bin, and Alice got up and answered the door. Three girls, their faces red from the cold, their hair mussed from the wind, came bouncing into the kitchen.

"Hi, we're ready to cook," Josie Gilmore said. "What are we making today?"

"Hello girls. Hang up your coats on the hooks and come wash your hands. We're going to make baked spaghetti, but first I'll fix you a snack."

"Yum. I love spaghetti!" Meghan said.

"Me too," Bree agreed. "What kind of snack?" She hung her coat on a hook and hurried to the sink.

Jane looked over at Alice, who was smiling.

"Come sit down, girls. I know Jane has cookies. I'll fix a plate."

The kitchen buzzed with life as the three girls talked at once, telling them about a cat that got into their classroom and climbed onto the teacher's desk.

"It started taking a bath right in the middle of our spelling test papers," Bree said, which sent the other girls into a fit of giggles.

Chapter Nineteen

*A*ll right, let's see what you've learned," Farley said. "Key of
G. One at a time, play a walking bass boogie pattern with
your left hand and solo over that using a blues scale. We'll start
on my left, with Noelle."

Noelle Perry thought for a moment, then started a walking
bass sequence. After a few bars, she played a run of syncopated
triplets up and down the scale, then she stopped and looked at
Farley.

"You've got the idea. Did you have to think about each note?"

Noelle nodded her head, then shook it. "At first I did, but
then I remembered hearing you play."

"Good. Remember, class, when you practice, it's all right to
think about the notes, the theories, the scales and chords, but
when you play, forget that and play from your heart. Hear a song
in your head and play what you hear. Feel a rhythm in your bones
and play the rhythm. That's jazz. That's boogie. That's blues.
That's freedom. Okay, Nathan, you're next."

Nathan began a bass sequence different from the one his sister played. Louise thought it sounded like "Chattanooga Choo
Choo." On top of it, he played a descending line in octaves that
bore little resemblance to the song, although listening closely,

Louise could imagine the train puffing along. The boy had a lot of talent. Watching him, Louise couldn't miss the joy on his face as he played. She'd noticed it when he played the cello too. In fact, many of the people at this music camp displayed delight and passion when they played. Few of her students showed the same kind of enthusiasm. What made the difference?

Louise's turn came. Not sure where to start, she played a succession of two-note dyads. She had no idea where she was going with the sequence. She began soloing over the bass with a syncopated riff on a blues scale, adding several grace notes for color. The results made a catchy tune. She repeated the phrase, then ended with a descending run, finishing on a tremolo on the I7 chord. Satisfied, she sat up straight and smiled.

Nathan began clapping. A few others joined him.

"Good job," Farley said. He went on to the next student, Daniel, a quiet young man in his midtwenties whose playing astonished Louise. His bashfulness disappeared. He played with confidence and spirit, as if his personality came out in his music.

When he finished, Louise clapped. He looked toward her and smiled.

He was the last to play and was about to pack up his things when Noelle went over to him and perched on the edge of his bench. He blushed and barely looked at her when she asked him about his piano playing. When she urged him to play something, he hesitated but finally gave in to her encouragement. He started with something simple but then demonstrated a rather complicated run for her. She tried it, her fingers fumbling. He showed her again, noticeably relaxing in the realm in which he felt comfortable. Noelle gazed at him with adoration as he played. Louise studied the couple closer. Noelle was an attractive girl in her early twenties. Daniel was a nice-looking, clean-cut young man. He had lovely blue eyes and a clear, honest gaze. Louise wondered if a romance was brewing between the two.

Bree stood at the counter, Meghan and Josie on either side of her, watching her press a whole white mushroom through an egg slicer. "Cool," Bree said, when neat, even slices fell out the bottom.

"Let me try it," Josie said, reaching for the slicer.

"Me too," Meghan said. "Although I hate mushrooms."

Jane laughed. "You'll develop a taste for them. Maybe even today."

Meghan made a face, indicating her distaste and doubt.

"They're okay," Josie said. "They're not my fave, though. My mom puts corn in spaghetti. It's yummy."

"Corn? I never thought of that," Jane said, making a mental note to try it.

"My mom buys mushrooms in cans. They're rubbery," Bree said. She popped a slice of raw mushroom in her mouth. "Not bad," she pronounced.

"Bree can finish the mushrooms while Josie chops the onions, and Meghan can chop the peppers." Jane set two cutting boards on the counter and showed the girls how to chop the vegetables. "I'll fry up the sausage. Be careful with the knives. They're sharp."

Josie made two cuts into the onion, then blinked and wiped her eyes on her sleeve. "This stings!"

"I'm afraid that's a problem with cutting onions," Jane said.

"My mom tried cutting them under water. It was so funny," Meghan said, laughing. "Little bits of onions were floating in the sink, and she couldn't see what she was cutting. She gave up."

"Why do onions sting?" Josie sniffed. Tears pooled in her eyes.

Jane set down her spatula and turned down the burner under the meat. She dampened a clean dishcloth and dabbed at Josie's eyes. "There's a chemical in the juice," she said. "When you cut the onion, it releases a mist of the chemical into the air. When it mixes with the moisture in your eyes, it becomes irritating. I've heard a lot of remedies. Most don't work and some are silly, like holding a match in your mouth or eating a piece of bread while you cut the onion."

"A match?" Meghan put a strip of bell pepper in her mouth and mimicked chopping with a matchstick. Then she giggled, and the other girls giggled with her.

"My grandma turns on a burner on her stove and cuts the onions. She says the flames burn up the onion fumes," Bree said.

"That makes sense," Jane said. "Let's try it. I already have a flame on the stove cooking the pasta. I'll turn on another burner. Let's move you."

She moved the cutting board closer to the stove but a safe distance from the burners. She turned a back burner on low. Josie moved her stool.

"Be careful you don't get too close to the flame," Jane warned her, watching carefully to make sure she wasn't in any danger.

"Remember, girls, you are too young to cook unsupervised. Don't ever do this when you're alone. An open flame could be very dangerous. Make sure you stay away from the burners, and always make sure that your hair is tied back and that you aren't wearing clothes that are loose or flowing. You don't want a sleeve to catch the handle of a pan or brush over a lit burner."

Josie made a cut, then started dicing. "Hey! That's better," she said.

"Good. Your grandma is a smart lady," Jane told Bree, who beamed at the compliment.

At the table, Alice sat dicing onions, since Jane intended to make a triple recipe. Jane glanced over at her sister. Alice looked up and smiled. She didn't appear to be affected by the onion mist. Jane didn't have a problem with onions either. Perhaps the Howards weren't sensitive to the chemical. Since she diced onions often, Jane was grateful for that blessing and the new hint. She'd invited the girls to teach them to cook. She hadn't expected to learn from them.

There was a tap on the door from the hallway.

"Come in," Alice called. The door opened and Garrett stood in the doorway. Behind him, Jane saw a petite blond woman.

"Sorry to interrupt," he said. "We heard voices, so I figured you were in here. I just wanted you to know I have Elaine and I'll take her up to her room, if that's all right." He beckoned his daughter forward and introduced her to Alice and Jane.

"We're so glad to have you here," Alice said. "The room is ready if you want to go on up. I'd come help, but I smell of onions," she said.

"No. Don't let us interrupt you," Garrett said. "As soon as Elaine unpacks, we'll be going out. I want to show her the town and take her over to Riverton to see where I'm working."

"Welcome to Grace Chapel Inn," Jane said. "Let us know if you need anything at all."

"Thank you," Elaine said. She looked at her father a bit hesitantly. He looked at her and smiled.

"We'll see you later," he said. He took Elaine's arm and ushered her out.

"I don't think I've seen him looking so happy before," Alice said after they left.

"I agree. Getting Garrett and his daughter together is worth putting on the whole weekend," Jane said. She checked the boiling spaghetti noodles.

"These are done. Look out, Josie. I'll carry this to the sink." She put on padded mitts and pulled the inner basket out of the pot, letting the water drain back in before she carried it to the sink.

"Who's finished?" she asked, turning to the girls.

"Me," Bree said, raising her hand.

"Do you know how to break eggs?" Jane asked.

"Yes. I cook scrambled eggs for my family all the time," she said.

Jane moved Bree to the table with a dozen eggs and a large bowl. She watched the girl crack an egg. Bree was careful not to get shells in the bowl. Jane left her to complete the task and returned to the stove.

"How are you coming?" she asked the girls. "Let's add the peppers and onions to the meat, then you can wash your hands. Josie, rub your hands on the metal disk on the sink and the onion smell will go away."

As Jane stirred the meat-and-vegetable mixture in the large skillet, the girls went to watch Bree crack eggs. Alice brought over a bowl of diced onions and peppers to add to the skillet.

"The girls are enjoying your lessons," she told Jane quietly. "Bree's mother and Justine told me they really appreciate the time you're giving their daughters."

"It's nothing," Jane said. "They're learning, and I'm getting help."

"I think it's wonderful that you are doing this to help Cynthia. I know she'll appreciate it."

"Well, we'll see. So far what I'm learning is how much I don't know about kids."

"Tomorrow night we'll play two pieces," Farley told his class Thursday afternoon. "The level-four guitars, fiddles and bass will join us for 'The Eyes of Texas.' They'll be playing and singing it. That's the same tune as 'I've Been Working on the Railroad.' Do you know that?" Farley asked.

There was a positive response from the class.

"Okay, listen up. I'll run through the first song in the key of

D, then you play it." He sat at his piano and started with a rumbly, leisurely walking bass. Louise knew she could play the bass with no problems. Then he added the melody, keeping it simple, with a few flourishes and arpeggios.

When the class played, Louise followed easily. The familiar song sounded different from any version she'd learned, but the loping gait, like a slow cantering horse, was easy to play. After three times through, Farley brought the song to an end.

"Good. Practice that a few times this afternoon. Tomorrow we'll add the other instruments. For our other song, with just our class, we'll play a bluegrass piece with a different flavor." He sat and played a simple bass phrase, repeating it over and over. He stopped and had everyone play it. The entire class kept the beat with no difficulty.

"All right, here's the whole piece," he said, launching into the song. Louise didn't recognize the tune, but the catchy beat had her toes tapping. Then Farley took off on a complicated set of riffs and patterns that made Louise wonder. She listened in a daze. Surely he didn't expect them to repeat what he'd just played.

"I improvised on the basic song. Write down these chords. Key of G with a four-four beat. Sixteen-bar blues." He gave them the sequence of verse, chorus, repeat, then inserted a bridge, then went back to the beginning, then ended with a tag. He explained the tempo and chords.

As he continued with the chorus chord progressions, Louise kept writing, but she felt like she'd stepped into a binary math class that made no earthly sense to her.

"Six minor, five, four, one," he continued. He finished the chorus then went on to the bridge. "This is where you can really ad lib." He rattled off a succession of chords. Louise wrote as fast as she could. The last line varied slightly.

"Louise, Nathan and Dan, I want each of you to play a solo. Louise, play a solo over verse two and give it some bounce. Nathan, chase Louise on the second chorus. Dan, you've got the bridge. Play it rubato—light and easy, with a lot of swing. Everyone else will carry the melody pianissimo during your solos."

Farley launched into the song. Louise followed along. The numbers began to make sense. One, five, two, six, equated to G, D, A, E. She scribbled a few notes on her score. She glanced over at Dan. His brow was knit in a frown as he listened and scribbled on his sheet. *Is he having as much difficulty as I am?* Louise doubted it. He'd played like a natural-born jazz pianist earlier.

Farley wanted her to play a solo. Why *her*? She'd struggled more than the rest of the class.

When Farley finished, they all played through the piece. Louise caught on to the tune. She liked the easygoing swing that took off into freestyle jazz. She loved the syncopation in parts of the song. In her mind, she heard a descant that she could play for her solo. She relaxed and began to enjoy the afternoon session.

"That's it for today," Farley said when they'd gone through it twice. "Louise, Dan and Nathan, please stay. I'll work with you on the solos. The rest of you can leave or stick around if you'd like. Oh, I almost forgot. If anyone wants to play a solo or duet at the student's celebration tomorrow night, let me know. We've got room for several."

As the others left, Louise played through the descant she'd heard in her mind. Her jazz riff sounded a bit like an operatic aria. The timing differed, but she'd have to be careful so she didn't slip into playing Strauss. She needed to count the four-four beat. She added a couple of minor notes. Next to her, Dan began playing the bass chords to her riff. She glanced over at him. He nodded. Emboldened, she played louder, letting the rhythm catch her. She repeated it three times to make sure she had it. Then she switched to the bass chords for the bridge and nodded to Dan. He let her play a few bars, then he jumped in with a solo unlike anything Louise had heard before. When he finished, she stopped and looked at him.

"I've never heard anything like that before."

"Oh." Dan looked dismayed. "Was it bad?"

"No. It was excellent. Have you heard the song before?" she asked.

"Not before Farley played it," he admitted.

"Well, that was brilliant. I wish I could hear music once and play like that," she said. "You have a natural talent."

He turned beet red. "So do you," he said.

"No, I have years of education and practice," she said. "Do you come here every year?"

He shook his head. "This is my first time. I found the music camp on the Internet. They offered scholarships, and I applied for one." He glanced over at Noelle, who was sitting at her keyboard, waiting for her brother. She was watching him and gave Dan a dazzling smile. He blushed, then looked back at Louise. "I'm glad I came," he said.

"Yes. I'm glad I came too," she said, and she realized she meant it. "You should do a solo," she told him.

"You think so? I composed a song. Would you listen and tell me if it's any good?"

"I'll be happy to," she said. "Maybe we can find another room to practice, where we're not so visible."

Farley came up behind them. He'd been listening. "There's a piano in the chapel," he said. "No one would disturb you there."

"Really? I don't recall seeing it," Louise said.

"It's against the back wall. It has a blanket over it. I'd like you to consider playing a solo too, Louise."

"I don't know. I need a lot of practice before I perform. You know that I'm totally out of my comfort zone, don't you?"

He smiled, and his eyes twinkled. "Yes. And you've adapted awfully well."

Louise was speechless. She wondered if her mouth might be hanging open. "Thank you," she said.

"You're welcome. Would you play the bass for Nathan?" He gave the young man his attention. "Ready?" he asked. Nathan nodded. Farley began snapping his fingers in time

"One, two, one, two, three, four." Farley gave her an upbeat. Louise started playing.

Nathan started and stopped. They repeated the beginning.

Nathan started again, then stopped. Farley walked over to him and bent over the keyboard.

"Like this," Farley said, running a simple blues pattern using the scale. "Now you do it," he said.

Nathan tried it again and managed to complete the bars.

"Good, good," Farley said. "Louise, you and Dan go ahead. I'll work with Nathan."

Louise nodded and stood. Dan followed her off the stage. Glancing back, Louise noticed Noelle watching Dan. Dan followed Louise's gaze. Noelle's face lit up.

"She's nice, isn't she?" Louise commented, looking over at Dan. He nearly stumbled.

"Y–ye...yes." He quickened his pace, passing Louise and making her hurry to keep up.

Chapter Twenty

an helped Louise fold and remove a beautiful handmade quilt from the spinet piano at the back of the chapel.

"Go ahead and warm up," Louise told Dan. "Play when you're ready." She found a folding chair and moved it near the piano.

Dan wasted no time launching into his song. His work surprised her. She'd expected something with a boogie beat, but his style reminded Louise of an old Miles Davis blues rendering. The easygoing tempo countered a melody that brought to mind several old favorites from Louise's childhood years. Her mother had loved "Stella by Starlight" and "On Green Dolphin Street." Dan's playing evoked tender emotion. Louise closed her eyes and let the music fill her senses with sweetness and memories. When he finished, she couldn't even applaud. She opened her eyes.

"Dan, you must play that tomorrow night. It's wonderful. Where did you learn to compose and play like that? You must have a wonderful teacher."

The young man turned red, but she could see he was pleased. "Thank you, Mrs. Smith. I don't have a teacher. I wish I did. I never know if I'm doing things the right way or not."

"Someone must have taught you to play."

"My mother, I suppose. I was homeschooled."

"Your mother must be a wonderful pianist."

"No. She doesn't play. In fact, she's tone deaf." He smiled. "She makes a joke about it, but she's my inspiration. We have my grandmother's old player piano, and I used to put in a roll and match my fingers to the keys. My mother bought me some piano-method books. I guess I taught myself. I don't read music very well. I play by ear."

Louise took a moment to digest Dan's story. This young man was a natural talent, perhaps a genius. She'd read about people like him. She'd worked with some amazing talents, but Dan had a special quality. His music came from somewhere deep in his soul, and listening, her soul responded. She wanted to play that way. Perhaps some day, in heaven, she'd be granted that gift.

Dan stood. "I need to go now. I promised Noelle I'd sit by her at dinner." He looked embarrassed. "Thanks for listening to me play."

"You'll play that tomorrow night, won't you?"

"If you think it's good enough."

"Oh yes. It's far more than good enough. Enjoy your dinner."

"Thanks."

She watched him leave, then sat at the piano and stared at the keys.

What Dan possessed, what Farley had tried to teach that week, was freedom. Freedom from method and theory and written music. Farley had said music was auditory, not visual. Louise knew and believed that, but she hadn't achieved such a level. She'd studied music and theory and taught others to read and sight-read.

Those were tools, but the master carpenter didn't need a blueprint to create a thing of beauty.

Farley wanted her to play a solo. What could she play? What did she know well enough to play without a score and improvise a solo arrangement? She played a few chords and let her mind wander over the music she'd played in recent months. Church music. Other than piano lessons, the only time she played on a regular basis was at church.

A tune popped into her head. She'd played several simple songs for Vacation Bible School during the summer. She loved listening to the preschoolers sing. Their voices held such sweetness and enthusiasm. She began playing her favorite. As she played, she could hear the words and the children's voices. *This little light of mine, I'm gonna let it shine.*

What was it Farley said? "Forget the music and the theory and let your heart play and your fingers dance over the keys"—something to that effect. How would he play it? A rocking beat with bass chords. She began to play. If she could pull it off, wouldn't Cynthia be surprised?

"I love your inn," Elaine Yeager said at breakfast. Jane and Alice were eating with the father and daughter, who were the only guests. "Your town is so cute," she said.

Alice smiled at the young woman. "Thank you." Alice thought of Acorn Hill as quaint and laid-back, but cute better described a puppy or a kitten. But then, Elaine was young, perhaps twenty-two or twenty-three.

"Where do you live?" Jane asked.

"Oh, I live in Queens. I commute to the financial district in Manhattan, where I work, so your town seems positively...rural. It's so charming. Dad took me to the Coffee Shop for dinner last night. Everyone's so friendly, and they all seem to know each other. 'Course, I guess there are places in Queens where people know each other, like the old neighborhoods, but Peter and I spend our extra time commuting to the city or going to Jones Beach."

"Peter is your husband?" Alice asked, noticing the wedding ring on her finger.

"Yes. We've been married a year."

Alice heard a knock on the back door and rose to get it.

"Good morning, Zeke," she said, opening the kitchen door.

"Mornin', Alice. I have tables and chairs for you."

"Wonderful. Come in. I'll get Jane. I think she talked to Penny about where to put them."

She left the door open for Zeke while she went back to the dining room.

"It's Zeke," she told Jane.

Jane stood. "Good. If you'll excuse us," she said to Elaine and Garrett. "Our tables are here."

Garrett stood. "Let me help." He followed Alice into the kitchen.

"I'll take this one," he told Zeke. "Where do you want it?"

"We'll put two in the sunroom and use the table that's already in there," Jane said.

Alice led the way, opening the doors for Garrett to carry the table through. He propped it against the wall as Alice started moving furniture out of the way.

Garrett helped her rearrange chairs against the walls so they could get the tables in. He set up the one he'd carried and left to get another one.

Zeke came through with another table. Alice hurried to move furniture in the parlor. Garrett and Zeke moved Louise's piano into a corner so they could set up two tables. The Eastlake chairs went against the wall.

By the time they finished, the downstairs had been completely rearranged. Looking around, Alice was glad Louise was gone. Louise liked everything neat and orderly. The rooms were anything but orderly, and Alice had a feeling they'd be worse before the weekend was over.

Alice answered the phone and heard a frantic-sounding Mary Jo. "I tried to reach Penny, but she's in school. I'm afraid I'm going to be late, and I've got the materials. I don't know what to do."

"I'm sure we can figure out a solution. Where are you?" Alice asked.

"I'm at the Potterston Hospital emergency room. Timmy broke his collarbone. He and Jimmy were horsing around."

Alice heard a deep sigh over the telephone. She looked at the clock. It was only eleven. "Oh dear. Poor boy. I'm sure he'll be all right though. I know how upset you must be feeling right now. How long do you think you'll be there?"

"They're ready to release him. They put his arm in a sling. He's supposed to stay quiet. Ha! I don't see how that's going to happen unless they put him in a straitjacket. They'd have to put Jimmy in one too."

Too bad they couldn't keep the child in the hospital for the weekend, Alice thought. Not that she wished anyone a stay in the hospital, but keeping a young boy still and preventing reinjury was hard on the child and the parents. However, a collarbone injury wasn't life threatening. She could care for the boy so his mother could lead the scrapbook weekend, but he'd be bored at the inn. All of these thoughts swirled through Alice's mind as she processed Mary Jo's dilemma. "I could get your supplies," Alice offered. "At least they'd be here when the ladies arrive."

"Oh, thank you. That would be wonderful." Mary Jo gave Alice directions to her house. "I should get out of here and be home by twelve thirty or one at the latest."

"Perhaps your husband could watch Timmy, and your sister-in-law could watch Jimmy and your other children. Anyways, I'll see you soon. Don't worry. We'll make things work," Alice said.

"Nurse Alice to the rescue," Jane said as Alice hung up.

"You heard? Timmy broke his collarbone. We have to do something."

Jane shook her head. "I'm so sorry."

"I volunteered to get her supplies, but I didn't volunteer to take care of the child. I knew that you couldn't handle this weekend without me."

"I hate to admit it," Jane said with a grateful smile, "but you're right. I'm sure volunteering was your first instinct."

"Any suggestions for handling the problem?"

"Did she call Penny?"

"She tried. Penny's at work at the high school."

"Maybe I can reach her. This is her event. Perhaps she'll have an idea."

"Meanwhile, I'll run to Potterston and pick up Mary Jo's materials. At least the ladies can get started. I'm sure some of them know how to make an album."

"I've seen the finished books. I can help," Jane said.

"You have to fix dinner."

"Thanks to you and my little chefs, the spaghetti dishes are ready to go in the oven. I'll be fine. Go ahead."

"I'll be back as soon as I can," Alice said, grabbing her jacket and heading out the door.

"I can't believe we're not having a class this afternoon," Louise told Cynthia at lunch. "One practice with the guitars and fiddles isn't enough. It's not like a symphony, where the sheet music is scored and every player has a defined set of instructions and knows exactly what to play and when. An orchestra might be able to put a piece together in one session, but this..." Louise shook her head in disbelief. "We're a bunch of amateurs, but Farley and the others seem to think we can work miracles. They need to set up the stage and the dining hall for tonight's concert, so we're done. Finished."

"I know. I heard. Are you playing with the class tonight?" Cynthia asked. "You don't have to, you know. I didn't realize until we got here and I started observing the different classes that this is completely different from the way you teach."

"That's putting it mildly," Louise said.

"Please keep in mind, Mother, that your teaching gives your students an appreciation of music and how it is composed. You give tools to play any kind of music. I hope you don't feel as if you've wasted the entire week. You could have been out sightseeing. We haven't visited the Empire Mine yet. I've heard it's worth seeing, and I'd love to visit it."

"I have to admit, I've learned a lot this week. I've gained an understanding of a different musical genre. Learning is never wasted, and besides, I've enjoyed an entire week with you. So let's go. I don't have to be here until after dinner tonight, and we have tomorrow free until the concert," Louise said. "Essentially, I'm finished."

Louise couldn't believe the camp was almost over. She tried to wrap her mind around what she'd accomplished, and she couldn't. She only knew she wouldn't look at music in quite the same way in the future.

As they drove from the ranch to the nearby town of Grass Valley, Louise thought about what she'd observed and learned during the week.

"After visiting the classes, what do you think about the music camp and the teaching methods?" Louise asked.

"I think I want to learn the fiddle," Cynthia said, glancing at her mother with a smile. "I don't know if I could learn it, though. The children here amaze me. They pick up the techniques so easily. I wonder if it might be easier to go from this play-by-ear method to learning the standard music reading and theory, rather than the other way around. I'm looking forward to hearing the classes perform tonight, to see how it all comes together."

"Yes. I've only heard my class, and I'm a bit of a perfectionist when it comes to my own performance."

"A bit, Mother?" Cynthia's gentle smile took any criticism out of her reply. Louise knew her own strengths and weaknesses. Her high standards kept her striving to improve but also bound her at times.

"You might be right about learning the ear method first. I've struggled to grasp this method all week. I have to admit, because of my training, my preconceived ideas are difficult to set aside. In a sense, the students and teachers are still reading music, just by a simpler number system that allows them to transpose more easily. It accommodates players who don't read music, so the accompaniment can transpose any piece easily to play along with other instruments. For the piano at least, they still have to learn the different keys."

"Could you integrate the two systems? Would you even want to teach this method?"

"Perhaps. I'm not sure, but I like the idea of encouraging my students to improvise more. For instance, they could learn and memorize a piece, then vary the rhythm or the time. They could play in a minor key or add a riff over the top just for fun."

Cynthia laughed. "A riff, Mother? Now you sound like the Blackthorn Brothers and the Lukens."

Louise smiled. She had picked up some of the jazz vernacular. Jane would get a kick out of that. Louise tried to envision a piano recital with improvisation. She wasn't sure she could stand to hear her students butcher Beethoven or Liszt or any of the classical composers. Perhaps she would teach her advanced students more Gershwin. Her younger students could improvise on simple choruses or nursery songs. If nothing else, they'd have a good time, and after all, music should be a form of pleasure and inspiration. Occasionally, when she played, she would reach a subconscious state where the music took over. At those rare times, music became worship and Louise felt transported into the very presence of God. The tune didn't matter. Perfection didn't matter. Only giving her soul to God through music and feeling Him smile on her humble offering. Was that what Farley experienced?

Chapter Twenty-One

*A*lice pulled up in front of a green and tan clapboard house in a modest neighborhood on the west side of Potterston. The houses looked similar. Bicycles, tricycles, balls and other toys rested in most of the yards, waiting for the children to come home from school.

A three-foot-tall chain-link fence surrounded Mary Jo's yard. Alice entered through the gate. At the sound of the creaky hinges, a short, elongated beagle came tearing around the side of the house, yapping furiously. Alice stopped. The dog stopped several feet away and looked her over.

"Hello there," she said in a gentle voice. The dog's tail began wagging. It approached her cautiously. She leaned down slowly and extended her hand. The dog sniffed her, then wiggled all over when she reached out and scratched its ears.

A small maple tree had shed yellow and orange leaves over the browning grass. Before Jane moved back to Acorn Hill, the lawn at home had looked shaggy like this much of the time. Yard maintenance took effort and attention. So did small children.

The front door opened. "Don't mind him," Mary Jo said. "His bark sounds ferocious, but he's an old softy. Come in." She held the door open for Alice.

Timmy was sprawled on the couch, engrossed in the bang-bang, shoot-'em-up antics of a TV cartoon. He showed no signs of pain, which didn't surprise Alice. In her experience, children were much more resilient than adults after an injury.

Mary Jo, on the other hand, looked like she'd been agitated by a washing machine. Her clothes were wrinkled and the buttons on her blouse were off by a buttonhole. She wore no makeup, and her hair was unkempt. Alice had seen harried mothers in the emergency room many times. Often, they looked like Mary Jo. Accidents didn't wait for mothers to get dressed and ready for the day. They usually happened when people were ill-prepared to handle them.

"Here are all the materials. Maybe Penny can get everyone started, although I hate to dump this on her. She's only been to one of my classes. I don't know what else to do. My regional rep is out of town, so I can't call her." Mary Jo ran a hand through her hair. "I'm a mess, aren't I?"

"You've had a traumatic morning. Why don't you make us a cup of tea, and we can go through what needs to be done?"

"All right." She turned toward the kitchen. "Come on back. Please excuse the mess. I didn't get the dishes done."

From the looks of the sink, the dishes hadn't been done for a couple of meals. Breakfast cereal and a carton of milk sat on the counter. The remains of a pizza had dried out in the box, which was open. Alice moved a sweatshirt from a chair and sat at the kitchen table.

"Ordinarily, I'd have this cleaned up by now," Mary Jo said. She piled bowls in the sink while the water heated.

After a few minutes of chatting, she carried two cups with hot water and teabags to the table, then plunked herself down across from Alice.

"Larry thinks I should quit doing the scrapbooking, but it does bring in a little extra money. I paid for all our Christmas gifts last year, and we took a real vacation this summer. Besides, I enjoy the parties. It's just juggling the kids and the house and all." She shook her head.

"Let's concentrate on getting through this weekend. Will your sister-in-law still watch your children?"

"She said she'd take all the kids except Timmy. She has two boys, and she doesn't have any way of keeping Timmy isolated and quiet. She's afraid something will happen to make his shoulder worse. She's probably right."

From Louise's and Jane's descriptions of the twin boys, Alice agreed. She thought about Mary Jo's bringing Timmy with her to the inn, but that didn't seem like a good idea. The small television Jane kept in the kitchen wouldn't keep a little boy entertained. Sitting with a bunch of women would be boring. Alice didn't know what to suggest.

Mary Jo's cell phone chimed a catchy tune. She took it out of her pocket and answered it. She stood and walked over to the sink. Even so, Alice could hear every word from the booming voice on the other end.

"Hi, honey. What happened now?" he asked.

Mary Jo straightened. Her chin came up, and Alice thought her back stiffened.

"Timmy broke his collarbone. I took him to the hospital. He's all right, but he's supposed to stay still and keep quiet for four to six weeks." Mary Jo hung her head, as if under a great weight. She pushed her shoulder-length hair off her forehead as she listened.

"I know you gave your word. I know you're obligated. I wish— never mind. I'll watch him this weekend, but I can't get home until five thirty. Can you take him with you until then? I'll pick him up."

Mary Jo's shoulders slumped. "Thanks, honey. I'm sending my materials ahead so they can start without me. I can't imagine taking Timmy with me. He'd hate it. I'll wait for you here. Please hurry home as soon as you can."

"I will. Hey, it's okay. Timmy will be fine. I broke my collarbone twice in the same place, and I turned out okay."

"Yes, you did," she answered. When she hung up, Alice saw tears in her eyes. She wiped her eyes with the back of her hand.

"I'm sorry," she said. "I hate it when my kids are hurt or sick. I should have been watching him closer this morning."

"You don't have to apologize to me. Mothers usually take their children's accidents harder than the children. No mother can watch her children every second. I'm a nurse at Potterston Hospital. I assure you that you can't prevent your children from getting hurt. It's going to happen, and it's not your fault. Now tell me what I need to do with your materials."

"Thanks." She sat down and her phone rang again. "Excuse me." She stood and answered the phone.

"Hi. I tried to call you. I forgot that you work."

Mary Jo listened for a few moments, then said thank you and hung up. She sat at the table again.

"That was Penny. Your sister called her. Penny said to bring Timmy to her house and her son will watch him until Larry picks him up."

"Penny's son is a wonderful young man. Bart'll take good care of Timmy."

"That's a relief. Do you want to take the materials anyway? Then everything will be there when the ladies arrive."

"Yes. Let's make a list of what I need to do." Alice took a small notepad and a pen from her purse and started writing as Mary Jo gave her instructions. Things would work out with God's help. They always did.

Two school buses were parked at the Empire Mine. The drivers stood outside in the sunshine, waiting for their passengers. Cynthia parked the rental car close to the entrance.

Although the sun shone brightly, a breeze cooled the air. Louise put on her sweater. "Do you want your jacket?" she asked Cynthia.

"I'm warm, but I'll take it along." She hung her camera bag over her shoulder. "I saw in the newspaper this morning that New England is expecting snow showers next week. I'm not ready for winter," Cynthia said.

"I wonder how Jane and Alice are doing. The scrapbook event kicks off this afternoon."

"I'm sure they're fine. They're two of the most capable people I know, Mother."

"Thank you for reminding me, dear. You're right."

The extensive buildings and equipment on the grounds surprised Louise. Many of the buildings were constructed of quarried rock, not unlike some of the old architecture in the East. Cynthia spent half an hour taking pictures of the mine-yard buildings, the head frame where ore was brought out on carts, and the various relics of the mining operations. Even with the school children running about, the park had a peaceful, leisurely atmosphere.

Cynthia picked up a brochure and read as they walked toward the museum. "The mine operated from 1850 until 1956, so it's no wonder it's so well preserved. The Empire Mine was the richest hard-rock mine in California," she read.

In the museum, they found a scale model of the complex and of the former massive underground mining operation. There were also gold ore samples and a large mineral collection. From there, they wandered the grounds. The principal owner, William Bourn, built a home at the mine and developed extensive gardens, water features, pools, a clubhouse and a greenhouse. A huge hedge of hydrangea bloomed profusely along the lawn. Louise and Cynthia wandered through the rose garden, which was still in full bloom.

"Wouldn't Jane love this?" Louise said as Cynthia snapped pictures. "Look at the imported trees." Magnolias, hawthorne, weeping birch and Italian cypress displayed a wide array of fall colors. "It's warmer than home right now, but I imagine it gets cold here in the winter. I wonder if some of these species would survive in Acorn Hill."

Cynthia laughed. "You're running out of yard as it is," Cynthia said. "You don't have the room for more trees and bushes."

Jane was in the kitchen when she heard cars pull into the parking area. She slipped off her apron and hurried to the reception desk as the front door opened and five women came into the hallway.

"Oh, look! This is positively elegant," a young woman in her late twenties exclaimed.

"Love it!" another young woman echoed. "It's so...so old-fashioned."

"It's Victorian," an older woman said. "Authentic, if I'm not mistaken," she added.

"Welcome to Grace Chapel Inn, ladies," Jane said, stepping forward and introducing herself to the group. They gave their names as well, but Jane had already picked out the three slumber-party girls, as she'd tagged them, and the two middle-aged women from Baltimore with no problem. The younger women were bubbling over with enthusiasm. "Let's get you signed in. Then I'll show you to your rooms."

"Take care of these ladies first," said Maggie, the older woman with her dark hair pulled back in a twist. "We're in no hurry. In fact, we'll be happy to wait in the parlor. Won't we, Joan?"

"Sure. May we leave our suitcases here?" Joan asked.

"They'll be fine there," Jane said. "Thank you." Jane guessed that the Baltimore women were about her age. Joan was tall and slender, with short red hair. Maggie was of medium height and had a charming smile.

The two women went into the parlor while Jane checked Liana, Kiran and Chanelle into their room. "If you'll follow me, I'll take you up." Jane led the way to the Sunset Room, where she and Alice had set up a rollaway bed to accommodate the three roommates.

"Neat!" Chanelle said. She was the tallest of the three. Her short reddish-brown hair reminded Jane of Alice's hair. "I'll take the rollaway." She plunked her suitcase on the bed. "It's closest to the bathroom, so I can get first dibs," she said, grinning at her friends. The bathroom was just a few steps from anywhere in the room. Jane suspected Chanelle was a person who put others first.

"There's a stack of towels in the bathroom. Let me know if you need anything else," Jane said. "The retreat doesn't start until after dinner, which is at five thirty, so you can get settled and relax here or look around town."

"Let's go look around town," Kiran said. "I've never been in this area before." Her blunt-cut black hair bobbed as she moved, and she seemed to be in motion all the time.

"Sounds good to me." Liana put her small bag on the left side of the bed. She reached up and rubbed her temples. Jane noticed she winced slightly, then turned and smiled at her friends. If she had a headache now, she'd be miserable later. The shortest of the three, Liana had a pert, upturned nose and light-blue eyes. The three told Jane they were college friends having a reunion.

Jane left them to settle in and hurried downstairs to the other women.

"I'm so glad to get away for a weekend," Maggie was saying. "I've allowed myself to get too involved with the art club and the museum renovation. I just can't keep it up anymore."

"You must learn to say no," Joan replied.

"You're a fine one to talk. Look at all you do."

"Thanks for waiting, ladies," Jane said. "I can sign you in and show you to your room now, if you're ready."

Maggie stood. "We're ready," she said, giving Jane a smile. "What time does the scrapbooking start?"

"This evening, after dinner," Jane said.

"Good. We have time to relax for a while. I love scrapbooking, so I was excited when Joan saw this advertised online, but I'm also looking forward to unwinding," she explained.

" You have a lovely home," Joan said after they had completed the necessary paperwork and were following Jane to the stairs.

"Let me help with your bags," Jane said, picking up the largest suitcase. She climbed the stairs and took the two women to the Garden Room.

"Charming," Joan pronounced. She set her bags on the floor.

Maggie went over to smell the fresh flowers in the fall bouquet. Then she glanced down. "Oh, chocolates. How delightful!" Four handmade truffles sat on a paper doily. She picked out a candy with a swirl of white chocolate on top and bit into it. The center had dark-chocolate ganache and orange cream. "Mmm. Divine. Just melts in your mouth." She picked up the small card tucked under the doily and read it aloud: "'Madeleine and Daughters Chocolates. Available at Time for Tea.' Is that in town? I must get some to take home."

"Yes," Jane said. "The shop carries all kinds of wonderful items. We serve the store's tea here at the inn. The chocolates are my mother's recipe. I'm glad you enjoyed your truffle."

"Loved it," Maggie said. She offered one to Joan.

"I'll have one later," Joan said.

"I'll leave you to get settled," Jane said. She told them the evening's schedule, then left.

Alice was carrying a box into the dining room when Jane got downstairs.

"Need some help?"

"Yes, please. There are four more boxes like this in my car," Alice said. She turned to go outside.

Jane followed and took one of the boxes. "Wow! It's heavier than I thought. Mary Jo carts around a lot of stuff for these parties, doesn't she?" Jane said, lugging the unwieldy box inside. "Are we setting her up in the dining room?"

"Yes. We need to put a couple of card tables against the wall so she can display her merchandise. She said she'll give demonstrations in here."

"Is she coming tonight?"

"She'll be here around dinnertime. Penny volunteered Bart to babysit Timmy until his dad can pick him up."

"What a sweetheart," Jane said. "Bart's such a good kid. Timmy will enjoy being with him. Our weekend guests have arrived." They heard a thunder of footsteps on the stairs. "That must be our threesome in the Sunset Room. They're here for a kind of reunion as well as scrapbooking. They're going into town."

"I hope they find something interesting," Alice said.

"In the mood they're in, they will. Believe me, they are primed to enjoy themselves."

"Good. They'll liven up the weekend," Alice said.

Jane cocked her head to one side. "Are you doubting the pleasure of scrapbooking?"

Alice considered. "I'm sure I'll enjoy it. We've got a great group coming, and I told Vera I'd participate, so I will. However, it sounds more painstaking than exciting." Alice walked back through the kitchen to get another box.

Right behind her, Jane said, "There's a great satisfaction in completing an album. It's like a piece of history preserved."

"You should be the one making a scrapbook, not me," Alice said over her shoulder.

"I have enough craft projects underway."

"True. So I'll represent the Howard sisters and make an album." Alice hefted a box out of her trunk and handed it to Jane.

Jane smiled. "You're a good sport. I think you'll be surprised at how much you'll enjoy yourself."

Alice picked up the last box. "After all this preparation, I hope you're right."

Chapter Twenty-Two

*L*ook at you! You look terrific!" Cynthia said. "Wait. I have to get your picture."

"Not in here. Maybe downstairs on the porch," Louise said. She took another peek in the full-length mirror in their room. Now she wished she'd bought the shoes to complete the outfit, but her practical side had prevailed. Where would she ever wear granny boots?

"You must wear my shoes," Cynthia said with a sly smile. She held out the same pair of old-fashioned shoes that Louise had declined.

"You bought them?" Louise asked in surprise. "But I can't wear them if they're part of your outfit."

"I have boots. I bought them for you. I knew they'd complete your look."

"Well, thank you." Louise slipped off her flats and sat on a chair, loosening the thin grosgrain ribbon ties that served as laces, crisscrossing on the shoe's hooks. She wiggled her foot into the slender shoe. It fit as if it were made for her. Fortunately, she and Cynthia wore the same size clothes and shoes. She put on the other shoe and stood.

"How do they feel?"

"Surprisingly comfortable." Louise went back to the mirror. She looked as if she'd stepped off a western movie set.

"One more thing," Cynthia said. "I also bought this with you in mind." She produced a bowler-style felt hat with a wide ribbon and bow in the back. "It's actually a riding hat. It'll look terrific with your outfit." She placed it on her mother's head. "Oh, I love it!"

Louise had to admit, the hat and boots looked smart with her denim skirt and western blouse. "I should hire you as my fashion consultant."

"You can wear it tomorrow night, too, when we go to the concert."

"Perhaps. We'd better go, so we won't be late." All of a sudden, butterflies began to swarm in Louise's stomach. She chided herself for being nervous. After all, tonight's event was not a real concert. The music-camp students would play for each other and their families, and perhaps a handful of locals, like their bed-and-breakfast hosts. She'd played before much larger groups. Besides, after tomorrow, she'd never see these people again. And Cynthia? Her daughter had grown up listening to her mother and father play the piano. However, despite her rationalizations, tonight's performance mattered, though Louise couldn't say why.

Jane carried the third large pan of baked spaghetti to the buffet table set up in the hallway. She'd estimated ten servings per casserole, but she misjudged the appetite of this group. There was still some antipasto salad and plenty of dipping sauce for the bread. Elaine Nichols stood in line with Garrett and Hope. Behind them, Liana, Chanelle and Kiran waited for seconds.

"That's *sooo* good," Chanelle said. "Do you give out your recipes?"

Before Jane could answer, Ethel came up behind the girls and got into the line. "Now, now, my niece is a professional chef," Ethel said. "Her recipes are her livelihood."

Jane winced at her aunt's blunt declaration.

"Delicious, isn't it? Reminds me of lasagna," Viola Reed said as she took a place in the line. She pushed her long paisley neck scarf around to her back to keep it out of the way.

"You're from the bookstore, aren't you?" Kiran asked.

"Viola *owns* Nine Lives Bookstore," Ethel said.

Jane rolled her eyes. Ethel seemed intent on securing her role as know-it-all. Jane hoped Ethel and Florence wouldn't vie for attention during the weekend. No one would guess the two women were friends by observing their rivalry. She set the hot pan on a trivet.

"Cool name. Is it because of your cats?" Liana asked. "They made sure to greet us this afternoon. I found a neat book on herbs."

"Yes, I named the shop for my furry friends. I hope you enjoy the book," Viola said.

"I'm sure I will."

"I'm worried about Mary Jo," Penny whispered, coming up beside Jane. "She hadn't shown up at the house before I left. I thought about waiting but figured I'd better get over here and help."

"You haven't heard from her?"

"Not a word. She was going to bring Timmy over."

"She hasn't called here. She'll come soon, I'm sure. Don't

worry. We'll manage."

Jane went back to the kitchen for herbed focaccia bread. She pulled a pan out of the oven as the door from the hall opened.

"Hi. Need any help?" Hope stepped into the kitchen.

"Not right now, but thanks for offering."

"Just holler if you do," Hope said, then she went back into the hallway.

Jane set a basket of the hot bread on the buffet table and looked around. Everyone had a plate of food. She counted heads. Everyone was there except Mary Jo. She hoped their weekend hostess would make it. Jane could pinch-hit if need be, but she didn't know the tricks of the craft or how to use the templates, stamps and punches that she and Alice had unpacked and set out on tables. Penny didn't sound like an expert, either.

As she set out a large pan of fudge-caramel brownies, the front door opened and Mary Jo came in, looking thoroughly frazzled.

"Thank you for attending our tenth annual Luken Music Camp Student Concert. I can't believe it's Friday night already," Matthew Luken said into the microphone. "Tonight is the windup of our camp, and you're in for a treat. Every year, the talent gets better and better. This year is no exception."

From the front sideline, standing with Dan, Noelle, Nathan and the rest of her class, Louise looked out at the audience. The tables had been removed from the dining hall, and chairs brought in. Cynthia sat in the second row next to Melinda Perry, her husband on one side and Doris and Jake Luken on the other, chatting like old friends. The room was packed with people. Louise saw cowboy hats and bolo ties, tiered full skirts and ruffled blouses. She felt as if she were about to perform for a crowd in a TV western. She smiled when she noticed Dan take hold of Noelle's hand and give it a squeeze.

After a trio performed "The Star-Spangled Banner" and one of the younger children led the Pledge of Allegiance, Matthew got back onstage. "Let's start out with the entire group. Ya'll come on up," he said.

The little ones went first and lined up at the front of the stage, where the microphones were set about three feet high. Intermediate classes were next, with advanced at the back of the stage. In all, nearly a hundred people stood together. The guitars began, and the fiddles joined in. None of the keyboards performed. There wasn't room. Everyone sang "Amazing Grace."

As they sang, Louise looked out over the heads of the students in front of her at the audience. Everyone joined in. She hadn't expected to come to a music camp and have a spiritual experience, but just at that moment, she felt the presence of God in the old converted stable. Whatever else happened, that moment was worth the entire trip.

"Come into the kitchen and let me fix you a plate of dinner," Jane told Mary Jo, who looked as if she needed to catch her breath.

"No time," Mary Jo said. "I need to get organized and start the first session." She slipped off her coat and looked around for a place to put it.

"Let me put that in the hall closet. Then come with me to the kitchen," Jane said, taking Mary Jo's arm and leading her. Jane hung the coat in the closet, and the two went into the kitchen.

"Thank you. Did you get the materials unpacked?" Mary Jo asked.

"Yes, and there's no hurry. Sit down."

"But..."

"Do you hear that sound out there?" Jane asked.

Mary Jo sat still and listened. She got a quizzical look on her face. "What?"

"Hear the laughing and talking? Everyone is having a great time visiting and getting to know one another. Besides, they're still enjoying their brownies and ice cream." Jane dished up a plate of food while she talked, then carried it over to the table. She set it down in front of Mary Jo. "Penny and Alice have everything under control." Jane sat down across from Mary Jo. "You have time to relax for a moment and eat."

Jane thought she was going to object, but she didn't.

"I *am* hungry. I skipped lunch today. I would have been here sooner, but..."

Jane held up her hand. "It's all right. You're here."

Mary Jo looked at her, then nodded. She bowed her head and said a silent prayer, then picked up her fork and began to eat.

She ate too fast, but Jane didn't scold her. She looked frazzled enough. She gulped down the food, thanked Jane, and stood, picking up her plate.

Jane stood and took the plate from her. "Take a deep breath," she said.

Mary Jo complied, breathing in deeply. She exhaled and

breathed again. This time her shoulders seemed to relax. Jane smiled.

"We set your material on tables in the dining room. Tables are set up in all the other public rooms as well. I think everything is ready."

"Thanks so much for everything you and Alice have done." After giving Jane a hug, Mary Jo exited the kitchen.

Watching her leave, Jane shook her head. She guessed Mary Jo was trying to be a good wife, mother and businesswoman. Jane suspected that the woman had too many plates spinning and was struggling to keep them balanced. Jane had seen several beautiful scrapbooks. She knew they brought joy to their creators and to anyone fortunate enough to receive one. She hoped Mary Jo knew that she spread joy with her little business, but Jane suspected that knowledge had been lost in the pressures of Mary Jo's busy life. Jane wasn't sure how she could help their scrapbook chum, but she would do what she could and trust God to do the rest.

After the ensemble opening, all the students took seats in the audience except the beginner's piano class. Louise relaxed and enjoyed the simple performance. A four-year-old girl soloed on "Twinkle, Twinkle Little Star" in a style all her own. As each student played a phrase, Louise picked out the nursery song from the freestyle notes, but each student had a unique interpretation.

One by one the classes mounted the stage, performed, and then sat down in the audience. The fiddles and guitars performed together. One class played a medley of Irish tunes. Louise hadn't realized that all Celtic songs seemed to start and end in a similar way, with a long, defining theme. Then the fiddles launched into a complicated jig or reel that made Louise want to dance.

Each class became more musically complex. Louise concluded that either the students were accomplished musicians or the odd teaching system worked. The students played with a degree of proficiency, but Louise wouldn't call them concert pianists. The one common denominator Louise observed from all of the players was joy. Many went up on stage displaying nervousness, but everyone seemed to finish with bubbly, infectious delight. Louise wanted to bottle that effervescence and take it home to her students.

Finally it was time for Louise's class to perform. Louise walked onstage behind Noelle and in front of Dan. Only Nathan appeared perfectly calm. In unison, they sat at their keyboards. Farley sat in his usual place at the upright piano. The guitars and fiddles joined them. At a downbeat, they began the boogie version of what Farley announced as "The Eyes of Texas." The song seemed to go on forever, with the various fiddle and guitar players taking solo parts. Louise got into the rhythm, easily keeping pace with the song. The last time through, Farley and the fiddle and guitar players sang the words.

As the song ended, and the string players left the stage to loud applause, Louise mentally prepared for the next song, which she barely knew. Farley gave them the upbeat, and they began.

The carefree tempo helped. She got into rhythm with the other keyboards. The melody sounded rich and full, coming from eight keyboards at once. Louise followed her notations for the first verse, then got caught up in the music. The tune came naturally. As they approached the second verse, Louise tensed. Her solo was coming, and she couldn't remember her part. Of course she couldn't remember. Nothing was written down. Nothing was arranged. She was supposed to improvise. She glanced over at Nathan. He looked relaxed. Dan was watching her as he played. The last bars of the chorus sounded.

Saying a prayer for inspiration, Louise let her mind go blank. She played the first notes of the second verse with the other keyboards, then ran a fast scale in triplets halfway up, arpeggio, descent and rise, tremolo and arpeggio. Her fingertips danced over the keys, pulling a tune out of thin air. Louise had no idea what she was playing, but her spirits soared with the notes. Then all too soon, the verse ended. She finished on a tremolo and faded back into the tune as Nathan picked up the solo over the chorus. She held her breath for him, but he played beautifully. Dan took the bridge, and Louise felt the music climb up and over a wide chasm, then descend once again to the verse.

Suddenly it was over. Louise didn't realize she was smiling until she caught Dan's grin and realized she was grinning too. Farley bid them rise, and they stood for applause, bowing to the audience. The class left the stage except for Dan, who stayed behind for his solo.

"Now we have an original composition by one of our advanced piano students," Micah Luken announced. "Dan is self-taught, and this is his first year with us. We hope he'll become a regular. Give a hand for Dan."

The shy young man transformed when he sat at a keyboard. Listening to Dan play his solo, watching the audience become enthralled in his music, Louise once again recognized the power of music.

Louise clapped enthusiastically as Dan finished. She was so caught up in her applause, she didn't realize Micah was introducing her.

"Our next soloist comes to us from Pennsylvania, where she teaches piano. She has an extensive classical background. In her career, she's played concerts and accompanied symphonies." Micah grinned. "I imagine our casual methods came as quite a shock to her. As you heard in the Master Piano class performance, she is also very versatile. Welcome Louise Smith."

Louise heard cheering and cringed a bit. She went up on the stage and sat at the keyboard. For a moment, she couldn't remember a thing about what she was going to play. *Vacation Bible School. Oh yes.*

In her mind, Louise pictured a little boy, mouth wide open, looking skyward, singing and dancing in place, poking his fingers in the air as he acted out the motions to the song with a group of preschool children at Grace Chapel. Totally oblivious to anyone around him, he'd sung for the pure joy of the song. Louise began a right-handed run of triplets and arpeggios with a tremolo, then made a fast descent into the melody, starting a rocking boogie bass with the song. "This Little Light of Mine," she played, forgetting the music, the notes, the arrangement, and playing for the pure joy of the song. Three times she played through the song, ending on a long tremolo. Standing to the thunder of applause, Louise looked out at the audience. Cynthia stood along with many others, clapping, looking stunned. Louise smiled. She still had it in her to surprise her daughter.

Chapter Twenty-Three

*A*lice glanced around the crowded living room. Everyone had found a place to sit. The three reunion friends perched together on a sofa. Joan and Maggie, Ethel, Florence and Viola sat on chairs, and the rest of the group sat on the floor. Even Garrett Yeager was there, sitting cross-legged on the floor next to his daughter. Hope sat on Garrett's other side.

The noise level had lowered to a soft hum as everyone waited expectantly for the event to begin. Patsy Ley made her way to the front of the room.

"Hi," she said, smiling at the group. "I'm not a scrapbook expert, but Penny asked me to give a short devotion about scrapbooking."

Everyone got quiet and turned to look at Patsy. Alice saw Mary Jo come to the doorway. She looked agitated. Alice sent up a prayer for Mary Jo's peace of mind, that her family would be fine without her and that she would be able to relax and enjoy the weekend. Mary Jo slipped into the room and sat on a chair against the wall.

"I know most of you, but not everyone. I'm Patsy Ley, and my husband is the assistant pastor at Grace Chapel. When Penny asked me to give a devotional, I thought about what kind of scrapbook to make. I don't have children, like some of you, which kind of gives you a built-in subject. I got out my pictures, which were in a box, and started sorting them. I found lots of flowers and butterflies and birds. I love nature, so that's my theme. Did any of you pick a theme?" she asked.

She got some nods and some shaking heads.

"Well, I like to figure out motivation, so I wondered why I took so many pictures of nature, and I decided it's because I see God in nature and that brings me joy." Patsy picked up her Bible and opened it to a marked passage.

"Psalm 8:3–4 and 9 says, 'When I consider your heavens, the work of your fingers, the moon and the stars, which you have set in place, what is man that you are mindful of him, the son of man that you care for him?...O LORD, our Lord, how majestic is your name in all the earth!'" Patsy closed her Bible.

"God's creation is so beautiful. When I see something beautiful, I feel joyful. God wants us to have joy in our lives. There are many verses in the Bible that talk about joy. And not just when everything is going well. In James 1:2–3, the Bible says, 'Consider it pure joy, my brothers, whenever you face trials of many kinds, because you know that the testing of your faith develops perseverance.' I think that's why scrapbooks of pictures and memories are important. We can look back and remember good times and even bad times, when God brought us through trials. I hope you all find joy in making a scrapbook this weekend. Thank you." Patsy took her Bible and went to the back of the room, where she stood against the wall.

Penny stood and looked around. She spotted Mary Jo, and Alice could see the relief on her face. Then Penny went up front.

"Thanks, Patsy. I'm glad you're all here, and now I want to introduce our scrapbook hostess, Mary Jo. She's going to tell us what we're going to do."

"Wow, look at this great turnout," Mary Jo said, looking around. "I can't wait to get to know each of you." She thanked Jane and Alice for letting everyone come to the inn, then explained about the worktables. With such a large group, they'd be a little crowded, but they'd work it out so everyone had her own space. They could leave their albums out the entire weekend and no one would disturb anything, she explained.

Hope helped Jane gather up the dishes from dessert. "You've got a big group here. You're going to need my help all weekend," Hope said as she set a stack of bowls on the sink.

"I appreciate your offer, Hope, but I want you to spend time on your scrapbook," Jane said. "If you help me set up the breakfast buffet in the morning, that'd be great. Then I'll be fine."

"I don't know that I want to make a scrapbook," Hope said.

"Did you bring photographs?"

"Yes, I have some, but not many." Hope turned away and tidied up the counter as Jane stacked dishes in the dishwasher. "I found some in a basket with my mom's things after she died." Hope shrugged. "When I was a kid, we moved a lot. I don't have many happy memories."

"I'm sorry, Hope. There must have been a few happy times. Maybe you'll discover some. Are you helping Garrett and Elaine?"

"They don't need my help." Hope quickly added, "I'm glad Elaine's here. She's very sweet. Garrett wants so badly to be part of her life. I hope they have a good time together."

Jane gave Hope a hug. "You're very special, do you know that? Some women would resent Elaine showing up."

Hope shook her head. "I was a little smitten with him at first, but I've come to realize that Garrett and I are just friends. Maybe he and Elaine can find something I never had with my folks."

"I hope you're right. Why don't you go join the others? I think Mary Jo is in the dining room showing the scrapbooking tools and papers. Maybe you'll see something that sparks your interest."

"I'd rather help you."

"Okay. Why don't you fill that bucket with ice and we can put sodas in it," Jane said, indicating a galvanized tub on the counter. "There's a bag of ice in the freezer."

"Sure." Hope found the ice and emptied it into the bucket, then filled the tub with cans of soda from the refrigerator.

"Where do you want this?" she asked while Jane poured snack crackers into bowls.

"Put it on the table I set up in the hallway. I put a plastic cover down, so it won't hurt the wood. Then go join the others. Soon as I finish this, I'm done for the night."

"Okay. If you're sure."

Jane watched Hope carry the heavy tub of sodas through the doorway. She wasn't quite finished for the night, but she didn't want Hope spending the entire weekend in the kitchen helping her.

"Are you still working?" Alice asked, coming through to the kitchen from the dining room.

Jane looked over her shoulder. "Almost done. I wanted to have the French toast ready to go in the oven tomorrow morning." She laid slices of bread on large, shallow baking pans. "I noticed it's gotten quiet out there. Is the party over for tonight?"

"Not quite. Garrett and Elaine are sitting in the library, talking." Alice glanced at the kitchen clock. It was ten thirty. "The three roommates put on sweat suits and fuzzy slippers, and they're out in the sunroom going through their boxes of pictures. They were best friends in college and they're making scrapbooks of their time together. They've gone around the inn and downtown taking digital pictures."

"It sounds as if they're having fun. No wonder they wanted to room together," Jane said. She lifted a large bowl and poured egg mixture over the bread.

"One of them brought a laptop computer, and they want to print out the pictures they're taking."

"My printer won't do quality photographs, but there's a place in Potterston that does quick prints," Jane said.

"That's what I told them. They were dismayed to learn we

don't have a high-definition television so they can watch the DVDs they brought along." Alice chuckled. "I think they intend to stay awake the entire weekend."

"I hope they don't keep everyone else awake," Jane said. She covered the large flat pan with plastic wrap and put it in the refrigerator. "There. I'm done for the night. Let's go up the back stairs so we don't disturb anyone."

⁊

Sausage links sizzled in an electric skillet. Biscuits baked on a rack in the oven above the French toast. Jane poured omelet batter into three miniature forms.

Jane heard a tap at the back door. Hope was standing outside. Jane waved her in.

"Hi. Boy, it's cold out there." Hope took off her coat and set it in a corner with her purse. She rubbed her hands together and smiled at Jane. "At least the sun is shining," she said. "I passed Garrett. He's out jogging." Hope walked to the sink, pushed up her long sleeves and washed her hands. "So I'm ready to help. Put me to work."

"I thought maybe you'd sleep in after last night. It went later than I expected," Jane said.

"Oh no. I always get up early. Habit. Besides, I told you I'd be here to help. What can I do?"

"You can fill the coffee carafes out on the table. The one on the right is decaf. It has a label. Then we can start another pot of each."

"I'm on it," she said, going through the doorway.

Jane flipped the mini omelets and put a circle of cheese atop each to melt, then pulled the biscuits out of the oven.

"Plates and silverware are ready," Alice said, coming into the kitchen. "I didn't know Hope was coming early to help."

"I didn't expect her this early either. Is anyone else up yet?"

"Joan and Maggie are up. They brought down their pictures this morning and settled at a table in the living room. The girls haven't come down yet. Neither has Elaine."

"The rest of the ladies will be coming soon," Jane said. "We'll be ready."

"I wouldn't make any more decaf," Hope said, coming back in the kitchen. "I don't think you'll have many takers. Just keep the regular coffee coming. Do you have tea and hot chocolate? Joan was asking."

"There's a carafe for hot water," Jane said, pointing to a tall, green thermal pitcher by the sink. "Alice will set out an assortment of tea bags and cocoa packets."

"That'll do it. What can I do now?"

Jane wasn't used to having an assistant. It took more thinking to delegate than to just do it, but she didn't want to hurt Hope's feelings. "There's an ice bowl in the freezer. The bowl of yogurt in the refrigerator will fit right in it. You can set that out, if you'd like. The fruit bowl and pastries can go out too. I don't want to put the hot food out until we have a bunch of guests ready to eat."

"Will do," Hope said, taking a bowl and heading out.

Jane hadn't worked with a professional waitress in a long

while, not since she'd left San Francisco and the Blue Fish Grille. She'd have to be quick to keep up with Hope.

"I feel positively decadent," Louise said Saturday as she sipped coffee and watched deer feed on the lawn outside the Blue Peacock Inn.

Cynthia smiled. "It's nice not to be on a schedule today. What would you like to do?"

"Relax," Louise said. She set her cup down and leaned back in the easy chair on the screened porch, where she and Cynthia were having coffee. She rolled her head to the side and looked at her daughter. "How about you? What do you need to do for your story?"

"The concert tonight isn't until seven o'clock. I volunteered us to take tickets, so we need to be there early. How about a nice drive in the mountains? It's supposed to be beautiful. Earlene told me there are some very western mountain towns, and neat shops and galleries."

"Sounds lovely."

Cynthia gave her mother a cat-in-the-cream smile. "I thought we'd do a little gold panning while we're at it."

Louise raised her eyebrow. "Gold panning? In a river?"

"That's the only way I've heard about. Who knows? Maybe we'll strike it rich."

Alice set her box of pictures at one end of a table in the living room. Hope had the middle of the table, and Garrett and Elaine were using the end. Joan, Maggie and Viola were using the other table in the room.

Opening the twelve-inch-square burgundy-leather album, Alice stared at the clear sleeves inside the book. She had no idea how to begin. Glancing down the table, she realized Hope was facing the same dilemma.

"I have no idea where to start. Do you?" she asked.

Hope shook her head. She began leafing through a basket of pictures she'd brought over. Hope had fewer pictures than Alice had.

"I don't even know where some of these pictures were taken," Hope said. She sounded dejected.

Mary Jo had entered the room. She came behind Hope and leaned over the table.

"Getting started is the hardest part sometimes. Is there any order to your pictures? Are they holidays or birthdays or something like that?" Mary Jo asked.

"Most of them are roads. My mom took pictures of roads through the windshield of the car. I don't know why." Hope sighed. "We were always on some road or another. We moved around a lot." Hope propped her elbow on the table and leaned on her fist.

"Lay them out and see if something strikes a memory," Mary Jo said. "Something like 'Roads I've Traveled' or 'Places I've Been.'"

Hope let out a short laugh. She looked up at Mary Jo. "Sorry. I didn't like traveling all the time."

"Do you know where all those places were and when you were there?" Garrett asked. "Sometimes I equate a place with something that happened that year. For instance, I was in the navy, stationed at Norfolk, when Elaine was born. We were out at sea, returning to base the day before she was due. As we pulled into port, I got a message from the captain to get myself over to Portsmouth Naval Hospital the minute we hit the pier. I was jumping off that ship before they even had it tied up properly. I believe I ran most of the way. Got there just as they wheeled her mother into the delivery room." He smiled affectionately at Elaine. "I paced that waiting room for forty minutes, and it seemed like an eternity. Then they brought you out and put you in my arms. I couldn't believe you were so beautiful."

Elaine looked at her father, her eyes misty, as if she'd never heard the story before.

Hope watched them, then looked away, as if embarrassed to be intruding on their intimate moment. She looked up at Mary Jo. "I remember most of these roads. I looked out the window and wished I were somewhere else. Usually the place we'd just left."

"Why not lay these out and put a little sticky note with each one, telling where it is and when. You could piece together sort of a road map and timeline."

"All right."

Alice thought Hope didn't sound too enthusiastic, but she started going through the basket, arranging the pictures on the table around her.

"A timeline is just what I need," Alice said. "I'll put my pictures in chronological order."

Mary Jo pulled a folding chair close to Alice. "You have the makings of a wonderful scrapbook," she said. "I have lots of old-fashioned stickers you could add to the pages. Is that you as a little girl?" she asked, pointing to a picture of two young girls in dress-up clothes.

"Yes, and that's Louise," she said, pointing to the older one with a huge straw hat with silk flowers hiding most of her face. "Our mother put on lots of tea parties and picnics for us."

"I'll bring in some of my tea-party embellishments," Mary Jo said. "They'd be perfect."

"Thank you," Alice said. "I admit, I'm lost when it comes to decorating."

After Mary Jo went to the next table, Hope said, "Your scrapbook is going to be beautiful. You and Louise and Jane had such an enchanted childhood. I'd have given anything for a backyard tea party with sisters or friends. You know, I think we hit every state in the union, except Alaska and Hawaii, in about seven years."

"Wow. You must have seen some interesting places," Elaine said.

"Not really. We stayed in cheap hotels and run-down apartments. We couldn't afford much. Once in a while my dad would get some money and we'd stay at a fancy hotel and dine at a nice restaurant. He'd buy my mother and me a new outfit and new shoes, but that didn't happen often."

"I always wanted to travel with my dad, but I had to stay home," Elaine said, looking at her father longingly.

"Your mother and I thought you should have a stable home,

honey. That's why you didn't go with me when I had to go out of town on jobs."

"You're lucky," Hope said. "I never went to the same school for a full year. I didn't make friends or play in the band or sing in the chorus. Your way was much better."

Alice could see Elaine wasn't convinced. Each of them thought the other had it better. She said a silent prayer that they would discover positive things about their childhoods as they assembled their scrapbooks.

Chapter Twenty-Four

*J*ane stood at the back of the dining room listening to Mary Jo demonstrate cropping techniques using special cutters.

"You can achieve several different looks using the same edgers. Here's one with smooth, rounded corners on the photograph, and the mat is scalloped." She held up a matted picture. "In this one I cut the picture to get a scalloped look against a plain background," she said, showing them a different example. "Now I can take this and add a braided border."

Mary Jo took two pieces of colored paper and cut strips of paper using the same edging scissors. Then she wove the strips together to get a braided effect. When she held the braid against the dark mat, it created a decorative finish. Jane was fascinated by the variety of sample pages Mary Jo had on display. Jane decided she needed to leave before she got caught up in another hobby.

She wandered through the rooms, looking at the activity at the various scrapbooking tables. Patsy, Florence and Ethel were set up in the library. Ethel had a pile of pictures of her daughter Francine's family. Ethel's two grandsons were grown and attending college. Ethel had photos and news clippings of Geoffrey at various law-school events and of Franklin, who was studying biology and had an internship at a marine-life aquarium. Jane hadn't seen her cousin's children since they were teenagers. She couldn't believe how they'd matured.

Patsy Ley was having a great time creating collages of nature scenes and wildlife around Acorn Hill.

In the living room, Alice was surrounded by Hope, Elaine and Mary Jo, who were helping her rather than working on their own scrapbooks. Jane was curious, but Alice didn't seem ready to share what she was making, so Jane went over to Viola.

"Hi, Jane," Viola said. "What do you think?" She held up several pictures of the interior of her house. "I took pictures of every room to make an album, in case I ever have a fire or loss, for insurance records. I've been meaning to do it, and a scrapbook seemed like the ideal opportunity. I can slip letters and memorabilia in with them. I took pictures of my mummer-mask collection. They're family pieces. And I've got pictures of the Mummers Parades in Philadelphia, with my grandfather and my uncles wearing the masks."

"That's a great idea," Jane said. Jane had seen Viola's mask collection. Viola had told her the history of mummers plays in England, which usually occurred at Christmastime or New Year's, when the amateur players wore masks to disguise themselves. Immigrants from England and Europe brought the tradition with them and began marching in a yearly parade in Philadelphia, wearing their elaborate old-world masks. Viola's masks were made with shimmery fabric and long feathers and decorated with sequins and beads.

"Excuse me," Maggie said. "I couldn't help overhearing. You collect mummer masks?"

"I have a few masks that were in my family. My family is from Philadelphia and always took part in the Mummers Parade every New Year's Day. They were in every parade since 1901, until a few years ago. I'm afraid that tradition is gone now."

"My family still takes part in the parade," Maggie said. "What is your last name?"

"Reed. Viola Reed." Viola studied Maggie, as if looking for something familiar.

"I'm a Lander," Maggie said. "I grew up in Philadelphia. I found some Reeds in my background when I was looking up my genealogy. I think one of the Lander daughters married a Reed."

"Really? I don't know a lot about my history, but my great-great-grandfather came over from England and settled in Philadelphia," Viola said. "Do you think we're related?"

"I think it's possible. May I see the pictures of your masks? Do you know what kind of club your family belonged to?"

"They were part of a fancy division." Viola stood and handed her photographs to Maggie. "I haven't been to a Mummers Parade in years, but I remember the pageantry and the bands and dancing. The masks predate my lifetime, though. A few of my relatives wore masks, but most wore fancy costumes and headgear and painted their faces like clowns."

Maggie studied the photos and began nodding. "My grandmother had a mask like this." She looked up at Viola and smiled. "We've got to be cousins. Probably distant, but I'm pretty certain we're related."

Viola sat down. "Wow!" she said. She regarded her newfound

relative. "That's...remarkable." Viola shut her mouth and stared at her cousin.

Maggie laughed. "I feel the same way. Speechless." She sat down too.

"Tell me about your family. Are you married? Do you have children?" Viola asked.

Maggie and Viola began sharing their backgrounds, so Jane left and went through the parlor to the sunroom. The three friends had pictures spread all over one of the tables.

"Hi, Jane. That breakfast was great," Kiran said. She patted her flat stomach. "I need to work out after your fabulous meals."

All three women were slender. From the energy they exuded, Jane doubted any of them had to battle weight. "We don't have any workout equipment, but you could take a nice brisk walk around town. I go jogging as often as possible."

"I went out early this morning," Chanelle said, standing straight and stretching. "It's warmed up a little."

"So what are you working on?" Jane asked, looking at the pictures spread all over the table.

"We want memory albums of the three of us, so we won't forget our friendship. I live in Illinois," Chanelle said. "Kiran lives in Harrisburg, and Liana lives in Denver. We hardly ever get to see each other anymore."

"Do you want me to take a picture of you together?" Jane offered.

"Would you? Get a picture of us working on our scrapbooks," Kiran said. She produced a digital camera.

Jane backed up so she could get them all in. She snapped several pictures, then handed the camera back.

"Thanks. I'm going to put these on my laptop and get copies made this afternoon," Kiran said. "Alice said there's a one-hour photo place not far from here in Potterston. I'll do that after lunch."

"Yes. They do a good job," Jane said.

"Great."

After talking a bit longer, Jane went back to the kitchen. She had a little time before lunch preparations. Pouring herself a glass of water, she sat at the kitchen table and took out her sketchpad.

Leafing through the pages, she stopped at a page with five small sketches of the girls cooking. She pictured the three girls surrounding the large bowl that held the crazy-cake ingredients, waiting to see magic happen.

With that image in her mind, Jane began a new sketch in the lower corner of the page. She was lost in a world of lines and details when the kitchen door opened.

"Excuse me, Jane. I don't want to disturb you. Can I get some ice?"

Jane sat up straight. "Hope. Sorry. I hadn't thought about putting out the sodas yet. I guess some people drink soda instead of coffee in the morning."

"We get a few who do that in the Coffee Shop. Just stay put. I'll get it."

Hope filled a container with ice and went out front.

Jane glanced at her watch. Ten thirty. Time had slipped away

from her. She needed to think about lunch and putting on potatoes for dinner.

She set the tablet down, still open to the sketches, and rose as
Hope came back into the kitchen. The waitress wiped out the ice
container and put it in the sink.

Hands on her hips, Hope came over to the table. "Would you
like some help with lunch?" she asked.

"No thanks. It's under control. How's the scrapbook coming?"

"It's interesting. I'm surprised at how many pictures I have
with my mom and dad. I don't know who took all the pictures,
but it's like my mom wanted us to look like a normal family on
vacation." Hope sighed. "Trouble is, we were always on vacation.
My dad kept getting us in debt and then he couldn't pay up, so
we'd move. I hated that. We were always looking to make sure
someone wasn't following us. I guess my mom hated it too."

"I bet your father hated it as well," Jane said. "It sounds as
if they went to a lot of trouble to make things look normal for
your sake."

Hope rubbed a finger around the sketches on Jane's tablet.
"Maybe. I never got to spend time in a kitchen learning to cook
like that," she said, pointing to the pictures. "You're sure artistic,
Jane. What are you going to do with the pictures?"

Jane started to close the tablet but realized that would seem
secretive or rude. "I don't know. I taught some girls a little about
cooking. They helped me make the baked spaghetti for last night.
I loved watching them."

"These are adorable. June's thinking about making new
menus. They'd sure be cute on the menus."

"I doubt June would want them."

"I'd be happy to tell her about them if you want. Unless you have other ideas for them." Hope looked embarrassed. "You probably do. I'd better get back to my scrapbook."

"I don't know yet, but I'll let you know if they're available. Thanks, Hope."

"Why? I just stuck my nose in your business."

"No, you didn't. I'm always critical of my work. Thanks for the encouragement."

Hope smiled. "You're welcome. Your art is as great as your cooking, Jane."

Hope left the kitchen with Jane staring after her. Jane sat down for a moment and looked at her notes. The recipes she'd picked out seemed inappropriate. The girls had fun cooking, but they'd suggested she should leave out the very ingredients that made the recipes special. The girls preferred the old standards that called for plain ingredients and that could be found in any cookbook...or in a package.

Jane took potatoes out of the pantry and peeled them, then put them on the stove to boil while she prepared pie filling. She measured two generous cups of chunky peanut butter and two packages of cream cheese into a large bowl and creamed them together with an electric mixer. She liked making peanut-butter pies as late as possible the day she needed them, so they stayed light and fluffy. They'd need to chill all afternoon.

Setting the mixture aside, she checked her lunch menu. Her cakes were ready and chilling in the refrigerator. Everything was prepared except for grilling the chicken, Swiss cheese and cranberry-mustard panini sandwiches. She would make a few chicken paninis with provolone, sweet peppers and marinara sauce for the less adventurous, then keep them warm in the oven. So far, the scrapbook ladies seemed willing to try anything she made. Obviously, a children's cookbook wasn't the right venue for her recipes. She'd enjoyed working with the girls and loved observing and sketching them. It seemed a shame to waste the drawings. Maybe June could use her sketches after all. Meanwhile, there were eighteen people looking forward to eating her gourmet cooking.

Ice-cold water, diverted from the north fork of the Yuba River, washed down the long sluice channel where Louise swished water around and around in an oversize pie pan with little ridges in the bottom. Gradually she washed the black sand and tiny bits of gravel out of the pan. Her hands burned from the cold.

Cynthia looked up from her panning and squinted against the afternoon sun. "Any luck, Mother?"

"Nothing. Just dirty sand and rock. What am I looking for, anyway?"

"Tiny bits of shiny gold flakes. I was told there's gold in here. I'd love to find some. Buying a little vial of gold flakes just isn't the same."

"No, but it would be easier on my hands."

"Remember, this is research for my project," Cynthia said.

"Yes, dear," Louise said, then jerked her pan up out of the

water. "I found some!" She slowly swished the water around in the pan. She'd seen something shiny. Now it was gone.

Cynthia came over. So did the man who'd allowed them to pan in his sluice for a small fee.

He peered in. "Sure enough," he said, pointing to a little dot of gold. He took a tiny vial of water and an eyedropper out of his pocket. "Shake the sand away. The gold is heavier than the sand. It'll stay put. Then scoop it up with the dropper and put it in the vial."

Louise did as he instructed. It took her a few tries, but soon she had a shiny dot of gold in the bottom of the vial. In the glass and water, it looked larger. She held it up proudly.

"Try again. Find some more to add to it."

Louise shook her head. "That's enough for me. Go ahead, Cynthia. I'll wait for you."

Cynthia shot her a saucy look. "You bet you will. I've got the car keys."

The sunshine was bright and temperature mild when Jane called everyone to the hallway for lunch. After Penny asked a blessing on the food and fellowship, Alice carried extra folding chairs out to the sunroom. The room quickly filled with the younger set. Two of the local ladies carried their plates out to join Chanelle, Kiran and Liana.

After Alice made sure everyone had lunch, she followed Mary Jo to the buffet table. She passed Penny and Vera, who were also headed for the sunroom.

"What smells so wonderful in here?" Mary Jo asked.

"Jane has a turkey in the oven for dinner tonight."

"No wonder. I could just stand here and breathe in the wonderful aroma." She picked up a paper plate and filled it with fruit, veggies and chips. She spooned some artichoke dip on top of the veggies and some ranch dip on top of the chips. Then she perched a sandwich on top of the fruit. "This is such a treat," she said. "I never get to sit and eat a full meal at home."

Alice didn't doubt that was true. She took a sandwich and a few veggies and dip, then followed Mary Jo.

Viola, Joan and Maggie were sitting in the parlor, talking about their families and their lives. Alice was thrilled that Viola had discovered an unknown relative. What a bonus to the weekend.

Mary Jo carried her lunch plate into the sunroom. She sat on an empty chair. "How are you ladies doing?" she asked cheerfully.

"Great," one responded. Several others indicated they were doing well.

Alice sat in the last empty chair, next to Mary Jo. "Have you talked to your husband? How is Timmy's collarbone?"

Mary Jo smiled sheepishly. "I've called at least ten times since I left yesterday. My husband told me not to call again. He said that Timmy's fine and I was interrupting their construction project. They're making a fort out of plastic building blocks. They ate pizza and popcorn and soda pop and a whole bag of chocolate-chip cookies."

"This is only day two," Penny said. "You have weeks ahead of you keeping him quiet. My son broke his collarbone twice," Penny said. "Keeping him quiet was harder on us than it was on him. He wanted to be out playing football and skateboarding. Just wait until your twins get older."

"I don't even want to think about that," Mary Jo said. "I'm just praying to get through this episode. I told my husband what you said about keeping Timmy's shoulder inactive, Alice. He made shoulder pads out of foam and cardboard and told Timmy it was football gear. Timmy insisted on sleeping in it. I'm so glad you're a nurse. If you hadn't reassured me, I would have stayed home this weekend. Actually, my husband said he's happy to have time with just one of the twins. He wants to do a dad-and-son night with Jimmy next, and he even mentioned taking Jasmine on a date night to get ice cream or something. I can't believe it."

"That's really cool," Kiran said. "My fiance doesn't want to take care of our children by himself when we have them. I think it's the diapers."

"My husband wouldn't do the diaper thing either. Not unless he had to, that is," one of the Acorn Hill moms said. "We've graduated to training pants. That's better."

"I don't know how you manage taking care of a house and family while working full-time too," another woman said. "I just have one child left at home, but I'm busy all the time."

"Yes, but you volunteer at the school and at church. And look at Mary Jo." She turned to look at their hostess. "How do you manage a house, four kids and working?"

"In all honesty? Not very well," Mary Jo said. "But it sounds like I'm in good company. You're all busy, yet you took the time to come this weekend. I really appreciate that."

"We came so we could have a little uninterrupted time to sort through our memories and put those special events in a scrapbook. Then, when times get tough, we can take out our pictures and remember how good life can be," Penny said. "You know, I had been feeling sorry for my son Bart. During the summer and after school, he works with his father in the construction business. He plays football and has a few other after-school activities, but most of the time, he's busy with work and homework and school. What you said about your husband spending time with Timmy is so important. Bart spends a lot of time with his dad. I have pictures of them putting on a roof, building a concrete foundation, framing a house and mudding drywall. In every picture, they are together, working as a team, and the looks on their faces..." Penny stopped and blinked back her sudden emotion. "I realized today looking at those photos that every minute they spend together is more valuable than any free time Bart could have."

"Wow. That's so cool," Chanelle said. "You're all just amazing. I've got my hands full with an apartment and a cat and a full-time job," she said, smiling.

Alice heard laughter and glanced toward the parlor. She caught a glimpse of Jane moving through the room. Alice hoped she'd covered her photographs well enough on her table in the living room. She'd be glad when she finished and the weekend was over. She felt like a sneak every time Jane went by the doorway.

Chapter Twenty-Five

*J*ane carried a pumpkin cake to the buffet table and looked around. She heard the sounds of voices and laughter coming from the parlor and the living room. No one seemed to be working. All the scrapbookers were busy visiting. She hated to disturb their conversations, so she took the cake back into the kitchen and cut portions of pumpkin cake and of fruit dump cake and put them on dessert plates. She topped each with a mound of whipped cream and a sprinkle of fresh nutmeg. She checked the coffee to make sure she had plenty ready, then carried the tray to the parlor.

Maggie and Viola were marveling over the similarities in their families.

"Have some dessert, ladies. I'll bring around the coffee later," Jane said, holding the tray in front of them.

"Did you hear that Maggie and I are related?" Viola asked.

"Yes. I was there when you discovered the tie because of your masks. It's wonderful."

"I'm so excited, I can't remember anything else," Viola said. "I'm going to take a long weekend and go to Maggie's for Thanksgiving. Isn't that grand?"

"What fun!" Jane was thrilled for Viola. Although they often included Viola in their festivities, and Viola loved to entertain,

Jane knew the holidays could be lonely without family around. She'd spent a few alone in San Francisco.

Jane refilled the tray, then went into the living room.

Hope popped up when she saw her coming. "May I help?" she asked.

"I don't want to disturb your conversation," Jane said.

"No, I think Garrett and Elaine should have some time alone. I'll get the coffee pot."

"Good idea. Start in the parlor," Jane said.

Jane offered dessert to the father and daughter, who were sitting by the fireplace. After they made their selections, she carried the tray to the library, where Ethel, Vera, Patsy and Florence had pulled chairs into a small circle and were holding court.

"Yum, those look wonderful," Vera said. "I think I want some of both."

"Let's split them," Patsy suggested. "You can have half of mine and I'll have half of yours."

"Excellent idea," Florence said. "Ethel, would you like to try half of each?"

"Oh yes. Then we'll know which one to get for seconds."

Vera laughed. "I like the way you think." She took a piece of pumpkin cake and split it with the fork, then offered it to Patsy.

Jane returned to the kitchen for more dessert. She was cutting the cake when Alice came in.

"You should have called me to help you. Let me serve those."

"The only unserved guests are in the sunroom. You can take a tray in there, and I'll put the rest on the buffet table, so people can have seconds. Hope is serving coffee and tea. How is the scrap-booking going?"

"Mine or everyone else's?" Alice asked. "Mine is going slowly, but everyone else seems to be doing great. Several of the ladies have taken time to help me."

"Good. You can work on it all afternoon. I've got dinner under control, and Hope is more than willing to help me."

"I hope she's enjoying herself. She's so used to serving, she rarely lets herself relax and have fun."

"I know. I won't let her overdo it," Jane said.

"I'm so full, I'm likely to fall asleep on the drive back to the inn," Louise told Cynthia as they walked a path along the river, back to the rental car.

Cynthia laughed. "If you think you can sleep on the moun-tain roads, you're welcome to try."

They'd dined at a bakery that made delicious breads and homemade soups.

"I should have passed up dessert," Louise said. "That carrot cake was heavenly."

"Well, we won't be hungry for dinner. Since we need to be at the concert early, this should hold us. Thanks for indulging me and going gold panning with me."

"My hands are still chilled, but I'm glad we came. These mountains are beautiful."

They reached a footbridge across the river. "Stay there,

Mother. Let me take a picture of you and the river." Cynthia backed up and stood on a rock several yards away. She aimed her camera. "Smile."

Louise complied while Cynthia snapped several pictures. "Let me take some pictures of you," Louise said when she finished.

Cynthia came back and handed her the camera.

"Go back on the rock. That will be a pretty shot with the town in the background."

Cynthia posed, and Louise took her picture.

"I'd like copies of the pictures you've been taking," Louise said as they got into the car. "This has been a week worth remembering."

"Has it, Mother? I'm so glad. I was afraid you weren't enjoying yourself, especially having to deal with the music style they teach. Your performance last night was superb. I'm so proud of you. I think you should play it in church."

Louise chuckled. "I'm not sure Grace Chapel is ready for boogie-woogie renditions of the hymns. Aunt Ethel would be horrified."

"Maybe. Maybe she'd love it."

"I doubt that. However, I will treasure this week—especially since we spent it together."

Louise thought she would ask Alice and Jane how to make a scrapbook out of the memories she'd collected. With copies of Cynthia's pictures, she could make one for her too, perhaps for Christmas.

Jane wrapped a thin slice of ham around a generous spoonful of cooked cranberry-apple-nut stuffing, making a filled tube that she secured with a long string of chive, tying a knot to hold it together. She set the bundle on a shallow baking dish already lined with ham and turkey bundles. Brushing the bundles with cranberry glaze, she put them in the oven to heat through while she finished her meal preparation with a tossed green salad with mandarin oranges, dried cherries and slivered almonds.

"I told Alice to keep working on her scrapbook," Hope said, coming through the door.

Jane turned toward her volunteer helper. "What about yours?"

"It's coming along fine. There's not that much to it. So what can I do here? I checked the buffet table and set out plates, silverware and napkins."

Jane tore pieces of curly leaf lettuce into the large stainless bowl. "I made a pear vinaigrette salad dressing. It's in the refrigerator if you want to get it out. I'll put it on the salad just before I serve it."

Hope set the bottle of dressing on the counter next to Jane. "Shall I put the scalloped potatoes out yet?"

"Sure. Put them in the chafing tray so they stay hot. The bundles will be ready in a minute. The rolls are in the warming oven. They can go out."

Jane watched Hope carry a dish out to the table. She wasn't sure what to do with all Hope's help. Jane was used to working with Alice and Louise, and they had a routine down. The Coffee Shop waitress was so efficient and so willing, she seemed to be a step ahead of Jane all the time

Hope swept back into the kitchen, picked up relish trays of pickles, olives, pearl onions and cherry tomatoes, and took them out to the table. She returned as Jane tossed the salad with the dressing. She handed the bowl to Hope.

"I'll get the meat if you want to get the rolls. Then we're ready," Jane said, removing the entrée from the oven.

The scrapbookers had gathered for the meal in the hallway, which crowded the large entryway, but it worked.

"Let us pray," Mary Jo said. She bowed her head. The group grew quiet as they bowed their heads.

"Dear Lord, we thank You for this wonderful home and the delicious food and ask You to bless it and our time together. May our efforts bring us thankfulness for our families, our homes and jobs, and all the blessings You've given to us. In Jesus' name. Amen."

"Thank you, Mary Jo," Alice said. "Before we eat, I want to invite you to attend church with us tomorrow. We'll be walking to Grace Chapel after breakfast."

"For those who'd rather stay and scrapbook, I'll leave coffee and goodies to keep you going," Jane said. "Now dig in, and enjoy. When you're finished, I'll bring out the peanut-butter pie and peach cobbler, so save room."

There was a murmur of appreciative sounds at the mention of dessert and at the spread before them.

"I hope you're planning to have more scrapbook retreats," Joan said. "I'd love an excuse to come back."

"Me too, and soon, I hope," Kiran said. "I want to make a scrapbook about my engagement next."

Jane had noticed the shining diamond ring on Kiran's finger. This retreat was going so well, she was up to doing another one. She glanced at Alice. Jane suspected Alice would do another one—if she didn't have to make a scrapbook.

"Dad and I want to go to church with you," Elaine told Alice. They were sitting in the living room after supper. They'd asked Hope and Alice to stay and talk to them while Mary Jo gave a demonstration in the dining room on how to make glittery velum snowflakes for embellishment. Elaine reached over and patted her father's hand. "We haven't gone to church together in a long time."

"Five years," Garrett said. "That was just before you graduated from high school. Then you went off to college. After your mother passed, I got out of the habit of going."

"We'd love to have you join us," Alice said.

"How nice that you can go together," Hope said.

"We'd like to sit with you," Elaine said, giving Hope a smile.

"I told Elaine that you got me going to church here, and your pastor's been meeting with me for Bible study at the Coffee Shop," Garrett said. "I didn't realize how much I've missed the fellowship and the preaching. I've got a lot of time to make up for." He took his daughter's hand and squeezed it. "I'm a lucky man. My daughter has turned out to be a beautiful woman, like her mother, and she's married to a fine young man. And they're going to make me a grandfather," he said proudly. His face beamed with his announcement.

Elaine smiled. "And our baby is going to need a big, strong grandpa. I'm so glad you suggested Dad call me. I've been praying for a chance to spend time with him and tell him in person."

Hope grabbed Garrett's hand. Her eyes sparkled as she smiled at her friend. "I'm so excited for you! That's wonderful. Congratulations, Elaine."

"That *is* wonderful news," Alice said. "You should put something announcing your baby in the scrapbook for your grandmother."

"Oh yes, that's perfect!" Elaine said. "Maybe I can get a little announcement card. I saw baby paper in Mary Jo's stock. I'm already planning to make a scrapbook for the baby."

"May I tell Jane?" Alice asked.

"Yes. You can tell anyone, now that I've told Dad," Elaine said, giving her father a hug.

Alice glanced at her own scrapbook project as she left the living room to find Jane. She'd made progress. She'd hand printed journal notes to add to the book. Over the weekend, many of the other scrapbookers had contributed something to her pages. She was glad she'd decided to make a scrapbook of the Berry-Howard house, but Elaine's good news and the restored relationship of father and daughter topped everything else.

"You look mighty fine tonight, Louise," Farley Blackthorn said. He stood inside the Festival Center, where Louise and Cynthia would take tickets for the Luken Family Scholarship Concert.

"Thank you, Farley." Louise thought Farley looked exceptionally fine in his black western suit, complete with boots and hat. With his dark hair and eyes, he looked like a western movie star. "Have you met my daughter Cynthia?"

"Yes, ma'am." He nodded to Cynthia.

"I interviewed Farley along with the other instructors for the book," Cynthia said. "The Lukens put together an impressive staff," she said. "I thought the instructors left after the concert last night. Are you performing tonight?"

"We do a reciprocal deal," Farley said. "Some of the Luken family will appear with us in Branson this spring."

"Have you known the Lukens for long?" Louise asked.

Farley nodded. Louise caught a glimpse of weariness in his gaze and his posture. "Long time. Since the oldest kids were knee-high and the family did the circuit—you know, county fairs, rodeos, tent meetings, that sort of thing. They always did a western gospel sound. Our mother, rest her soul, hated us doing gigs. We were supposed to join a symphony. Hurley on violin, Sheldon on bass."

"And you on piano. You're all good. Why didn't you?" Louise asked.

He tilted his head and looked Louise straight in the eyes. "Music calls you, you know? It gets in your head and in here." He pounded his fist against his heart. "Music moves you. Some makes you want to dance and sing or get out and do something. Some takes you to a mountaintop, and you sit and stare and drink in the wonder of it all. Some makes you want to cry. I was twenty-two years old. My brothers were in their twenties. We didn't want to cry. We wanted to sing and dance. We wanted to live." He grinned. "When you played that solo last night, which was terrific, by the way, didn't it get your blood pumping?"

Louise smiled, pleased. "Yes. I enjoyed playing last night. I have to admit, Farley, this week has been quite an experience. Going back to teaching and playing hymns in church will seem a little flat after this. Though I find my music very satisfying."

"Just don't forget to have fun with it," Farley said.

The door opened as the first guests arrived. "Is this where the Luken family's playing tonight?" the woman asked.

"Yes ma'am," Cynthia said.

"I'd better get backstage," Farley said. He tipped his hat. "See you ladies later."

"Good-bye, Farley," Louise said as he walked away. She wasn't sure they'd see Farley or any of the family and instructors again. They were expecting a large crowd.

"Farley thinks your playing is terrific, Mother," Cynthia said, grinning. "So do I."

"*Hmm*," was all Louise responded. His offhanded compliment meant a lot to her. Farley knew how to have fun with his music. She looked forward to hearing him play again.

Chapter Twenty-Six

*A*fter dinner, Jane poured a cup of coffee and went into the parlor, where Vera and Penny were working at a table. Pulling up a chair next to Vera, she sat down.

"Good to see you finally coming out of the kitchen," Vera said.

"Anyone want some coffee or soda or anything else?" Jane asked.

"We can get our own, Jane. You just sit and relax. You've already spent too much time waiting on us," Penny said.

"May I see what you're doing?" Jane asked.

"Sure," Penny said, handing Jane a couple of plastic-covered pages. One page had a racetrack background and pictures of Penny's husband and son building and painting a soapbox racer. In the center picture, the two posed in back of the midnight-blue car with yellow and red flames and lightning bolts. Along the side were the words *Holwell's Comet*.

Another page showed the father and son mudding a room together. Over several pictures, the room got whiter, and so did the guys. In the last picture, they were leaning on each other, smiling, showing their white teeth. They were covered from head to foot with white spackle. Penny had mounted the pictures on a dark background, then sprinkled the page with white dots.

"These are great! Zeke and Bart are going to love these. Do they know you're doing this?"

Penny beamed at Jane's compliment. "Zeke knows I'm working on an album, but he doesn't have any idea what I'm putting inside."

"That's fabulous. What a team. But I don't see any pictures of you with them," Jane said, frowning.

"I made another scrapbook with all of us. This is for Bart for Christmas. I want him to have these special memories with his father."

"Maybe you should make a duplicate for Zeke."

"I thought about having the pages photocopied to make another album."

Vera set her scissors down. "I'm making duplicate albums for Polly and Jean." Vera held up two identical pages. The sisters were young teenagers, dressed up for Easter in one picture and running around the beach in shorts and T-shirts in another. "That was the year we went to South Carolina for the Easter break. We got home just in time to go to church on Easter. I have other pages for each of them. I'm just duplicating the ones with both of them in it."

"They'll love the scrapbooks. Now I wish I'd made one. I don't know of what, but they're beautiful," Jane said.

"You could do all your beautiful food creations, or your garden, or your jewelry," Vera suggested. "Or you could take up photography as an art form."

"I'll have to give that some thought. And now that I've had

a break and a cup of coffee, I have some eggs to boil." Jane stood and gave them a quick salute. "See you later."

～

Sunday morning, Jane set a pan of savory ham bread pudding in one of the chafing dishes to stay warm. Liana Drake came up to her.

"Is it all right to wear casual clothes to church?" she asked. "None of us brought dresses."

"Pants are fine. Tell your friends not to worry."

"Oh, good. I really want us to go to church together. Thanks." Liana went to tell her friends.

Jane usually wore skirts and tops, but she thought today she'd wear pants to make their guests feel more comfortable.

Garrett and Elaine came downstairs dressed casually. Jane greeted them as they arrived for breakfast. Most of the local ladies had stayed home to get ready for church. Mary Jo was going to church with Penny's family.

Viola came in with Ethel to have breakfast.

"Are you and Joan and Maggie coming to church with us?" Ethel asked.

"Not today," Viola answered. "I want to spend as much time as possible visiting with Maggie. We have a lot of catching up to do, you know. I'm going to take her and Joan to see my bookstore and meet my cats."

～

Lloyd came to take Ethel to church. She suggested that they walk with the scrapbook ladies.

"Are you sure, Aunt Ethel? You still have the sniffles," Alice said.

Ethel gave a dismissive wave of her hand. "It's the weather. I feel fine."

The group walked from the inn to Grace Chapel. Hope, Patsy and Florence met them at the door.

"We're so glad you decided to come," Patsy said. "I saved a couple of pews for you."

She led the way down the aisle, with Florence bringing up the rear. The pews were near the front.

"We're right behind you," Patsy said, introducing them to Henry Ley, her husband, and to Ronald Simpson, Florence's husband. Ethel moved back with the Leys and the Simpsons, so she could sit beside Lloyd. Alice and Jane took the pew in front of the group, beside Mary Jo, Penny and her family.

"Good morning," Pastor Thompson said from the pulpit. "Florence tells me we are honored to have a group of guests with us from a scrapbooking weekend at Grace Chapel Inn. Welcome. We hope you enjoy worshipping with us this morning."

During the service, Elaine's sweet soprano voice blended with her father's deep tenor singing the hymns. The three roommates got into the spirit of the singing when the organist substituting for Louise began to play "I've got the joy, joy, joy, joy down in my heart." One of them started clapping, then the other two joined her, and soon the entire congregation was clapping in time to the song. Every time the verse said, "down in my heart," the three shouted, "Where?" in unison.

"There certainly seems to be joy in this congregation this

morning," Rev. Thompson said when he got up to preach. "Perhaps I need to take up scrapbooking."

That remark earned him a laugh, which set the tone for the sermon.

"That song reminds me of one of my verses for today. Isaiah 55:12 says, 'You will go out in joy and be led forth in peace; the mountains and hills will burst into song before you, and all the trees of the field will clap their hands.' So thank you for clapping and singing joyfully. You gave my sermon a boost," he said.

Alice settled in to savor another of Rev. Thompson's excellent sermons. *Joy* certainly described the scrapbooking retreat. So far, Viola had met a cousin she had never known before, and Garrett had not only reunited with his daughter but learned he was going to be a grandfather.

"The Bible talks a lot about joy," the pastor said. "Doing a word search in the King James Version on my computer, I found 167 references to joy. James 1:2 tells us to 'Consider it pure joy... whenever you face trials of many kinds.' The passage goes on to tell us why trials are a good thing in our lives, but not many of us can feel joyful when we're going through tough times."

Alice marveled that Rev. Thompson had selected the same verse from James as had Patsy for her talk to the scrapbookers. She was still thinking about the pastor's closing verse as she walked out of church with the others. "I will turn their mourning into gladness; I will give them comfort and joy instead of sorrow" (Jeremiah 31:13).

Jane scooted ahead to set out some snacks and fresh coffee for everyone. Alice hung back, letting the scrapbookers speak with

Rev. Thompson before she thanked him for his thought-provoking sermon and followed the others down the path.

The sun shone brilliantly, warming the day. The scrapbook crowd chattered merrily on their way back to the inn. Alice noticed Liana hanging back from the rest, waiting for Alice to catch up to her.

"Hi. I wondered if we could talk," she said. From the somber look in her eyes, Alice knew something was wrong.

"Of course. Shall we let the others go ahead?"

"Yes. Thanks."

They watched the group enter the backyard of the inn. Chanelle looked back for a moment, then turned and went on.

"You're troubled," Alice said.

"Yes. I heard Mary Jo say you're a nurse. I...I have a medical problem. I found out right before I came." She stopped and took a deep breath. When she looked at Alice, her chin trembled. She gave her head a shake, as if to rid herself of the burden. "I've been having headaches. The doctors couldn't figure out why. When the headaches started affecting my vision, I had an MRI, and they found a small tumor in my brain."

"I'm so sorry," Alice said.

"Yeah. Me too." Liana gave her a brave smile. "The doctor says it's probably benign, and they can get it out, so I'm really lucky."

"But it doesn't feel lucky," Alice said.

"No. I just completed my master's degree and started a new job. My husband and I were hoping to start a family soon. The headaches were so bad, I had to quit my job. Now everything is on hold."

"Have you told your friends?" Alice asked.

"No. I didn't want to spoil the weekend. I have medicine that controls the headaches. The doctor said I could put off the surgery for a couple of weeks so I could come. Kiran is getting married next spring, and I'm supposed to be her matron of honor. Now I just don't know. That sermon today...it was meant for me. I needed to hear that there's still joy. I always thought my faith was strong, but now I'm not so sure."

"I believe that faith can't shine unless there's friction to polish it," Alice said. "I'm afraid that sounds trite, but I think it's true."

"I want to shine for my husband, who is so supportive. I know he's worried. The doctor said I should be fine, but it's a delicate operation, and things can go wrong. I don't want to end up being a burden." She turned serious, luminous eyes on Alice. "I'm scared. Have you ever taken care of someone who's had a brain tumor?"

"Yes, I have. Several times, in fact. The doctors are able to do amazing things these days. If your doctor said the tumor is operable, then you have a good chance of complete recovery."

"That's what he said." She straightened her shoulders. "I'm going to believe him and trust that everything will be fine. Your pastor said the Bible tells us to consider it joy when troubles come. I thought, I must not be much of a Christian, because I'm supposed to be joyful and just trust the Lord, but I don't feel joyful about this. Then what he said made sense. I'm to think about my struggle as a good thing because God is going to help me learn perseverance. I think I can do that. I'm glad your pastor gave that sermon. I felt like God was talking just to me, telling me I'm not alone, and He's going to help me get through this thing."

"God speaks to us in many ways," Alice said. "I love it when I get a message that I know is just for me. That tells me God is listening, and He wants me to know He won't ignore my prayers."

"That's how I feel. I'm going to tell Chanelle and Kiran this afternoon. I know they'll be upset for me. That's why I wanted all of us to go to church this morning."

"Can I pray with you?"

"Yes, please."

Alice put her hand on Liana's shoulder, and they bowed their heads. She could feel the sun like the warm hand of God anointing them. "Heavenly Father, please send Your comfort and grace to ease Liana's fears and calm her spirit. Give her strength when she tells her friends, and let them see her faith as she walks through this dark valley. Help her to look for the joy that can only come from You. Draw her close and give her courage to face what lies ahead. In Jesus' name. Amen."

Liana whispered "Amen." She lifted her head and looked up. When she looked at Alice, her gaze held deep resolve.

"Thank you, Alice. I'll be all right now."

"I'd like to keep in touch with you," Alice said. "May I?"

"Yes. I'd like that."

Alice only paid partial attention to her scrapbook. Liana was in the sunroom with the door closed, telling her friends about her tumor and upcoming surgery. Alice couldn't concentrate. She offered silent prayers for the three friends. Hope came over and sat down beside her.

"What's the matter, Alice? You seem so quiet and troubled," Hope said.

Alice looked up at her friend and smiled. "I'm fine. I was thinking about someone who's having problems, that's all."

"Ah. It's our three girls, isn't it? I noticed the short one, Liana, seemed sad after church. I kind of wondered if their gaiety wasn't hiding some pain. I see that all the time in the Coffee Shop."

"You have the gift of mercy, Hope," Alice observed. "That's why your customers love you so much, besides your beautiful smile and friendly attitude."

Hope looked stunned. "You think so?"

Alice smiled. "Absolutely. You sense when people are troubled."

"I suppose that's true. I remember knowing that my mother was sad, even when she was pretending to have a good time. I don't know what's wrong here, but God does, so I'll add the girls to my prayer list," she said, looking in the direction of the sunroom. She turned back to Alice. "How's your scrapbook coming? You've been working really hard on it, and I could tell you didn't want Jane to see it. I tried to give you some extra time. I hope it helped."

"Is that why you keep hopping up to help Jane? So I can work on this book?"

"Yes, sort of. You know, I'm not big into crafts, and I was dreading going through my photos. I'm surprised, though. I've got some great pictures with my folks. We did have some good times, just the three of us." Hope shrugged. "It's easy to wish things were different. I saw that with Elaine and Garrett. She wishes she'd traveled more. I wish I'd lived in one place. You know what I think?"

"What?"

"I think we both just want to know our folks loved us. Elaine has years ahead of her to spend with Garrett. My folks are gone, but now I have this scrapbook that shows they cared. I can see it in picture after picture. So I didn't have it so bad."

"Good for you."

"So how about you? Can I help you finish your book?" Hope asked. "Or I can go help Jane some more," she said, grinning.

"I'm almost finished. Everyone's been helping me, and it looks pretty good, if I do say so myself. I've got pictures of this house from the time my great-grandfather built it, until we turned it into a bed-and-breakfast. And I'm nearing the end none too soon." Alice looked at her watch. "Louise and Cynthia should get home in a few hours."

"Wow! That's cutting it close." Hope stood and stretched. "In that case, I guess I'll look around and see how I can be helpful."

"I might have been wrong," Alice said. "No, I don't think so."

"Wrong about what?" Hope asked.

"About your gift. I think you've got two of them. The gift of mercy for sure, but you also have the gift of service. You have a servant's heart."

"I hope that's a good thing," Hope said.

"Oh yes. It's a very good thing. You probably need to learn how to say no though."

Hope laughed. "You hit that nail on the head."

Chapter Twenty-Seven

*J*ane helped Mary Jo pack up her materials in the dining room. As she put edgers and punches in a box, Jane couldn't believe how little was left.

Penny and Hope had organized a work party of the local scrapbookers, who were collecting trash and stacking folding chairs. Jane appreciated the help. Louise and Cynthia would get home soon.

Garrett and Elaine had left. He was driving her home, then returning the next day.

Liana poked her head into the room. "We're ready to leave," she said.

Jane left Mary Jo to finish. "Would you like receipts for the room?" Jane asked, walking to the reception desk.

"That's not necessary," Chanelle said.

"But we could put them in our scrapbooks," Kiran said. "I'd like it as a memento." She looked at Liana. "I feel like we've started a whole new chapter in our friendship," she said.

Liana nodded. "If it's not too much trouble, receipts would be great."

Jane split the bill in thirds and printed out a receipt on Grace Chapel Inn letterhead for each of them. "I hope you'll come back to see us again," she said

Liana smiled. "Thank you," she said. "I'm so glad I came. Chanelle and Kiran are *the best* friends anyone could have. Just staying here this weekend and going to church together gave me a needed boost."

Alice came out of the library, where she'd been straightening furniture. "I'm glad you came," she said. "I'll be praying," Alice whispered when she gave Liana a brief hug and a smile.

Liana gave Jane a hug too. "Thanks for everything."

After hugging everyone they could find, the girls said good-bye and carried their suitcases out to their car.

"It's starting to snow!" Liana exclaimed, looking up at the sky. "I love snow!"

"Oh my. Fred's weather front barely waited for us to get done. I hope Zeke hurries to get the tables out of here," Jane said, waving good-bye to the girls.

"I hope it stays off the roads until Louise and Cynthia get home," Alice said.

Zeke's pickup truck pulled into the driveway as the girls drove out. Bart was with him.

"Penny called and said you're ready to get rid of tables and chairs," Zeke said.

"Your timing is impeccable," Jane said, holding the door open for them.

They stomped their feet to shake off the dusting of snow before they entered the kitchen.

Penny and Hope carried a folded table into the kitchen. Vera followed behind with another table. "We've got them broken down," Penny said. "We'll bring them in, and the guys can load them."

"Great. We'll be done in no time," Zeke said, taking the first table. Bart grabbed the second one and they carted them out to the truck.

Penny turned to Jane. "If you'll come tell us where the furniture belongs, we'll put things back to normal, except for the piano. Bart and Zeke can do that."

Mary Jo came into the kitchen with a box. "I think I'm packed up. Penny, I need to go back to your house and get my suitcase."

"My guys can load your car too. I'll be headed home in a minute," Penny said.

"In that case, I'll wait for you."

Within a few minutes, the house was restored to order. Looking around, Jane couldn't believe they'd just completed a scrapbook marathon.

"And life resumes," Alice said, standing next to her.

Jane glanced out the window at the snowflakes. "One storm blows out, and another blows in. This one will be a lot more peaceful, though. I plan to curl up in front of the fireplace with a cup of coffee and a good book."

"Sounds heavenly," Mary Jo said. "Maybe someday, after the kids are grown, I can look forward to doing that."

"I hope you don't feel as frazzled as you did when you arrived," Alice said.

"I don't. After listening to everyone and seeing their scrapbooks, I realized that all of us have problems and stress. My stresses are also my source of joy. Thanks for helping me remember that," she said.

"You're welcome, although I don't know what we did," Jane said.

"You opened your inn and your home. You showed us true hospitality. That's enough," Mary Jo said. "I hope you'll consider doing another scrapbook weekend."

"We'll consider it," Alice said, smiling.

Chapter Twenty-Eight

They're here," Alice said as she shrugged into her coat and grabbed two extra parkas by the back door.

Jane slipped her coat on and stepped into boots. She followed Alice out to the driveway where Cynthia had just parked. Alice handed her a coat as she got out of the car, then passed one to Louise. Fat flakes accumulated on Cynthia's hair before she pulled up the parka hood.

"Thanks, Aunt Alice. You're a lifesaver. It was sixty-five degrees this morning when we left Sacramento."

She went to the back and opened the trunk. Jane and Alice each grabbed two suitcases, leaving Cynthia and Louise to bring the smaller bags.

Inside the kitchen, they removed their coats. "Do you have to go home tomorrow, Cynthia, or can you stay for a few days?" Jane asked.

"I'm off until Wednesday, but I'd planned to drive home tomorrow and get caught up on some work." She looked out the window. "If this keeps up, I may wait it out."

"I'm putting you in the Garden Room. We cleaned it and changed the linens right after the guests left. You can stay as long as you want," Jane said. "I'll put your bags in there."

Cynthia followed Jane into the hall. "I'll get mine, if you'll take Mother's bags. She won't admit it, but I know she's worn out."

"Travel is exhausting," Jane said. She grabbed Louise's large suitcase and a smaller one and started up the stairs.

"So how did your scrapbook weekend go?" Cynthia asked, following her.

"Very busy. We had sixteen scrapbookers, plus the hostess and us."

"Nineteen people? Where did you put everyone?"

"Most of them were local. Seven guests stayed here, but everyone ate meals here. You should have seen it. We had tables and chairs everywhere." Jane chuckled. "I'm glad your mother didn't see how we pushed the furniture back against the walls."

"No kidding. Poor Mother's been through enough this week." Jane paused at the first landing. "Was it bad?"

"No." Cynthia smiled. "She's amazing, you know. She handled it like the pro she is, but the camp was quite a challenge."

"Your mother is a Howard. A challenge just makes Howards toughen up," Jane said, grinning. "I can't wait to hear all the details. Come down when you get settled."

"What are you doing, lugging my suitcases?" Louise said, coming up the stairs behind them.

"I thought I'd drop them off on the way to my room," Jane said, feigning innocence.

"I'm not an invalid, you know," Louise said. She was carrying two smaller bags.

"How well I know it," Jane said, heading up the second flight of stairs.

"See you in a few minutes," Cynthia said, turning toward the Garden Room.

"Are you hungry?" Jane asked her sister. "I've got tons of leftovers."

"Didn't you have many people come?" Louise asked.

"We had a good group, but I cooked too much."

"As it happens, I'm starved for your cooking. I'll be back down as soon as I get into something comfortable. And warm. I'm chilled to the bone."

"I'll put the tea on," Jane said, setting her sister's suitcases inside her bedroom.

Cynthia went to the carriage house and walked Ethel over to the inn to have supper with them. As they took their places around the dining-room table, Ethel sniffed delicately but insisted she was fine and would brave any weather to see her grandniece.

"Have you been ill, Aunt Ethel?" Louise asked.

"I started coming down with a cold, but Jane made a pot of chicken soup for me, and I feel much better."

As Jane and Alice carried food to the table, Ethel declared, "Oh joy, a resurrection supper! I'm glad you're serving leftovers," she said. "I barely tasted all the food, with such a crowd here."

Cynthia laughed at her great-aunt's comment. "I've never heard leftovers described so colorfully," she said.

Jane had reheated baked spaghetti, ham and turkey rolls, and savory ham bread pudding with mushroom sauce. She'd steamed the leftover veggies and covered them with warmed artichoke dip, and put out a bowl of cut fruit.

"The house appears to have survived," Louise said, looking around. Everything looked undisturbed, although Ethel had alluded to a sizeable group. Louise wondered how many people constituted a large crowd. Ethel did have a tendency to exaggerate. "How about you two?"

"We managed fine," Jane said. "Didn't we, Alice?"

"Yes." Alice glanced at Jane, then looked at Louise. Since she didn't elaborate, Louise figured she'd have to pump them for details later.

"We want to hear more about your trip," Ethel said. "How was California? Warmer than here, I'm sure."

"Most of the week, I didn't need my sweater," Louise said. "We stayed at a lovely Victorian bed-and-breakfast. The owners decorated their inn to match the period of the house. It was quite luxurious," Louise said.

"Surprisingly so, considering the rugged landscape," Cynthia said. "You should have seen the ranch. It was straight out of a Clint Eastwood movie."

"I'd describe it more like a Roy Rogers and Dale Evans movie," Louise said. "They geared the entire camp to accommodate families. The main building, where we ate and had classes and performed, was an old converted stable."

"A beautiful stable, I might add," Cynthia said. "The kind that housed about fifty horses."

"I admit, the building was quite adequate. The food was country cooking served cafeteria-style," Louise said.

"Good cooking," Cynthia added, "though not as good as yours, Aunt Jane. They fed us well."

"People actually camped out in trailers and motor homes and tents," Louise said. "I toured the bunkhouse. Some single people, a few small families and lots of teenagers stayed there. It was like a long, converted barn. They'd made individual rooms with several iron bunk beds in each. The girls had one floor and the boys had another, and they were well chaperoned."

"The talent amazed me," Cynthia said. "You should have heard some of the little children playing fiddles and keyboards."

"One bashful young man in my piano class has a wonderful natural talent for playing the bluegrass-style music. You should have heard him play a piece he composed. He was wonderful," Louise said.

"As a matter of fact, you can hear him," Cynthia said, jumping up. "The camp recorded the student concert and gave us each a CD."

Jane got up. "If we're finished, let's move to the parlor so we can hear it. I'll bring tea and dessert in there."

"I'll help you," Alice said. She went into the kitchen.

Louise and Cynthia went into the parlor. Louise was surprised how neat the inn looked after the busy weekend event. She could tell her piano had been moved, however. It wasn't in exactly the same spot as when she'd left.

Louise hadn't listened to the CD of the students' concert yet. She was eager to hear how she sounded, since she'd improvised her entire piece.

Alice carried in a teapot and cups. Jane brought a platter filled with a variety of desserts.

Louise chose a cup of herbal tea. She didn't want anything to keep her awake tonight. She took a small piece of peanut-butter pie and some pumpkin cake. It looked delicious.

"Everything looks normal," Louise said. "It's hard to believe you had such a crowd of scrapbookers here this weekend."

"Louise, you would have had a heart attack at the mess here," Ethel said. "They pushed your piano into a corner, and the furniture was shoved aside to make room for the tables. I'm just glad it wasn't my house."

Jane looked at Alice and rolled her eyes. Alice shrugged. Louise caught their silent exchange and raised an eyebrow. Jane and Alice burst out laughing. If they'd meant to spare her, they'd failed. They could always count on Ethel to broadcast the truth and even embellish it a bit.

When everyone was settled, Louise set her tea aside, stood and walked over to the piano. "Before we listen to the CD, do you mind if I play a little classical music? I've missed my piano," she said. She lifted the lid, then sat down at the bench. Everyone was watching her. Without getting out any music, she rubbed her hands together and then poised them over the piano keys.

Louise began a delightful rendition of a Bach prelude from the *Well-Tempered Clavier*, Book I. Alice sipped her tea, then closed her eyes, listening. Jane sipped her coffee. Ethel tilted her head. Cynthia was watching her, smiling...waiting. She knew what was coming. Suddenly Louise changed, moving from the soothing classical music to a walking bass rhythm. After a few bars, she took off with a fast piano riff. She hadn't planned it in detail, but she let her fingers improvise and she felt the music.

She glanced at her sisters and her aunt. Alice had set her tea down and was staring at her, openmouthed. Jane was grinning and moving her shoulders in time. Ethel looked dumbfounded. Their reactions encouraged Louise. She kept playing, getting a little bounce into her hands and feet and shoulders as she played. After a rousing boogie-woogie rendition of Bach, she settled back down into the classical prelude, and concluded on a classical note. She wondered how the composer would react to her improvisation. She didn't know if he'd be smiling or turning over in his grave.

Alice, Jane and Cynthia jumped up and clapped.

"Bravo!" Alice said.

Ethel got to her feet and clapped too, though Louise suspected she did it because of the others.

Louise stood and took a bow. Cynthia gave her a big hug.

"So that's what you learned this week," Jane said. "Wow! I like it."

"That reminded me of years ago, when Bob was alive and we went to hear a jazz concert," Ethel said. "You played every bit as well as they did, Louise, and they were professionals; however, I cannot say it suits you. I do hope you don't intend to pursue that line of music."

"I don't know, Aunt Ethel. I discovered a new love for rhythm and blues and jazz. I believe I've become a convert."

"Oh dear. I hope you don't plan to play the organ in church that way."

Louise laughed. "I played this style on an old pump organ at the ranch. Farley complimented me."

"Farley? Who's he?" Ethel wanted to know.

"Farley is one of the Blackthorn Boys, and they are quite famous. He taught Mother's class," Cynthia said.

"I promise I won't begin a new music career at this stage of my life, Auntie. I'm quite content to run the inn and teach my students. But I thoroughly enjoy the energy and freedom of the music I learned this week."

Exhilarated and pleased with her sisters' reactions, Louise sat on one of the Eastlake chairs and picked up her tea while Cynthia put in the CD.

Three unschooled voices sang the national anthem. Louise smiled, listening to them. They sounded very nice. Then guitars and fiddles played a verse of "Amazing Grace," and the entire camp joined in singing. As she listened and remembered standing at the back of that stage, singing with everyone, a lump formed in Louise's throat.

One by one, the classes played, and several in each class played a solo. Louise felt as proud of these students as she did on recital night, listening to her own students play. The depth of her emotions surprised her.

Cynthia sat on the edge of her chair. "Mother's class is next." She smiled as the sound of the keyboards, guitars and fiddles played "The Eyes of Texas."

Louise set her cup on the table and leaned forward. They sounded good. Better than good. Her foot started moving in time.

"Wow! That's terrific," Jane said.

"Wait. It gets better," Cynthia said.

The song ended, and the next one began. The bass chords began in perfect unison. Louise listened for mistakes. She heard a couple of minor timing problems, but the sound was full and the rhythm was good. Her head began moving with the time.

"Listen. That's Mother," Cynthia said.

A syncopated solo riff played over the top of the melody. Louise listened critically, like a judge at a music festival. "Not bad," she said out loud. "Listen to the next part. It's Nathan. He's ten. He plays guitar and cello too."

Louise listened as Nathan's solo played over the top of the chorus. Then Dan's bridge solo began. "This young man stole the show," she said. She couldn't wait to hear his solo composition.

Alice and Jane clapped. "That was fantastic," Jane said.

"You played without music?" Alice asked. "Did you have time to memorize everything?"

"They don't use written music at the camp, and she didn't memorize it," Cynthia said, gazing at her mother proudly.

"Now Dan plays his composition," Louise said.

It seemed odd listening to Dan on a CD, when just two days earlier, she'd stood by the stage, praying for him as he played. Hearing him now, Louise wished she could hear him again and perhaps work with him and encourage him. He had such potential. He played with such joy.

The song finished. A voice on the CD announced Louise's solo.

"Okay, this is it. Listen now," Cynthia said. She smiled and her eyes sparkled as her mother's playing came over the speakers.

Watching her daughter, then looking at her sisters and aunt, Louise saw the delight on their faces. They enjoyed "This Little Light of Mine" as much as she'd enjoyed playing it.

"I've got a CD of your class sessions for you too. Bonnie gave it to me for you. They give one to every student, so you'll have the songs and techniques."

"What a pleasant surprise," Louise said. "Thank you, darling. For the entire week. I had a blast."

Cynthia removed the CD and put it in a clear plastic holder. "A blast? Oh dear, I'm afraid Mother learned a whole new language this week."

Louise laughed. "You're never too old to learn something new."

Louise wondered if Alice, Jane and Cynthia would like the autographed CDs she'd bought for them for Christmas. She'd gotten one of Farley's piano CDs for Cynthia, a Luken family gospel music CD for Alice, and a CD of Nainsi Donovan's Celtic fiddle music for Jane.

"Alice has something to show you too," Ethel said. "I've wanted to see it all weekend."

Alice stood. "I do. I'll get it. Louise, why don't you scoot your chair close to Jane so you can look at it together?"

"I've also waited all weekend to see this," Jane said. "Alice was quite secretive."

Louise raised one eyebrow. "Alice? Secretive?"

Cynthia moved chairs next to the couch so she and Ethel could see too.

Louise sat next to Jane. Alice returned and placed a leather album in Louise's lap.

"This is your scrapbook," Louise said. She opened the cover and looked at the first page. A large oval photo of their house occupied the center of the page, surrounded by a frame with large decorative script detailing the completion of the William and Elizabeth Berry home, one of the finest examples of Victorian architecture in Acorn Hill.

"Where did you get this?" Louise asked, looking at Alice.

"Carlene went through the old *Acorn Nutshell* archives for me. Then she used a special script font to print the lettering," she said.

Turning the page, they found a copy of the original article, with a grainy picture of their house. William and Elizabeth Berry stood on the porch. William was holding their son, Matthias.

"That's Mother's father," Jane said, pointing to the baby. "And our great-grandparents. The house was brand new."

The next page had a picture taken in the dining room. Elizabeth Berry was serving lunch to a group of ladies. The newspaper caption announced, "Acorn Hill Garden Club dines at Berry home."

"This is fabulous," Jane said. "Mother's grandmother must have started our gardens. I wonder if any of our trees date back that far. Some of them are very old."

Page after page showed pictures of the Berry house, embellished with old-fashioned stickers, decorative trim and small formal cards giving descriptions of the occasions. Elizabeth had loved to entertain. There were pictures of church picnics on the lawn and a formal photograph of the sisters' grandparents, Matthias Berry and Sarah Pitman, on their wedding day. These were followed by formal pictures taken at a reception in the garden. Gradually the pictures became more informal. There were many pictures of Madeleine as a baby and as a toddler. Very few pictures were taken inside the house. Most were out in the yard.

"There's Daniel's wedding," Ethel said. "Didn't he look handsome? Madeleine looked like a princess. I was there." She leaned over and peered at photographs of the wedding party. "There I am," she said, pointing to a child, dressed up for the occasion. "I felt like I was in a fairy tale," she said. "Madeleine treated me like a grown-up. After her parents died and they moved into the house, I visited them often." She pointed to the next page. "There's Daniel holding Louise. You were such a cute baby."

Alice included several pages of photographs of Louise and Alice as children. Then there were pictures that included Jane, but their mother no longer was present. Jane grew quiet as they flipped through those pages. Finally, she said, "The absence is obvious. Mother was so filled with life. The pictures after I was born seem empty."

"That's not what I see," Louise said. "They're just different. In the history of a family, people are born and they die. Then new generations carry on. Mother had a very bubbly, loving personality that showed in everything she did. So do you. Look at your baby pictures. Look at the joy and life going on around you. That is because you are in the picture."

Louise turned the page. Daniel Howard stood on the steps of Grace Chapel in his Sunday suit. His three daughters stood with him. Louise looked quite grown-up. Alice was still a young teenager, and Jane stood in front, with long pigtails, dressed in a colorful sundress. After that, there were several pictures of the family together, at graduations and holidays and at Louise's wedding. Then came pictures of Daniel performing weddings or attending church functions. Several newspaper articles chronicled his career as the pastor of Grace Chapel and an influential resident of Acorn Hill. Only a couple of pictures included Alice, Louise and her family, and Jane all together. Then Daniel was gone and the pictures skipped to the new era. Scenes of change showed the transformation into Grace Chapel Inn.

Louise turned the last page. It showed a close-up of their plaque, surrounded by snapshots of recent activities. Through tears, she read the handwritten entry:

A legacy to the Berry-Howard family. Grace Chapel
Inn has become—

"A place where one can be refreshed and encouraged
A place of hope and healing
A place where God is at home."

Louise slowly closed the book. "Beautiful," she said.

"Alice, what an amazing scrapbook. Your pages are works of art. We must put this out where everyone can see it. The pictures and everything about the house are wonderful, but all the embellishments and comments you added are priceless." Jane got up and hugged her older sister. "Thank you for putting this together," she said.

Cynthia turned to Jane. "We've talked about Mother's week and Alice's scrapbook. How about you? Did you have a chance to do anything this weekend besides cook?"

"Me?"

"She was drawing," Ethel said. "She was sketching in a notebook when I went in the kitchen for a glass of water."

"Really, what kind of sketches? I'd love to see them."

"Oh, nothing really," Jane said. "Just...doodling."

"We've shared our secrets," Alice said. "Now it's your turn."

"Oh, all right. I'll get my doodles."

Jane got up, left the parlor and returned a minute later with a sketchbook. She handed it to Louise.

"When Cynthia told you about the possibility of her getting her own book imprint, I thought perhaps I could help her by developing a family cookbook."

Cynthia gave Jane a surprised, pleased look. "What a great idea," she said.

Jane shook her head. "Not really. It didn't exactly turn out the way I expected. I got out a few recipes that were simple to make and I thought kids would enjoy. Well, if you need a lesson in humility, try to impress a group of youngsters. I learned that they don't like fancy food and that I don't know much about kids' tastes."

Cynthia laughed. "Working with children's books, I've discovered kids really do like things plain and simple. So what happened?"

"I invited several young girls over to try out my teaching methods. They did great, but they did not appreciate my embellishments to their favorite foods. They like packaged macaroni and cheese, plain cheese pizza, cake from a mix with lots of chocolate...basically, leave out the good stuff and they're happy. I'll stick to cooking for our guests," Jane concluded, grinning. "They appreciate my creative genius."

"Poor Jane," Louise said. "Those girls will grow up and develop a taste for finer food."

"The scrapbook ladies loved your cooking," Alice said.

"Yes, and that soothed my injured sensibilities," Jane said with a laugh.

"*Humph!* In my day, children ate what they were given and considered themselves fortunate," Ethel declared, frowning. "Children these days have no manners."

Jane reached over and gave Ethel's hand a squeeze. "Thanks for defending my cooking, Auntie, but it's all right. I wanted to know if my recipes would work in a children's cookbook, and I found out. They don't." Jane shrugged. "Sorry, Cynthia. I tried."

"It was a marvelous idea, Aunt Jane. Your sketches are fabulous. What are you going to do with them?"

Jane laughed. "A few of them might make an appearance at the Coffee Shop. Hope suggested June might want to use some of them on her new menus. I'll be sure to warn her not to fancy up her children's entrees, though."

"They don't know what they're missing. You can try them out on us anytime," Alice said.

Cynthia looked uncomfortable.

"What's wrong, dear?" Louise asked.

"Well, I appreciate fine cooking, Aunt Jane. Don't get me wrong, but..." She gave her mother, then Jane, a helpless look. "I have to confess, I like packaged macaroni and cheese. It's, well, it's easy for a single person, you know," Cynthia stammered and looked apologetic.

Jane burst out laughing. "All that work, and all I needed to teach the girls was how to open a package and boil water."

"Yes, well, it's not quite that simple," Cynthia protested.

"Ahem," Ethel said, clearing her throat.

All eyes turned to her.

"I find a little cooked chicken added to packaged macaroni and cheese makes a fine meal...in a pinch, of course," Ethel said, tilting up her chin in a defensive gesture.

"Really?" Jane said. "Perhaps I should try it. I could add slivered almonds and asparagus or broccoli, or..."

"No!" Alice and Louise cried in unison. At their horrified looks, Cynthia began laughing.

"All right." Jane raised her hands in mock surrender. "I'll leave out the broccoli."

Baked Spaghetti

SERVES EIGHT TO TEN

12 ounces spaghetti noodles (Use a kitchen scale to weigh, or estimate ¾ of a one-pound package.)
4 tablespoons butter or margarine
1 cup grated Parmesan cheese
4 eggs, well beaten
2 cups cottage cheese
1 pound ground beef or bulk Italian sausage
1 cup chopped onion
1 cup diced green peppers
2 cups sliced fresh mushrooms (optional)
2 cups canned diced tomatoes with juice
1 6-ounce can tomato paste
2 teaspoons sugar
2 teaspoons oregano or Italian spices
2 teaspoons basil
1 teaspoon garlic salt
1 small can sliced olives, drained (optional)
1–2 cups grated mozzarella cheese

Cook spaghetti according to package directions. Drain and stir in butter to melt. Add Parmesan cheese and eggs. Form spaghetti into a crust in a greased nine-by-thirteen-inch baking dish. Spread cottage cheese over crust.

In a skillet, brown ground beef or sausage, onion, green peppers and mushrooms until meat is browned and vegetables are tender. Stir in undrained tomatoes, tomato paste and spices. Add drained olives. Spread mixture in baking dish. Bake thirty minutes at 350 degrees. Sprinkle mozzarella on top. Return to oven five to ten minutes, until cheese is melted.

About the Author

Award-winning author Sunni Jeffers grew up in a town much like Acorn Hill. After raising their children and running a business in a large city, Sunni and her husband moved to a small farm in northeast Washington State where deer, moose and elk graze in the hay fields, and hawks and eagles soar overhead.

Sunni began writing after her children left home. Her novels reflect the inspiration and hope she has found through faith and a relationship with Jesus Christ. Sunni served on the national board and the Faith, Hope & Love Chapter of Romance Writers of America. When she isn't writing, she likes to entertain and spend time with her children and four grand-daughters. Tea parties with all the trimmings, cooking and reading are favorite pastimes.

Sunni loves to hear from readers. E-mail her at sunnij@sunnijeffers.com and check her website www.sunnijeffers.com.

Tales from Grace Chapel Inn

Once you visit the charming village of Acorn Hill, you'll never want to leave. Here, the three Howard sisters reunite after their father's death and turn the family home into a bed-and-breakfast. They rekindle old memories, rediscover the bonds of sisterhood, revel in the blessings of friendship and meet many fascinating guests along the way.